THE FUTURE'S ADVOCATE

The Future's Advocate

BY E. G. CARR

HERALD PUBLISHING HOUSE

Copyright © 1975
HERALD PUBLISHING HOUSE
Independence, Missouri

Library of Congress Catalog Card No. 74-82187
ISBN 0-8309-0121-3

Printed in the United States of America

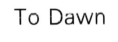

To Dawn

Chapter One

"Are you comfortable, Mr. Westering?" Evan hesitated momentarily before acknowledging the question with a brusque nod. Meticulous tailoring and contoured couch notwithstanding, lying on one's back in a space suit was little removed from being in an iron lung.

It had an additional disadvantage in fact, in that while an iron lung would at least be firmly on the ground, his present perch was some one hundred and fifty meters up, poised at the tip of the massive Tri-saturn which was soon to quite literally blast him from the earth.

The close-out technician didn't seem overly concerned with his reply in any case, being far too occupied with his immediate task of securing the connections between Evan's pressure suit and the module's life support and telemetry systems.

Evan closed his eyes and relaxed with conscious effort. For all of his many hours of training, and for all of his previous flights, no panacea was yet available for the cold agony of waiting out a countdown; being aware of every one of those seconds and minutes which came so slowly and yet passed in a blur. Time was like that, he mused: the future yawned ahead like an endless corridor, while all of the past was as yesterday. Situations like this just seemed to accentuate that principle.

He grimaced as the dull monotone of the voice of Launch Control continued to check off each system. Every new connection seemed to be linking his very being to that mindless, all-seeing, all-knowing ground control system. It was bad enough to just lie there being afraid, but to do so knowing that the cold data of his fear was being watched and recorded imparted to him a curious feeling of nakedness.

He stirred irritably; he felt extremely useless during this period of the launch. The day had passed when an astronaut participated in preflight operations to any degree. All he had to do was just lie there and appear normal. As long as his physiological readings were acceptable, he was perhaps the most ignored component in this monstrous machine. He smiled impishly as it occurred to him that it would be an interesting experiment to just hold his breath for a time and see what effect it would have on the countdown.

"T minus two hours and still counting." The procession of marching minutes was once more before him. The technician seemed to have completed his tasks, for he loomed once more into view, pausing momentarily to peer intently into his face. Evan winked, but the lack of response informed him that the man could not see him, possibly because of the light reflection from his visor. He was probably just checking the helmet glass for signs of misting. After a moment he turned away, apparently satisfied.

Evan became introspective again. Here he was, still

on the ground, and already he might as well have been a thousand miles away in space. The technological fence was up; he was no longer Evan Westering but an animal set apart—very much apart, in fact, for he was one of the three men who would travel farther away from Earth than man had ever been...into far reaches of the solar system that had never as yet known the presence of man, over distances at which Earth would seem reduced to the brightness of only a tiny star, and even the sun would be discernibly smaller and colder.

Evan was infinitely grateful that he was selected for this trip, because although it had not actually been spelled out in so many words, there would not be another one like it. The project had already been considerably reduced in scope and was being continued only because of the momentum it had obtained. With the economy continuing on its downward slide and the new military rumblings from Europe, Congress had approved the final grant only by the barest margin. It had led to newspaper quips suggesting that the crew should carry with them a canoe, as on their return the pickup vessel may already have been repossessed.

The humor held a glimmer of ugly feasability. The mission was to be conducted over a period of some seven years; and what with the rate of change to which people were becoming accustomed, this period was quite long enough to allow the space travelers to return to a completely changed world—a world to which, Evan mused, one might not even care to return.

The space program was under a cloud in quite a literal sense, for the interference of man in the upper atmosphere—particularly with his use of high altitude aircraft—had resulted in the disappearance of blue skies and the substitution of a milky-white contrail layer which was unquestionably affecting the environment.

Of course in spite of all the data collected the argument still raged as to whether the alarming increases in average earth temperature were due primarily to the hothouse effect of the contrail layer or the massive thermal contribution of the myriads of nuclear power stations in use.

It was almost incredible that man should be at the one time so conscious of the effects of his monstrous technology and yet so powerless to reverse it that he should resort to arguing with himself over causes in order that he might delay any real decision.

On the other hand, man had begun to move. Only a few days ago a worldwide moratorium had been called on the use of all supersonic commercial aircraft (it was quite improbable to expect it to encompass military uses), and there were efforts being made to extend the ban, however unlikely, to the use of aircraft operating at even lower levels.

Such shattering decisions as this, even if they would inevitably be only temporary, tended to place a rocket launching in a bad light, and once again it was only the specter of monumental waste which prevented the mission from being indefinitely postponed.

At least the manned space program was going out with a blaze of glory, for this was by far the most ambitious mission yet attempted. It was to comprise a huge elliptical orbit around the sun. Huge, of course, was a relative term because it was huge only by human standards. It would be quite wrong to regard it as some kind of grand tour of the solar system, because the main objective of the mission was simply to make a relatively close fly-past of the planet Jupiter, and, it was hoped, an even closer sweep past Ganymede, one of Jupiter's moons. With a diameter of three thousand miles, it was larger than Earth's moon and was regarded as a likely stopping place on some later mission for a more detailed study of the mysterious cloud-enshrouded planet.

The way things were going on Earth, the possibility of the later mission seemed somewhat remote, and that in turn made this mission superfluous. There were many other facets of the mission, of course—astronomical observations and the like—but somehow even Evan was aware of a sense of anticlimax, as if the world's enthusiasm for the mission had declined markedly.

After all, the whole project had been almost prohibitively expensive, and prognostication about the whole space program was generally pessimistic. This led to some reasonable doubts in the minds of the three crew members as to whether it was really worth giving so much just to one mission. It would be almost seven years before they returned to earth, and that was a rather large slice from anyone's life—especially where it involved separation from one's family and friends.

A tenuous radio link would always be maintained, made difficult and cumbersome by the long round-trip time of the signal of as much as one and a half hours, but Evan was doubtful that he could fully blank from his mind the fact that at times on the journey they would be almost five hundred million miles from Earth.

And yet he still called himself an astronaut! Evan grinned. How presumptuous it sounded! Man was venturing barely out of the inner circle of planets within his own solar system, yet he considered himself a mariner among the stars. It could be likened to a man standing on the wet sand of the seashore and then claiming to have ranged the seven seas.

But right or wrong, they were going, and no amount of comparison with the mind-staggering dimensions of the universe could take from Evan's mind the awe with which he regarded the task ahead of them.

Evan's craft, Magellan 1, was to rendezvous and dock with Magellan A, the giant wheel-shaped structure which had already been in orbit around Earth for several months. Evan would link up his command module nose-first to the central hub of Magellan A. The large service module and plasma engine would be behind him, ready to power the great spinning ship along her way.

The other spacecraft would come then. Magellan 2 would bring the other two men, Harry Bennet and Kurt Haller. Before coming aboard, they would attach their third stage engine behind the plasma engine, for their liquid fueled rocket would be required to push the Magellan to its initial escape velocity—a task the plasma engine could not be expected to do.

After a relatively normal escape from Earth orbit, the final stage booster would be discarded and the plasma engine would be brought into service to accelerate them along Earth's path, creeping slowly ahead of it in a solar orbit which would eventually reach an apogee coinciding with the position of Jupiter.

After only a brief encounter with the gigantic planet and its attendant moons, the plasma engine would again be brought into operation in a retrograde maneuver which would eventually slow the Magellan and cause it to begin the long, slow, curving "fall" back toward the sun.

When it finally plunged back past Earth it would carry too much energy to allow the recovery of the main ship, and the three crew members would be obliged to repair to Evan's command module which would leave Magellan and take them down the reentry corridor after they discarded the service module and plasma engine.

The main body of the Magellan would ultimately perish in the fiery heat of the sun—a fate which could quite well be shared by its occupants if there were any slipups at this crucial stage.

Evan's part in the scheme was an important one. Although he was the only passenger aboard his craft, the first two stages were almost three times as large as the other ship, and Magellan 2 was unusually large in any case. The major part of Evan's ship was the plasma engine, which would power them through most of the voyage.

The correct functioning of this vital and incredibly

sophisticated machine was Evan's main responsibility throughout the mission. He would literally live and sleep with it; while the other crew members would sleep in the outer rim of the ship during their hibernation, the flight engineer was to remain in the central hub alongside his charge.

In the event of any malfunction of the engine he would be the only one to be automatically revived, the others being awakened only at his discretion. The long-term effects of zero gravitation were still relatively unknown, but Evan's bodily functions would be monitored continually, and in the event of any unforeseen effects becoming apparent, he would be revived and permitted also to take up a position within the rim which had been provided for him against such an eventuality.

In fact it was almost certain that this would have to be done, in spite of all the research that had gone into the prevention of muscular atrophy and cardiovascular problems which seemed to attend weightlessness. Nevertheless, it was desirable that Evan should be at his post for at least the initial stage of the mission.

The engine module was completely self-contained because, on their fiery return to earth, this portion of the ship would be required to carry the entire crew along with, it was hoped, the voluminous data of their quest. Evan was spaciously accommodated at this stage, but it would not be so on their return.

The engine module was therefore a ship within a ship, with its own power and control systems, and carrying sufficient reserves of food, water, and recycling systems to be able to maintain the three members of the crew in hibernation within it for the duration of the return half of the journey should the necessity arise due to some accident or malfunction of the mother ship.

In spite of its great bulk and the fact that it was nuclear-powered, the plasma engine was nowhere near as fierce a machine as were any other of the propulsion and attitude systems of the ship. At best, it was capable of producing only a puny several kilos of thrust.

Its main virtue resided in the fact that it was capable of maintaining its thrust almost indefinitely; indeed, the engine would remain in constant operation throughout almost the entire duration of the mission, powering the craft on its long sweeping path for the first half of the journey and then slowing it gradually on the return half.

Relative to the centrifugally produced gravity around the rim of the craft, the effect of this thrust would be negligible and would pass almost unnoticed by the crew.

The correct operation of the plasma engine was an extremely critical factor in the overall mission. The Magellan carried no retro systems whatever but was fitted only with small thrusters capable of making only attitude changes should they be desired for the purpose of making observations. Such changes in attitude would be required from time to time during the trip, but they would be far from being arbitrarily decided. Any change in attitude of the plasma engine relative to its course would create changes in its trajectory which would have a cumulative effect on the duration and course of the whole mission, and this had to be taken into account. In the absence of retro systems the control of the plasma engine was a mind-boggling feat, for it was necessary for the thrust and attitude of the plasma engine to be controlled with such precision that on its return to earth years later it would arrive along a specific corridor which would allow its occupants to safely disembark.

This was a feat which could be accomplished only with the use of rigid computer control throughout the mission.

The consequences of failure in this respect were rather specific: either a fiery death into the environs of the sun or an equally appalling possibility of missing the earth by a great distance and entering into an almost eternal orbit around the sun from which there could be no hope of rescue.

Evan would have little to do with these delicate operations, but he would have limited powers in regard to momentary attitude changes as the necessity arose. When the time came for making detailed examination of an alien surface during the flypast, ground control was at an acute disadvantage due simply to the round-trip time taken by a radio command signal to travel to the ship located on the other side of the sun and for the acknowledgment to return.

Under such circumstances it was imperative that these attitude changes be handled by someone on board the ship. The subsequent corrections to the ship's trajectory would be handled later from Earth.

Evan was also the central figure in any emergency,

as he had control over all the automatic functions of the ship in the event of any malfunction occurring in space. This was primarily the reason why he was to remain at his central post for as long as possible.

"T minus forty and counting."

Lost in his thoughts, Evan suddenly realized that a large chunk of time had slipped past. He wriggled himself slightly to settle more deeply into his couch. The countdown was proceeding with a normality which assured him in some subliminal way that lift-off would be right on schedule. It was a good omen, and he felt a sudden thrill of anticipation at the imminence of his departure.

The close-out team had gone now, although he had been unaware of their departure. He felt a few muffled bumps against the side of the ship and knew that the access arm was being slid back. He could no longer walk from his perch now if anything should go wrong, but the escape tower would be armed and would carry him clear automatically in that unlikely event.

The final thirty minutes passed much quicker. With six minutes to go, Launch Control spoke to him directly for the first time.

"Hello, Magellan 1, we are still go for Launch. It looks like a good one...five minutes fifty and counting."

"Thank you," said Evan, "I think you're right."

His voice betrayed nothing of his feelings, but they would know. His heart rate would be telling them everything.

Things were happening rapidly now. He heard the

access arm being fully retracted. At T minus three minutes the firing command button had been pressed and the incredible series of computer-controlled sequences began racing toward the moment of firing.

Evan closed his eyes and breathed deeply, determined that by an effort of will he could calm his racing heart.

Then the moment arrived—the distant shuddering rumble as the main engines ignited and commenced building up power for the longest ten seconds of his life. The "launch commit" signal flashed momentarily on the data-logger before him, and he felt the hold-down arms finally release their vice-like grip.

He closed his eyes again as the gigantic ship performed its first maneuver, a slow, gentle tilt away from the gantry which Evan always considered to be by far the most disconcerting sensation of a launch. Ten seconds later he felt another change as the rocket, having safely cleared the tower, began the precise roll and pitch maneuver that was to set it on its unerring course over the Atlantic.

The massive acceleration was beginning to get to him now, as his fierce steed, growing lighter by some twelve thousand kilos every second, roared faster and faster through the ever thinning atmosphere.

Three minutes later and over eighty kilometers above the earth, the first stage engines fell away and the second stage proceeded to hurl him even higher, still perfectly on course. In less than fifteen minutes he was safely in orbit.

It was the first time he had been up like this, entirely on his own, and it was unexpectedly lonely. The view was too perfect to be wasted on only one person. He felt a great desire to turn to someone and say, "Just look at that," but there was no one, and he was filled with both wonder and frustration.

Confirmation from the ground—it had indeed been a perfect shot. He was now dealing with Mission Control at Houston. Evan acknowledged only briefly; he was too busy now to talk unnecessarily—at least he *should* have been busy. For a few moments he was not. Freed from the crushing emotional stresses of the countdown and launch, he took the opportunity now to gaze happily down at the view below him.

His boyish face rather belied his years; to an uninformed observer he could well pass for eighteen or nineteen. Fair hair which would normally have fallen loosely about his shoulders was tucked carefully into the hairnet that he would be obliged to wear constantly while he was weightless.

The impression of boyishness did not carry over to his eyes. Gray-blue in color, they held a deeper seriousness, due in part perhaps to the refining fire of his intense training for the mission. His manner was bright and outgoing; he was instinctively friendly, although equally capable of brief flashes of anger or belligerent stubbornness.

But right now he was supremely happy. . . and it was more than just the first elation of weightlessness; his mind was clear, and his body glowed with that strange exhilaration that follows the mastery of fear. Earth *was* beautiful—contrail layer notwithstanding—a radiant jewel set against the blackness of space. There was a feature of this panorama that always impressed itself upon him whenever he gazed on it, a detail which never manifested itself in even the best of photographs. It was the awesome immensity of the surrounding space.

To gaze upon Earth in such a context as this was to understand it with a reverence which simply could not be duplicated—a type of compassion, Evan thought, and he found himself swallowing uncomfortably against the swelling lump in his throat.

It was to him an alluring and elusive mystery, that joy and pain were so little removed from each other that one could gaze upon such a thing of indescribable beauty and want to cry. Whatever view the Creator took of man's despoilation of Earth and its resources, He must surely have been behind the space program. Man had to be permitted this one thing before he destroyed himself. . . . He had to leave Earth, turn, and look back. From that instant he was without excuse.

He was also happy to be busy again and freed from the numbing inactivity of the prelaunch period. He had an unusually large quota of work to handle prior to his rendezvous with the huge orbiting wheel which now awaited him. The docking procedure would have been quite a handful even for the three-man crew, but for this mission it would be carried out by only one man. Certainly, the operation would be almost entirely automatic, but this fact alone created the need for a checklist which would occupy a good two hours of Evan's time even prior to the rendezvous.

He removed his helmet, and after stowing it with meticulous care, pressed his nose again to the thick glass of the tiny observation window in an effort to see more clearly the striking panorama below him. For the moment at least, his mind was not on the job.

On the ground, the activity continued. The countdown was now well advanced on Magellan 2. Launch-controller Clarke regarded the televised picture of the gleaming floodlit monster with mounting satisfaction. Once the Magellan 1 docking was complete that smooth kind of precedent would be established that seemed usually to guarantee future success.

The rendezvous had been made, and in only a matter of minutes the locking catches would be snapping shut on Evan's craft. With this hurdle cleared, the launch of the second rocket became a certainty.

Clarke thought of the two intrepid men waiting in their tiny capsule. There was Harry Bennet, the youngest astronaut in the program, although only slightly younger than Evan. At twenty-four he was a quiet, confident, and somewhat uncommunicative person, but a man well chosen for the mission. He and Evan had cemented a firm friendship during their training period, although he was serious and inclined to moodiness. Evan was much more outgoing by nature, with an energy and enthusiasm which bordered on the aggressive. The jesting complaint of his father had often been that Evan was afflicted with an overbearing compulsion to convince everybody about everything—a trait that often created problems for him.

Clarke smiled to himself as he considered these two extremes. He himself had joked about them in the canteen that very morning. "If they were to meet some Jovians out there," he had quipped, "they would conclude on examining Bennet that the human mouth was an obsolete organ comparable to the appendix, while in Westering's case it would be considered a receptacle for housing the human foot."

Kurt Haller was the flight commander. Older and less intense than the other two, he had the kind of genial good humor that would serve him well in accommodating the behavior of the younger men. He was much more experienced in prolonged space travel than the others, having spent almost a year in an orbital laboratory at one stage. He was also familiar in a very practical way with the deep-freeze hibernation that they would experience during much of the mission. He had submitted himself as a guinea pig for the first tests on the time-release type oral capsule used to induce the initial torpor while the biological functions were being slowed down. He had spent two months in the suspended-animation state, the longest time that any person had been so tested. Neither Westering nor Bennet had been tested in this way, so it constituted an entirely new experience for them.

Kurt was not altogether happy with the amount of testing that had been carried out in this field. As successful as the test had been, it represented only a small percentage of the time which they would actually spend in this condition, and all the facts were not yet in. The recent speeding up of the program had resulted in several such shortcuts. Kurt had registered his misgivings about the tests, but beyond that he had remained tight-lipped; the mission was going, and he was going too!

Clarke found himself marveling at the bravery of these men. Westering and Bennet were probably driven, each in his own way, by a degree of idealistic madness typical of their youth, but Haller had no such incentive. Unlike the others he was a family man, with a wife and two daughters. His everyday conversation revealed in glowing terms his plans for their future—a future in which he obviously intended to participate. Certainly no one could accuse him of grandiose sacrifice or a subliminal death wish!

And yet this man had set his face toward the mission without hesitation in spite of the fact that he was more aware of the likely cost than anyone else. He had the most to spend.

Kurt's professional cool was apparent even in his heartbeat which was barely above the resting rate in spite of the impending blast-off.

Clarke shared Kurt's concern as did several other people on the program. Not that these things were discussed, of course; everyone knew that the allocation for the mission had barely escaped the knife. It was a matter of gratefully accepting the employment that the venture offered as it was, or of having no mission at all—and that would be a serious situation for many people who stood little chance of reemployment in these difficult times.

"Sixty minutes and still counting, Magellan 2; we

expect confirmation on Magellan 1 docking any moment now."

"Thank you." The polite reply was Haller's.

Clarke leaned forward on his console, chin on hand, and studied the image on the screen, his fingertips rapping quietly on the desk top in an unconscious manifestation of the more troubling thoughts that were crossing his mind. The television image of a rocket on its launch pad was a quite familiar sight to him now, but in spite of its ostensibly simple appearance he could not shake from his mind its true complexity and the predisposition to failure that this created.

The most disturbing fact, quite apart from the rather sketchy testing, was the lack of any backup protection for these men. Even if at the initial stage the Magellan reached escape velocity on the wrong trajectory there was no plan for bringing them down again. It would be quite useless even to attempt to build a rescue ship. Within the several months that would be required to set up such an operation the Magellan would have traveled such a distance that it would be impossible even to catch it, let alone correct its course. It had been intended to carry a lifting body aboard the Magellan for the use of the crew in such an eventuality, but even this proposal had been shelved in the light of cost considerations.

The space program was about to close either on a major accomplishment or a bitter tragedy. Clarke was not at all sure that either of the alternatives was really worth the money.

"Hello, Houston, this is Magellan 1."

Bennet's head snapped up sharply as the communication interrupted his pondering.

"Go ahead, Magellan." The reply had come from Craig Simms, the voice of Mission Control at Houston.

"Docking's complete. Everything checks out happy. How about that."

"You're four minutes late, but I guess we can put up with that. Do you mind if someone else comes too?"

Evan's chuckle came across with surprising clarity. "Sure, but tell him to knock three times. . . . I don't want to let just anyone in."

There was a short delay, and Evan spoke again. "I'll be transferring to the main ship in a few minutes to have a look around . . . so don't call me, I'll call you."

"That sounds okay, Magellan. You'll listen in on us though, won't you?"

Simm's comment apparently did not warrant a reply, because none was forthcoming. Evan would be anxious to make the excursion into the main ship before the others arrived, but he would ensure that the voice communications were piped through the ship.

"Magellan 2, we have confirmation of docking." Clarke relayed the information, knowing fully that the others would have already overheard the exchange.

"Thank you, Launch," said Kurt Haller.

Evan slid silently through the connecting conduit into the center of the mother ship. He found himself in the spacious annex at the center of the long, dimly lit tubular corridor which formed the single spoke across the wheel-shaped ship. The annex was located within a great metal sphere about twelve meters in diameter at the center of the ship.

The annex did not occupy the entire contents of the sphere, for opposite the access conduit, on the other side of the annex, was the hatch leading to the service center housing the life-support systems and power supplies for the main craft.

An air vent beside his head delivered a blast of cool, antiseptic-smelling air, and the whole ship seemed to whisper reassuringly of its preparedness for the mission. The corridor was about three meters wide, extending to about five or six meters at the annex. It was provided with three rubber-coated cables spaced around its circumference and stretching off into the darkness in either direction toward the outer rim some thirty meters away. The corridor was heavily cluttered with equipment along one side, and at each extremity could be seen the small circle of light formed by the viewing window in the access hatch to the outer rim cabin.

He cast himself carefully across the annex and came up against the service room hatch with slightly more of a bump than he had expected. He cast around anxiously for the support cable and clung to it for a moment as it gently twanged him to a halt. He was going to have to be careful until he became used to being weightless in such a large area as this. While he was without weight, the mass of his body still had to be reckoned with before he could launch himself around too vigorously.

From his position he could see through the circle of

triangular windows surrounding the access conduit, and part of one of the thruster assemblies on his command module was visible. Also visible was Earth, and it momentarily startled him as it was in quite a different position—up above his head rather than below his feet as it had been when he was back in his cabin. He watched in fascination as it continued to roll around, appearing successively in each of the circle of windows until it once more passed under his feet. Because his body was also in rotation the spin of the craft was almost unnoticeable unless he looked at the whirling panorama outside.

Cautiously, he began to make his way along the cable toward the corridor stretching away below his feet. He had hardly moved a couple of meters from the center of the ship before the acceleration of his body began to move him toward the wall of the corridor. He let go of the cable and began a long slow slide, bumping gently over the deep padded interior of the ship. Checking his progress carefully with the cable, he realized a good thirty seconds had passed before he dropped through into the main rim cabin and several more seconds before he had stopped bouncing about the padded walls and floor as he fought to gain his feet.

He finally settled for a hands-and-knees position on the floor which seemed stable enough for him to at least become accustomed to the strange rotational "gravity." It was something like a weak moon gravity in that it at least directed him gently against the floor, but beyond that it had some quite unpleasant qualities which made it difficult to live with.

While he remained in this position, everything seemed fairly normal; but any sudden movement, particularly turning his head, produced a momentary disorientation quite sufficient to topple him off balance. The weakness of the force tended to complicate the problem, as it prevented any real purchase on the floor with his feet as he tried to correct his wild stumbling. It was obvious that the deep padding was an essential feature if the astronauts were to avoid a multitude of minor injuries.

He remained on his knees for a moment listening to the soft "white" noises of the ship. He could faintly hear the short spurting sounds of the rim attitude thrusters as they fought to rectify the imbalance caused by his jumping around. As large as the ship was, it was nevertheless affected even by quite small changes in its dynamic balance. Evan was becoming rapidly convinced that he was going to prefer the weightlessness of his station beside the plasma engine to this curious centrifugal gravity.

He began a cautious advance along the gently curving floor, still on his hands and knees, and then found that he made better progress in a hands-and-feet attitude. In spite of a complete absence of spectators, he still felt rather ridiculous in this position.

The cabin narrowed to claustrophobic proportions, forming a small tunnel which served as access to the various self-contained sections of the ship. He found himself suddenly and unexpectedly gazing through a glass panel into one of the hibernation chambers. It caught him somewhat off guard, and a cold chill passed over him as he looked upon it. Illuminated only by its eerie ultraviolet light it looked more like a bizarre coffin than a life-preserving device.

He knelt with his nose against the glass for several minutes, preoccupied with the thought of the years of living death that men would spend in that unnatural habitat.

His reverie was broken suddenly by a voice communication from the ground. Magellan 2 was departing in ten minutes, and it would not be long before he had company. He continued his excursion around the rim, traveling with the peculiar bouncing crawl at which he was now becoming adept. He passed another of the hibernation chambers, but on this occasion he pointedly avoided looking at it, knowing that it would disturb him again.

"Five...four...three...two..." Evan reached the small annex at the other end of the spoke as the final seconds of the launch passed. He sat on the floor and listened to the succession of terse reports passing between Magellan 2 and the ground as the journey began.

The liquid-fueled final stage booster which the Magellan 2 men were bringing with them comprised a particularly large restartable type engine which would provide the long, smooth burn required to set the much bigger craft on her way. It would be restarted a couple of times if necessary until Magellan was on a course entirely satisfactory to Mission Control before it was discarded to allow operation of the plasma engine.

Evan began to hurry. It was important that he be ready for the others when they came. They would be obliged to go EVA in order to get from their vessel to

29

the mother ship, and Evan had to be on hand to assist them. He had traveled several meters down the tunnel again before a snatch of the relayed voice communication caused him to halt. He had not been particularly listening and he partly missed its content, but he detected that something was wrong. It was Harry Bennet's voice, and he had said something which sounded like "I'm sorry, Houston, but we can't tell you."

Evan's brow furrowed as he tried to make sense out of the remark. Bennet had obviously been answering a question put to him from the ground, a question which for some reason had not been relayed to the main craft. There was only one reason why Mission Control would narrow the communication like that—there was some sort of trouble! It was probable that he was not supposed to have received Harry's answer either, but someone on the ground had fumbled the switches.

He began to turn around in the tunnel but stopped again in an effort to catch another remark from Bennet. The nearest speaker was in the annex behind him, and the wall padding tended to attenuate the sound in the tunnel considerably. He did not get the tenor of the remark because it was obviously cut short.

He crawled back into the annex and sat down on the floor again in front of the speaker. A couple of minutes silence confirmed his theory that he was being bypassed by voice communications. They must have been rather occupied on the ground, Evan thought, because they would have at least advised him of the difficulty if they had had the time.

He began the hand-over-hand climb up the cable

toward the center of the ship, but Simms spoke to him before he got there.

"Hello, Magellan, sorry for the silence.... We had a small problem with Magellan 2's final stage. It's not serious...stand by, please."

Evan launched himself neatly across the central annex and into the access conduit. Once in his cabin he signaled Earth immediately.

"Hello, Houston, what's the trouble?" There was no immediate answer, so he repeated the question.

"No sweat, Magellan, we had a delayed start on the last stage......ullage failure we think...they're safe for the moment... looks like a decaying orbit, though, and we'll have to correct that—that's all."

Evan exhaled slowly The orbit could indeed be corrected quite easily, but the very nature of the failure was disconcerting, and in spite of Houston's statement it was serious; that engine would have to be restarted several more times yet, and it was crucial that these starts be precise. The faulty starting would already have left Magellan 2 in a lower orbit than required. The rendezvous was going to be later than planned.

The ullage rockets on this unusual last-stage booster were grouped around its rear end, outriggers from the main body of the craft. They were small restartable engines, four in number, which were used momentarily before the firing of the main engine to provide a slight acceleration sufficient to direct the liquid fuel toward the engine.

Telemetry advised what had happened; two of the ullage engines had indeed failed to ignite. The cause of

31

the failure was unfortunately not known.

Evan wiped the corner of his mouth and realized as he did so that his hand was shaking. The elation of the trip was beginning to wear off, and he was being reminded that there could be many incidents during the voyage which could carry the seeds of failure...or of death.

The problem did not reemerge, however, and the docking of Magellan 2 took place without further incident...albeit a little late.

From this point on, the Magellan was but one ship. She was fueled, manned, and in spite of all misgivings ready for her great adventure.

Inside the ship an air of gentle but anxious gaiety prevailed. Even Harry Bennet allowed himself the luxury of a little tomfoolery in the giddy environment of the rim cabin. There was work to be done, too—almost all of it in the form of system checks. The men worked quietly and professionally; their procedures had been honed to a high pitch of efficiency long before the mission. They had already passed through the furnace together, and they were now at the point of psychological preparedness for the dangers and uncertainties that lay ahead.

They were off to visit Ganymede together.

Chapter two

The Magellan was three days out of Earth orbit and dead on course. The final stage engine had been successfully restarted on four occasions, the first burn to escape velocity and then three shorter firings intended to adjust the course to its phenomenal degree of accuracy. The ullage rocket problem still existed, but it was a consistent fault and was therefore easily taken into account.

In any event, the problem was now dispensed with; the troublesome engine had been jettisoned, and the Magellan was beginning to draw away from it very slowly under the power of the plasma engine.

Evan regarded the diminishing last stage from one of the central annex windows and felt a flood of relief. He had tremendous confidence in the reliability and predictability of the engine which now propelled them. It operated with a gentle and unspectacular efficiency far removed from the ham-fisted brute force of the liquid fueled rockets and, unlike them, he knew himself to be its master.

Although the separation had taken place over four hours ago, the rejected engine was only about one hundred and fifty meters away. It would be quite a long while yet before their companion was no longer in sight. The relative speed between the two ships would gradually increase, with the Magellan moving eventually into a higher orbit. The booster on the other hand would continue in a slow arc back toward the sun.

It didn't deserve such an ignominious end, Evan thought; for all of its failings, it had at least ended up doing the job it was intended to do. He raised a finger to his forehead in a grave salute before he turned and began to propel himself, much more confidently now, toward the rim.

He plopped into the cabin in a sitting position. They had discovered, not without considerable amusement, that there were practical advantages in dispensing with the more conventional means of locomotion. He loped through into the galley where Harry and Kurt were already eating their final meal preparatory to hibernation.

Evan sat down Roman-style at the low table, and began eating his own meal, using the ridiculous all-purpose eating utensil that had been provided for each of them. The weak gravity, for all its faults, made a dramatic improvement over the usual eating conditions in space, allowing them to enjoy a meal of much more conventional appearance in a relatively normal manner.

They ate silently. The fact that it was their last meal somehow gave it a death-row quality. Evan would have brought the matter up, but with rare foresight he elected to say nothing; it was simply in the air.

It was Kurt who created the opportunity. He finished eating first and retreated noisily from the table until he sat with his back against the wall.

"Well," he said, patting his stomach, "the condemned man ate a hearty meal."

Evan smiled somewhat sheepishly. Kurt was grinning at them broadly in spite of the sinister implications; he had caught both of the other two staring vacantly ahead at the wall, each with the same dour expression. Harry remained serious, completely overlooking the intended facetiousness of the remark.

"Yes," he said, "I feel a bit the same way. I guess that now we are winding down we are finding more time to think about that sort of thing."

Kurt started to protest, but Bennet continued speaking, addressing the top of the table rather than anyone in particular.

"You start on one of those common, everyday things like eating a meal, and then all of a sudden you realize that nothing is common or everyday anymore. You realize that you have involved yourself in something a bit too lightly, and you begin to think about it in the way that you should have long ago. You ask yourself 'What am I doing here?' Here we are in a multi-billion-dollar kerosene drum heading off on a wild escapade which has all kinds of stated purposes but a true purpose that none of us even understand." He looked up suddenly at Evan. "It just may not be right?"

Evan felt a strange pang of fear. It didn't sound like Harry Bennet speaking, and for a moment he was unsure of his reply. His stomach had suddenly tightened into a knot; surely Harry wasn't beginning to crack before the mission was even fully under way!

What should be done in a situation like this if he was?

Kurt took control of the conversation again quickly, speaking gently, although his voice had taken on a firmer quality.

"I know what you're doing here. You are here because you are an acknowledged expert in photography, astronomy, and astral navigation. You're here because the people who paid for this multi-billion-dollar kerosene drum as you call it figured that you would be one who could make the best use of it." He extended an arm to point at Evan, still sitting with his mouth full and wearing a slightly stunned expression. "He's here for the same kind of reasons, and so am I. If you're just asking the old question about whether man is really entitled to do the things he does or whether he always spends his money in the right way I'm afraid you'll have to wait until the history books are written about our age before you can even start working on the answer."

Evan stole a cautious sideways glance at Harry, who was sitting gazing intently at the tabletop. He sat for so long that Evan began to wonder if he had even been listening. But eventually he spoke, slowly and thoughtfully.

"I think maybe that's the very thing that bothers me; we always seem to have to wait until all the consequences are in before we begin thinking seriously about anything. We already have our history books, and yet we don't seem to have learned much. I realize it *is* possible to list quite a few specific technological benefits that have accrued from other vastly expensive scientific gambles, and yet..." He gestured vaguely toward the window in the direction of Earth. "I cannot quite persuade myself that that's all they have in mind."

Evan stopped eating long enough to interject, "That all sounds like trying to answer a question that no one has really asked of you."

Harry spread his hands in almost a despairing gesture. "But they do! Can't you see? They do! You don't really need me to persuade you that there are more than three people on board this ship. Every man, woman, and child who even remotely comprehends this mission is traveling with us. As Kurt says, many of them have even paid for a ticket. And they're not just Americans; they represent every nation on Earth."

"I think I see your point," said Kurt, scratching the side of his face, "but what exactly are you trying to make out of it?"

"Simply this," said Bennet, talking faster now. "As I consider all those people, and who they are, I cannot see that they are so profoundly with us in spirit just because of some technological spin-off that's going to give them smaller transistor radios or better automotive lacquer. Why, they don't even believe that we are really going to find out much more about the solar system. The most uninformed layman knows that the principal cargo brought back from space missions has not been answers but more questions. The myth that we can go anywhere or do anything on the technological express collapsed at least a decade ago. The trouble is that it won't slow down enough for us to get off."

Evan's eyes widened noticeably. That was an

extraordinarily long speech for the usually tight-lipped Harry Bennet!

"So they spent their money for nothing?" asked Kurt, smiling. "Or do you also profess to know what the people who sent us really want?" He raised his eyebrows. "If it's anything other than what's written in the mission program, then no one has mentioned it to me."

Bennet shook his head impatiently. "That's what I'm trying to say. We are technicians, and as such we can do nothing much other than collect technical data. We have machines to do that."

"A man is a much more efficient payload," said Kurt. "But it's not technical data that people want. They want...well they want us to tell them how everything *looks* from out here."

Evan interjected, still with his mouth full, "I haven't the foggiest notion what you mean."

"Well," said Harry, slowing down a little, "take for instance those first photographs from Apollo Eight, the ones that showed Earth for the first time as a little round ball in space. Didn't you feel different about it when you first saw it?"

"I was fairly young then, and so were you," Evan grinned, "but I guess you're right."

Bennet finally looked up. "They didn't really *need* to photograph it, did they? I mean we already knew what it would look like. We could have had an artist paint a more spectacular or more colorful picture of it without ever leaving the earth. But men went up there, and when they came back, we all looked over their shoulders, and we looked at it through their eyes, and we saw that it was different than what we had expected."

"It certainly did make a better photograph in those days," said Evan.

"I still don't think you understand what I mean." Harry was beginning to sound irritated. "People have been taught that economic growth and technology were going to save them from their lot, no matter what. Look back at that planet; just look at it! You can see the fruits of our technology from four hundred thousand kilometers away!" He kept pointing at the window until the others felt obliged to turn and look, if only to humor him.

"So what has man done now?" Harry continued. "He's wrapped all his money and technology up in one big tin can and thrown it into space. He's giving technology just one last chance to go 'out there' and have another look from even farther back—one last look. When we get back to Earth people will want us to tell them how it looked. . . what we saw. . . what we now know. . . what we have become. . . ." He concluded with a palms-up gesture that signaled his laborious explanation was finally exhausted.

Kurt had continued smiling throughout Bennet's long discourse, a fact that was obviously deC railing Harry's train of thought. His reply was still quiet.

"What you are trying to say is that out of our vast and unprecedented experience on the mission, people will expect us to arrive back on Earth imbued with all of the wisdom of the ages and then some, just because we have been away from it for a while. If that is why they sent us, then I can only say that they sent the wrong people. They should have sent your artist to paint it, or a poet to write about it, or a philosopher who could carry out the first truly objective philosophizing about it, away from all earthly hindrances."

Evan was regarding Kurt curiously, unsure of what was happening, unsure if he was being entirely serious. Kurt leaned forward and lowered his voice still further.

"Perhaps it's even more than that; perhaps they expect us to find some*one* or some*thing* out there. When we meet it they will want us to speak to it for them . . . plead our case . . . tell it why we have done the things we have done . . . ask it where we went wrong—perhaps ask it to forgive us, give us another chance. Perhaps the people of Earth just want an advocate of some sort. You know, they might even be disappointed if we were to come back without a heavenly light surrounding us."

Evan sighed wearily and rolled his eyes to the ceiling. "I can only say that it's lucky you two didn't start talking like that back on the ground or they would have found another mission for you both. They would have handed you over to the Salvos! Now look, you're trying to see us as having some kind of awesome responsibility, when in fact all we really have to do is a job. Let's not make ourselves out to be more important to the world than we really are." He shuffled around to sit against the wall beside Kurt, who was now considering them both more seriously.

"Look," he continued, "say this mission is a complete fizz, and we all float away somewhere and

40

never come back. Do you think they would just call off the human race? They'd be sad for a while of course—all that money wasted and such—but there isn't one living soul back there who could be said to really need any one of us in the way that. . ." Evan caught Kurt's eye and realized that the humor was quite gone. His remarks were poorly worded, and he tried to redirect them in midsentence, "in the way that we're talking about, I mean. . .like philosophers and so on. We'd always be important to families. . .I guess. . .but in the long run we would be as thoroughly forgotten as anyone else."

The hurt had not completely left Kurt's eyes in spite of his attempt to quickly smile through it. A sensitive spot had been touched, and Evan couldn't think of any way to correct it.

It was time to drop the subject, and Evan went back to his meal. Kurt left to check out his hibernation module, and the other two ate for a while in silence. After some minutes Evan spoke.

"That was a rather long speech for you."

"Yes."

"Something bugging you?"

"No."

"You had me a bit worried when you started talking like that—about what we're doing here and so on I mean. I thought you were dropping your bundle." Bennet did not reply but continued eating.

"Are you really having second thoughts about the mission?" Harry raised his eyes and gave Evan a cocker-spaniel kind of look. Then they both laughed.

"Perhaps I have been a bit uptight," Harry

conceded, "but we might as well get used to it; we are all going to be a bit vulnerable in this environment." He raised his eyebrows. "Haven't you worried a bit about it yourself?"

"No," Evan lied.

"Well, other people can be a bit touchy. Kurt's Achilles heel is the fact that he's left his family for seven years, and you weren't particularly bright telling him how little they needed him."

Evan wiped his mouth vigorously with his paper napkin. "Heck! I didn't mean it that way and he knows it. I only reminded him about them, that's all—he would expect to have to do that from time to time anyway." He crawled over to the food dispensing unit and dropped the napkin into the disposal. "Just the same," he added, smiling sheepishly again, "I think I'll go and help him check out his capsule."

The bedding-down operation proceeded smoothly. Kurt Haller would be the first of the three to go into hibernation. He lay in his chamber peacefully, already partially sedated by the time-release capsule which he had swallowed some twenty minutes earlier. His hibernation chamber had not yet commenced its refrigeration cycle; in fact it would not do so until its occupant had been asleep for an hour and all his biological readings had been checked out. Once begun, the entire operation was automatic, and Kurt simply had to lie and wait—not an unpleasant task because the drug tended to create a degree of euphoria in the subject. Sleep would come peacefully and easily.

While sleep would advance upon him gently, it would continue to deepen far beyond the point of normal sleep and, coupled with the drop in bodily temperature, would take him to a point which, to a casual observer, would be indistinguishable from death. The amount of energy required from the ship's systems to maintain this state would be extremely small; and herein was the whole reason for the procedure. The resources of food and energy required were reduced to the merest fraction of what would be required if the men were to be transported in the conscious state over such a long period.

Evan watched the older man through the window of the chamber and noticed that it did not seem quite as sinister now that this quietly self-confident man lay within it.

It only remained now to check on Harry Bennet's bedding down and do a visual examination of the ship. Then he would be free to go into hibernation himself.

His own chamber would be much larger, because he would have the whole command module cabin to himself. It was fitted out with all necessary systems to maintain the same suspended-animation state for him as for the others. A third chamber awaited him in the rim, but with luck he would not have to use it.

He arrived at Bennet's chamber to find him already reclining in the couch. The main light was on, flooding out the eerie blue of the ultraviolet. Bennet did not appear to see him arrive outside the observation window, but lay gazing fixedly at the ceiling. A small indicating panel near Bennet's head revealed that all of the suit monitoring systems had been connected and checked out.

Evan could not help being disturbed by Harry's unnaturally glassy expression, but he concealed his feelings carefully as he pushed open the hatch and slid into the confines of the chamber.

"Hi, that was quick," he said. Bennet flinched, obviously startled by the intrusion, but he smiled with some visible effort.

"Not really; You were probably so busy ear-bashing Kurt that you haven't been watching the time."

Evan glanced at his chronometer and nodded. "You're right. I did punish him a bit....For someone over thirty-five he puts up with it rather well—not like some others I know. Are you going to take your capsule?"

"I took it about ten minutes before you came. Are you talking about your father?"

Evan grinned. "Yes...that wasn't a bad guess."

"Oh, it was easy; you have a voice which comes on whenever you're complaining about him. You've been squabbling again?"

"I didn't realize that I gave so much away," said Evan as he began to leave. Harry would be coming under the influence of the drug fairly soon, and it was important that he be resting quietly.

"I'll have to go now and make some preparations of my own." He was completely through the hatch before Harry spoke.

"Evan..."

"Yes?"

"Don't go for a minute."

Evan put his head back through the hatch. "What do you want?"

Harry looked embarrassed. "Could you stay and talk for a while?"

Evan felt another pang of fear. There was something of a frightened child in Harry's voice that was entirely out of character. By rights he should leave and attend to his own business, but the expression in Harry's eyes convinced him he should stay.

He slid back into the chamber without comment and seated himself beside his friend. He reached above Harry's head and switched off the main light, plunging them into a deep gloom which gradually changed to a bluish color as their eyes began to accommodate the ultraviolet. They sat in silence, each listening to the quiet whispering sounds of the ship; each unsure as to what should be said.

It was Harry who eventually spoke. "I'm sorry, Evan, but for some reason I'm feeling very unhappy about the mission all of a sudden—almost a premonition you might say."

"Don't forget," Evan reminded him, "you haven't taken that hibernation drug before, and it could be having some undesirable side effects."

"Maybe, but I was feeling a bit this way even before I took it." He forced another smile. "You're probably right, though; the drug could well be accentuating some vague feelings I already had. Do you mind staying though? Just for a while?"

Evan could hardly refuse. "No, that's okay."

"What were you talking to Kurt about?" Harry asked, trying to sound conversational.

"Well, as a matter of fact we were talking religion, so—since you are a healthy agnostic—you probably wouldn't be interested."

"Why don't you try me?"

"Oh, it was more or less a continuation of the discussion you started yourself, except that we had moved on to talking about what may well be the only answer for man—the Kingdom."

"Ah, yes, I know about that. God's going to come down and pull the fuse just before it all goes bang, isn't he?"

"It's not quite like that."

"Do you really know what you're talking about?" Harry's tone was only mildly provocative. "From what I know of most faiths, including yours, there are as many different ideas about that as there are religions, and your people don't even agree among themselves."

"That's true," said Evan, warming to the subject, "but many of them go wrong at only one specific point—as you do. They all look at it as something that is going to sort of plop down from heaven and fix everything. . . and as long as it's somewhere in the future they use it as they've always used it—as an excuse to do nothing."

"And your solution?"

"Well, we believe—my church that is—that the Kingdom starts with people who are willing to live in accordance with the idea, and this means if it's ever going to come about we have to be working on it right now."

"What do you imagine this eventual 'triumphant' kingdom to be like?" Harry had some difficulty with the word "triumphant," and it was obvious that the drug was taking effect.

"I don't really have the foggiest, and I don't particularly care either. The greatest problem that people had in the past was that they figured they knew all about it. Because it was always somewhere in the future they saw it in the terms of their present day. Then, when the concept was entirely outdated, they refused to give it up and fought about it."

"And that's what you've been doing with your father—fighting about it."

Evan chuckled. "Yes, you're right again. As a matter of fact we came to such an impasse that I spent the last night of my leave before the mission at a motel rather than sleep at home—terrible place—lots of traffic, flashing signs outside. . ."

"How is it," Harry spoke slowly and deliberately, "that Christians talk about a kingdom that is all sweetness and light and love, yet they disagree over it in one family to the extent that they don't want to live with each other?"

Evan dropped his chin to his chest. "Touché! But you must have heard of the generation gap."

"No, that's not the point; we've talked about this before, and as I see it the disagreement is simple. Your father believes in a literal, dramatic return of Christ while you, when you are pressed, don't."

Evan nodded slowly. "That's about the size of it I guess."

"But you're still going to set the world straight, right?"

Evan could feel himself becoming trapped. "You are

47

an agnostic, so you can't take sides on the issue."

"You didn't answer my question."

"It depends on what you mean by 'setting the world right,' I guess, but yes—given time, people will eventually come around."

Harry made incredulous snorting noises. "You've got to be kidding. How long do you think we have? You know as well as I do that the world is on a collision course with so many problems that no one down there dares to think even five years ahead anymore. If this God you talk of is going to have any say at all in what happens to his Earth, he's certainly not going to have it if he leaves the job to 'Christians.' About all he can expect to do is put his foot in the door before man slams it shut."

"Now I know what the drug's doing to you." Evan grinned. "It's making you argumentative."

Harry smiled. "I think you're right. I feel better for it though. I know it's a rather strange subject for me to get involved in, but I must confess that in this circumstance it does seem to have more relevance than usual."

"Well, it's been said that there are no athiests in foxholes; perhaps we could add to that there are no agnostics in space."

"I wouldn't go that far," Bennet parried. "I just said that if there is any hope for Earth at all, your father's theory seems to hold the most promise."

Evan frowned and pulled his knees up under his chin, his favorite thinking position. "But don't you see how unfair it would be? I mean, everyone would think quite differently about what would be a Shangri-la for him. Some poor underfed Asian would see it as regular meals, his own plot of land, and no more wars. On the other hand the average member of an affluent society like ours—my own father for instance—would see the good life as a continuation of everything he has now, but with a gilt-edged guarantee. Neither would understand the other's life-style, yet the very fact that they are so different is wrong to start with." He spread his hands in a questioning gesture. "But who is wrong? Do you know that my father doesn't approve of the space program? He says it misdirects money, wastes resources, pollutes the planet, and generally makes God cross!

"And yet on the other hand he sees his stewardship as holding down a well-paid job, looking after a luxuriously appointed house, and generally attaining all the conveniences available. He thinks these are his right.

"Now he knows very well that this can't last, but he thinks somehow God is going to step in at the right moment and manage a transition into the Kingdom just in time to spare him any discomfort."

"I like the sound of that," said Harry.

"Yes, but if we're all about to be swept up into this glorious reward as he says, who is going to be able to explain to that poor Asian why my father had the best of everything in life—largely at the expense of the Asian who received none of the benefits, yet they finally end up in the same place?"

"As you said before," Harry was now speaking with his eyes closed, "I don't have to take sides in your argument, but I don't think that either argument is really all that convincing. What I do have to live with is the fact that if neither one is really right, we face a pretty bleak future back on Earth, with man either starving, polluting, or warring himself to death. If God really is going to set it right, we should see some pretty smart footwork in the very near future."

They sat together again in silence, Bennet with his eyes closed and Evan with his knees still up under his chin and lost in his own thoughts. Harry had a point; it was easy enough to talk about growing consciousness but another thing altogether to realistically face the inexorable unfolding of events on Earth. He was frightened, too, just like Harry, and he sensed very strongly the despair which his friend suffered. Whether he entirely agreed with his father about the nature of the Kingdom was relatively unimportant at a time like this; at least he shared a hope. The silent figure beside him was aware of that hope, and he was trying desperately to share in it.

Harry spoke again, although he was now having some difficulty ordering his thoughts. "I'm going to be all right now, Evan...everything's all right. You can go if you want to...."

Evan glanced again at his chronometer; he was running well behind schedule and needed no further invitation to leave. He patted Harry's shoulder gently before backing away. "Sleep well; I'll see you soon. When I get to my station we'll keep voice contact for a while if you like."

"Thanks, but I'll be all right. You can go now."

Evan slid back into the tunnel and secured the hatch with a fair amount of haste. Harry was quietening down now, and that was good. How foolish, he thought, that they should have used that sedative without foreseeing that it could adversely affect some people. This knowledge did nothing for Evan's peace of mind, particularly as he considered the fact that he himself had not had previous exposure to it. "Too bad," he said aloud as he crawled back up the tunnel, "if I want someone to talk to *me*."

He visited Kurt again and found him looking much as he had left him earlier. He tapped lightly on the glass and Kurt responded by opening his eyes and inclining his head briefly in acknowledgment. He would be feeling pretty drowsy and was not wasting any effort.

Evan continued his progress around the ship on his scheduled tour of inspection. He was hurrying now, because he was at least a half hour late. Considering the years ahead, that period of time seemed unworthy of concern, but it was foreign to his training to be so far out of step with the program. He was even a little surprised that Earth had not checked up on the reasons for the delay.

He returned eventually to the annex at the end of the spoke and began to draw himself carefully hand-over-hand toward the center of the ship. He could feel his feet moving slowly away from the cable under the gentle influence of the thrust from the plasma engine.

When he arrived at the central annex he found the acceleration to be more noticeable, and he had to consciously work against it as he pushed open the hatch into the service room. There wasn't much to be done in here other than simply to look around. As he entered it was warmer and noisier than the rest of the ship, and this was mildly comforting. He had never been in this room before, yet he was entirely familiar with it because of the elaborate mock-ups which had been used for his training back on Earth.

In a weightless condition it seemed to be bigger, possibly because all parts of it were accessible to him. The room was actually a large hemisphere of about eleven meters diameter with its base resting against the spoke. It was heavily cluttered with air conditioning and life-support systems.

The visual inspection revealed nothing of note, and he had not expected it to. In any case the entire ship was under the surveillance of the data-logging central computer, and Mission Control would be as familiar with the operational condition of the ship as he himself—if not more so.

Still, the inspection was something that had to be done, and no detail of it escaped his attention. He slid out into the annex again and secured the hatch. The sudden abatement of the equipment noise left him in a sudden uncomfortable silence. There was no doubt about it—it was a little too quiet.

He shrugged off the thought: he knew what was bothering him. . . . In a little while he would be the last person awake half a million kilometers out in space, and the silence added yet another dimension to the enormous loneliness of this position. He let himself fall slowly across the annex to the access conduit into his cabin. He did not enter immediately, but almost as an afterthought moved across to one of the annex windows for one final look back toward Earth. It was a totally unnecessary action, done more to delay the inevitable than anything else, but it was a view well worth stopping for.

The booster was a lot farther away now, and still directly behind the Magellan. It must have gained some slight rotational momentum during jettisoning because it was now on an angle relative to his viewing position, and two of the troublesome ullage engines were visible at the tail end. Almost directly behind it was the earth, looking only moon-size now.

In spite of the speed at which they were traveling, the panorama held him in a spell of frozen beauty, as if the whole strange world in which he now lived had somehow paused for him to consider it. As the scene slowly rotated before him he pressed his head closer to the glass in an effort to see the moon, which was outside of his field of vision. The black curtain of space would be spread with countless stars, but the harsh reflection of the sun from the discarded rocket engine prevented his seeing them either.

Harry had been right; the earth did somehow seem different from out here, and he found himself feeling uncomfortable again as he thought of the conversation in the galley. Harry had a way of being right about a lot of things, and he knew that the subject would cross his mind many more times before the mission was over.

From his vantage point he could see the great bulk of the command module in which he would be housed. From its rear end a long thin pencil of blue light pointed back toward Earth, indicating the silent stream of ions that were propelling them onward toward a fantastic speed.

He turned from the window with a rapid and decisive movement and made his way again to the access conduit. Within minutes he was in his cabin with the hatch closed and secured. The cabin was now under the control of its own life-support systems, as were the hibernation chambers of the other two men. He strapped himself back into his couch and made immediate contact with Bennet.

"How are you, Harry?" There was a long delay before Harry's voice came back to him, rather incoherently.

"Everything's all right now; I'm all right; you can go now. . . ."

Evan closed the switch without answering. He was about to make contact with Earth, but he paused and flipped another switch.

"Kurt?" He listened for several seconds, but there was no reply; Kurt was asleep. He would not be sleeping all that deeply at this stage and in fact could probably be wakened, but Evan did not persist.

He called Earth and received an immediate answer.

"Did you wonder where I was?" he asked.

"No," came the reply. It was Simms speaking. "We could see that the others were a bit slow bedding down so we didn't want to bother you. Bennet is still awake."

"I know," said Evan, smiling. He was not going to let them think they knew more about the state of things on board than he did, even if it was quite true. "I'm shutting down service systems now. Will you check me, please?" On receiving the affirmative reply he began the procedure for preparing the ship for the long first half of the journey. All nonessentials such as air conditioning and lighting were to be shut down on the rest of the ship, and eventually even the air would be removed.

The air conditioning in Evan's cabin was relatively quiet in operation and he could readily detect the overall quietening of the ship as each successive system closed down.

The Magellan did not use the low pressure pure oxygen atmosphere throughout the main body of the ship, primarily because of the heightened fire risk entailed as the occupants moved about on their everyday chores. The hibernation modules, however, including Evan's cabin, would use such an atmosphere during the sleep period, and for this reason their compartments had to be carefully sealed against the normal atmospheric pressure of the rest of the ship.

Only well after the commencement of the hibernation period would the atmospheric pressure of the mother ship be slowly reduced so as to minimize air losses. The transition from normal air to pure oxygen was accomplished slowly and automatically. It had already commenced in the rim hibernation chambers and would soon begin also in Evan's cabin, although the change would not be particularly noticeable to him.

The main body of the craft would be a very forbidding place after a little while. Apart from being dark and almost airless, it would be extremely cold, especially at the outer extremes of the orbit where the sun would be over five times the normal distance away.

Evan completed shutting down the service systems and began to attend to details closer to his own impending sleep. He reconnected the suit umbilicals and telemetry channels which would serve to keep Mission Control informed on his condition. This done, he lay waiting for confirmation from Earth that his efforts were satisfactory.

The control panel before him was alive with information, indicating and recording the progressively changing conditions within the ship as the shutdown continued. Ironically, it would continue to do so even after he was asleep, because the ship's monitoring systems were perpetually awake. The occupants of the ship would rely ever increasingly on these watchful eyes as the ship moved farther from earth, and the time required for a corrective instruction from Mission Control gradually increased.

The information on the panel was of little interest to Evan now, for his work was nearly done, and it remained only for the Houston technologists to advise him that all was well, and that he too could go into hibernation. As he lay quietly, he watched the harsh glare of the sun creep slowly around his cabin as the ship turned endlessly on its axis. His couch was comfortable and the atmosphere inside the cabin was warm and quiet; it was going to be easy to settle down in this womb-like environment.

A message from Mission Control broke the silence. "Hello, Magellan. Everything is looking very good down here. Do you have any worries?"

"No, thanks. Are the others asleep?"

"Haller is well asleep, but Bennet could still be awake. We wouldn't trouble him though."

Evan thought for a moment but still spoke impulsively. "I have a medical query."

There was a short delay before the answer arrived. "Did you say you had a medical query?"

"Yes."

"Stand by, Magellan." There was another delay and a different voice answered. "Hello, Magellan—do your worst."

Evan laughed. "It's not all that serious, but could you tell me what the normally expected side effects of the hibernation drug should be?"

"It's very slow acting, and as long as the patient is relaxed the onset of effects should be almost unnoticed. They would simply be drowsiness and perhaps a sense of euphoria."

"Would they cause depression?"

"Put it this way," came the reply. "That hasn't been an observed symptom during tests."

"Such as they were," Evan muttered.

"What was that?"

"Forget it," said Evan. His hand strayed nervously to the switches on the communications panel, as if to reassure himself that Harry was not party to the conversation. "Would it be likely to cause any irresponsible attitude or reaction in the subject while he is still mobile?"

Simms spoke again, cutting across the other voice. "Have you had trouble, Evan?"

"No, not really. Kurt seemed to react pretty much as

you describe, but Bennet seemed depressed and agitated."

The second voice returned. "Can you describe his reactions a little better than that?"

"I'm not at all sure how to describe them. He seemed to be preoccupied with matters not directly involved with the mission. . . .He spoke about. . .well, . . .premonitions and the like."

"Was he irrational?"

"Not at all. In fact he was rather uncomfortably lucid. I stayed and talked to him for a while and he seemed to relax."

There was another long delay from the ground. Obviously the problem was being discussed. Simms eventually answered.

"Hello, Magellan," the voice was falsely optimistic. "The general feeling down here is that Harry is only suffering a few jitters. The way you describe him checks out pretty well with what we have already observed; he is not resting well at all. You did the right thing in staying with him."

"Did the drug have anything to do with it?" Evan persisted. He was sharply conscious of the feeling that they were trying to placate him.

"Frankly, Evan, we just don't know, but if he was calmed by your being with him, it doesn't sound very serious even if it was the drug."

"I'm glad you mentioned that," said Evan, not a little sarcastically, "because it sort of occurs to me that if I am adversely affected also there isn't going to be anyone here to hold *my* hand."

"We'll hold voice contact as long as you like."

"That's not going to help much if I become irresponsible, is it?"

"We have no fears on that score, Magellan." The fact that he was again being called Magellan signaled that the conversation was ended, so he let it drop. He shifted to a more comfortable position and began securing himself firmly to the couch with his safety harness. He took the small capsule from a pocket at the front of his suit and popped it into his mouth in as matter-of-fact a manner as he could muster. Being careful not to chew it, he flushed it down with a small plastic bubble of water stowed at the side of his couch. It was done now, and he resolved to concern himself with it no further. He grinned. Come to think of it, his interrogation of the people at Mission Control probably hadn't gone over too well. It was a pretty useless sort of argument in any case; he was on his way now, and there was nothing Mission Control could do.

He had known about these problems for a long time, but chose not to mention them. It was much easier to be critical now . . . now that he couldn't be fired.

He called the ground again. "I've taken my medicine."

"We copy that, Magellan," came the immediate reply. "Are you comfortable?"

"Yes, thank you."

"We won't worry you any further now unless it's necessary. Everyone down here wishes you the best of luck and a safe journey. We'll be keeping an eye on you."

"Thanks, Houston. Would you mind passing a message to my father?"

"By all means, Evan. What's the word?"

Evan smiled as he answered. "Tell him that he just may be right."

"Is that all?"

"Yes, thanks. Bye-bye."

"Good-bye, Magellan."

He reached above his head and flipped a switch. The cabin fell deathly quiet as the background noise from the communications channel vanished. He switched on the ultraviolet, although in his cabin—so brightly illuminated from outside—it was not visible.

The effect of finishing the contact with Earth was just a little too traumatic, and he eased it by flipping on the canned music, something he had not done up till now. The mere intrusion of the sound made him feel better, and he closed his eyes, consciously relaxing each muscle in sequence until he was entirely relaxed. In the weightless state it was not easy to tell whether he was fully relaxed or not.

He opened his eyes again. From his position in the center couch he could see most of the rest of the ship through the observation windows. The giant spoke stretched away from him and if he put his head forward a little he could see to the outer rim. He studied the view for a while, idly trying to visualize where different sections of the ship were relative to his position.

It would help a little, he thought, if there were even some illusion of speed. The stark, white outline of the ship seemed to be set so sharply against the darkness that it was easy to convince oneself that all movement in the universe had ceased, frozen at this instant forever. He shivered slightly at the chilling thought, then quickly dismissed it, realizing that he had resolved not to become morose, as Bennet's reaction had clearly warned.

He concentrated instead on some of the positive aspects. Some very difficult and dangerous maneuvers had already been carried out successfully, and for the time being at least the heat was off.

He flipped off the background music—he didn't need that either—and he lay relishing the silence. He was beginning to feel drowsy now, and he felt assured that sleep would come easily.

He reached to the communications panel and opened a switch very gently.

"Harry?" There was no answer.

Chapter Three

"Hello, Magellan."

Evan's head snapped forward in alarm. He had been dozing comfortably, and the unexpected communication startled him—at least he *thought* there had been a communication. Maybe it was only a vivid dream. If it was a communication, it must have come on the emergency channel, as he had closed the main one.

He felt numbly for the communications panel and replied cautiously. "Houston?"

"Hello, Magellan; we're sorry to have to disturb you." The tone was both anxious and apologetic.

"Disturb me! You scared the daylights out of me; I was nearly asleep."

"Yes, we know that, but we seem to have a bit of a problem that you should know about." Evan was looking at the data-logging panel directly in front of him; it showed all systems to be perfectly normal. His mind was decidedly befogged and the remarks from Earth seemed annoyingly irrelevant.

"There's no sweat here, Houston; you must have a gremlin down there."

"There's no trouble aboard Magellan, Evan, but we

are getting some rather weird telemetry from the final stage booster."

That didn't sound like sufficient reason to wake him up, and Evan allowed some of his irritation to show in his voice. "I don't have that item on board, Houston; we threw it away—don't you remember?" His question was not acknowledged directly; the reply was a lightly veiled order. "We've discussed the matter here, Magellan, and the feeling is that you should have a look at it for us."

Evan was becoming more annoyed. "Look, Houston, it may be news to you, but I can't see the booster from here unless we do an attitude change."

"We don't want to do that at this stage, but we do suggest that you go into the main ship and take a look from the annex. Try to conserve your energy as much as possible to avoid any premature side effects from the drug."

Evan cursed to himself. They seemed to know about the drug all of a sudden. He commenced the procedure for reuniting his cabin systems with the rest of the ship. There was little pressure differential at this stage fortunately, and it would not be a lengthy operation. To waste time arguing over the necessity or otherwise of carrying out the operation would only allow the pressure differences to proceed still further.

The noises of the ship gradually returned as the air conditioning and life-support systems sprang to life once more. Evan watched the data-logger screen dispassionately, and as he did so he began to recover his cool. The situation was obviously serious or he would not have been interrupted in this way. They were being pretty patient with him really.

"What kind of information are you getting back?" he asked.

"It's a little difficult to say; she was holding antenna alignment quite well, and then we lost it rather suddenly—as if she was disoriented. We don't know the reason for it, but then we couldn't explain that ullage failure either...."

"Could they be related problems?"

"That's what bothers us, Evan. The effect was rather consistent with an explosion. There's a lot of unburned fuel left in that thing, and this is why we'd like that visual check."

"Is it likely to be a hazard?" The question was not a fearful one—just a request for information.

"Well, it's as simple as this....If anything has happened to shift that thing out of position, we have a more than academic interest in exactly where it went."

The serious inference was not lost on Evan. There was danger that the booster could collide with Magellan. With its antenna alignment lost it had literally "gone missing" as far as Houston was concerned, and there was no way of determining its position or the direction in which it was moving.

A green light appeared suddenly on the panel. "I have the okay to open the hatch now, Houston. Will you stand by please?" He unsnapped his safety harness and unplugged his suit connections. He bumped his head against the wall of the cabin as he moved away from the couch, and this served to remind him that his faculties were not all that they should be. He steadied himself momentarily before operating the air valve to open the hatch. There was a sudden, explosive hiss of air as the hatch swung inward to reveal the access conduit.

He had his head and shoulders well into the conduit before he realized that it was very dark at the other end; he had failed to switch on the main ship lights. He frowned and shook his head in annoyance as he backed into the cabin and switched them on. He just had to concentrate; he was not thinking at all well, and at a time when he was required to be very alert!

He emerged into the annex with exaggerated care, making use of the mild acceleration to keep him against the wall. Even as he advanced slowly toward the row of windows he saw something flashing out there. He could see the reflection against the edge of the window.

Although forewarned to some degree, he was quite unprepared for the sight that greeted him. The giant booster was not just out of position—it was cartwheeling rapidly in space, flashing like a giant scimitar as it intermittently caught the light of the sun. Evan shook his head in fogged disbelief; it was incredible that the engine could have been accelerated to such a degree without breaking in half.

The reason for its behavior was only too apparent; a large side panel at the lower end was missing entirely, leaving a gaping hole in its side and distorting the bell-shaped engine outlet into an irregular oval. One of the ullage engines had completely annihilated itself, and in so doing had sent the whole craft into a wild spin.

Another vital fact took a short time to register with

him, but when it did, his mouth turned dry. The frantically spinning monster was a little closer—not much, but quite sufficient to be discernible. That was all he needed to know, and he scrambled back into his cabin with as much haste as his drugged condition would allow. He was slightly breathless by the time he contacted Earth.

"Hello, Houston."

"Go ahead, Magellan."

"That thing of yours...it's waggling all over the place. One of the ullage engines has exploded and given the whole gizmo a king-sized kick in the pants."

"Is it a hazard, Magellan?" Evan hesitated for a moment, realizing that he was not entirely sure.

"I think so, Houston. It appears to be closer." He waited impatiently while the information was digested on Earth. He was perspiring profusely, and the atmosphere in the cabin seemed to have become unbearably heavy. "Too much activity," he muttered to himself. It was going to be difficult to stay awake for all that much longer.

"How are you feeling, Evan?"

He wanted to say "lousy" but that would hardly have been a professional response.

"I'm having some difficulty concentrating, but I think I can manage for a bit longer."

"That's good, because it looks as if you may have to get some more information for us. We want you to tell us two things, Okay?"

"Yes, Houston."

"Here they are." Simms was speaking slowly and

deliberately. "First, try to ascertain if it is moving on a collision course. Do you copy that?"

"Yes."

"Second, try to estimate its closing speed and rate of spin."

"It's turning over in its length about once a second, Houston, but I'd have to go and have another look regarding the other items. Will you stand by, please?"

From the annex window he tried in vain to estimate the relative movement between Magellan and its dangerous companion. There was simply nothing working in his favor. Against the vast backdrop of space there was no visual reference with which he could effectively align himself, a problem further complicated by the continual rotation of the whole scene. Added to this was the factor of the hibernation drug which was now impairing his concentration to an alarming degree.

"I'm sorry, Houston," he explained back in the cabin, "but I just can't determine the information you want. The only things I can say with some certainty are that it is coming closer and it's coming faster than we can outrun. Whether we are going to collide I can't yet tell."

"Stand by," said Houston. "We'll tackle it another way." There was silence from Earth for an unbearably long period of time. Evan could feel his consciousness striving to slip away, and he battled desperately against it. Eventually Mission Control intruded again.

"Hello, Evan, are you still okay?"

"Yes, but only . . ."

"Look, Evan, we realize it must be getting pretty

hard for you, so we're going to try and handle things as much as possible. Now here's what we want you to do. It's not much, and once you've done it you can settle down again, and it won't matter if you sleep."

"Okay, Houston, but make it quick."

"Good. We're about to shut down the main engine and do an attitude change. We'll roll the whole ship ninety degrees and give you visual contact from your cabin." The readout in front of him showed that the maneuver had already commenced. "While we're doing that we'll get you to set the camera up to give us a view out the window. Okay?"

"What about the spin of my ship?"

"That's no problem; we can stop the action down here just so long as the camera pans it. A succession of shots like that should give us enough to work from. Now...secure your cabin again for hibernation, will you?"

Evan sealed the hatch again with as much haste as his failing dexterity would allow, then reconnected his suit and loosely fitted his seat harness.

The control panel continued to indicate the slowly changing attitude of the ship, although there seemed to be no other indication of change.

There were some rather obvious risks in the action that Mission Control was taking. Cutting the main engine would leave the closing speed of the booster constant, and no one knew whether the time could be spared to roll the ship into the new position. Yet to indiscriminately change course in the vague hope of avoiding a collision might well carry Magellan into the path of the runaway rocket. This was the wisest course.

A flash of light caught his eye and caused him to turn his head. It was the reflected light from the Earth as it began to show through his cabin windows. He watched it as it rose slowly, passing from window to window and giving him the first visual indication of the change in the ship's attitude.

An additional flash of light also appeared, but a far more terrifying one. There was no cause for doubt in Evan's mind now; it was clearly getting closer with every passing minute. He could read the identifying signwriting on its side now as it spun menacingly toward him. His first reaction was to tell Earth that he feared a collision, but it was a little way off yet and he would do better to simply set up the camera as he had been asked.

This he did, mounting it on the bracket at the head of his couch which had been provided for the purpose. The bracket had been placed to provide visual contact with the astronauts during the closing stages of the mission, but it had not been placed with a view toward televising through the window. Evan discovered to his despair that it was not possible to arrange it in this way. He was obliged once more to unstrap himself and disconnect his suit in order to find some alternative mounting.

"What's the trouble, Magellan?" Ground control was becoming concerned with the delay. Evan ignored the question and fumbled among the equipment that cluttered the cabin in a vain effort to wedge the camera into a suitable position.

"We have a picture, Magellan, but it's moving about too much. . . . Use the mounting pedestal at the head of your couch."

"I tried that. . . . It doesn't work." Evan snapped. "Just give me a chance, will you?"

Mission Control waited quietly. He discovered eventually that he could use the pedestal simply by mounting the camera in the opposite direction. It was too loose, but he succeeded in tying it down with its own connecting cable.

An excited interruption came from Earth. "Hold it there, Evan, we just saw it go past—hold it there."

He reconnected his suit and slipped his harness on loosely while he waited for Mission Control to collect information.

"We have a couple of shots of it, Evan," he was finally advised, "and it doesn't look good. We haven't confirmed the approach precisely yet, but it looks as if we may have tipped the ship the wrong way."

Evan gritted his teeth in exasperation. For all the directions in which they could have turned it they had chosen the wrong one! The thrusters mounted at various points around the ship were intended only for attitude changes and would be quite incapable of shifting the entire ship out of the collision path. The main plasma engine would manage a little better, but it would have to be facing the right way. It was becoming obvious even to Evan that starting the main engine would only carry Magellan farther into the path of the booster. His voice shook as he spoke. "I think it's going to hit us, Houston. You'll have to try for another attitude change." He closed his eyes in response to the burgeoning tiredness which was beginning to engulf him.

"Negative, Magellan—we haven't time. We have a decision coming up now. Stand by, will you please?"

Evan forced his eyes open and peered myopically at the terrifying spectacle outside. It didn't seem as close as all that, but then he couldn't make much sense out of anything now. The whole scenario was becoming progressively more unreal—a kind of cold, numbing dream in which all of the elements were becoming increasingly detached from once another.

Simms spoke to him as if from a great distance. "You're going to have to go it alone, Evan . . . stand by for separation."

The content of the message burned into Evan's brain, rending the drug-induced fog like a veil. They were going to try to rescue him alone and leave the Magellan to her fate! He summoned all of his remaining faculties to bellow a reply.

"No! . . . no, not yet . . . try to wake Harry!"

"Negative, Magellan."

"Let me call him . . . please!"

"Stand by for separation, Magellan." They were warning him of the coming explosive shock.

"Oh, no you're not!" Evan tore the seat harness from his body and launched himself across the cabin. The suit umbilicals suddenly became taut and swung him in a fierce arc against the wall. He tore them away also and made for the hatch. His wild urgency seemed to give him new dexterity and he operated the hatch valve with one swift movement. It swung open again; there was immediate response from the ground.

"Check your hatch, Evan—we've lost differential."

He ignored the communication and began working with a cool efficiency which belied his true condition. He opened a switch on the communications panel and spoke in a firm, level voice. "Bennet, do you read me?" He waited for a few seconds. . . . "Harry, do you read me? Wake up!"

Ground control continued to call him, apparently unaware that Evan had himself sabotaged the operation and prevented his separation from the mother ship. Someone would catch on soon, of course. He solved the problem by simply switching all Earth channels off. With this distraction removed he called Bennet again.

"Harry! Wake up!" This time Bennet responded with a grunt, and Evan followed it up quickly. "Can you hear me, Harry? Wake up!"

Harry's voice came back . . . heavy with sleep. "I'm all right now . . . everything's all right now . . . call me later." Evan struggled for a moment to make sense out of the remark, but he could not.

He tried again. "Harry, you must wake up and come here, We're in a lot of trouble . . . please listen to me . . . can you understand me?"

"I'm all right now—you can go if you want to."

"Harry! For pity's sake try to understand . . . you've got to get out!"

There was no further reply.

Evan spun around and literally hurled himself through the access conduit. There was little to be achieved by calling Harry any more and even less in calling Kurt—he had to go and get them himself, even if he had to carry them. He hit his head on just about every obstacle along the way, but he was now quite devoid of feeling. He covered the distance along the spoke in what surely was record time and, in spite of his condition, succeeded in opening the hatch and dropping into the rim with remarkable speed. He blundered against the hatch of Harry's hibernation chamber and tried desperately to open it. It was completely unyielding.

This was an unexpected development. He struggled vainly with the locking wheel for a full minute before the cause of his difficulty suddenly dawned upon him. The interlocks! He sat back suddenly against the wall of the tunnel. He had forgotten the interlocks! He felt his face drain of blood. He had forgotten the interlocks!

Harry's cabin had begun its depressurizing cycle and the automatic pressure-operated safety devices were in operation to prevent anyone inadvertently unlocking the hatch while the dangerous difference in pressure was present. He had reversed the cycle for his own cabin, but in his drugged haste he had not thought to do the same thing for Harry and Kurt. He was numb with shock. He had goofed, and the consequences for the other men would be death!

He threw himself against the hatch in senseless anger, striving by sheer force to drag it from its hinges, a feat which he well knew to be entirely impossible. Harry could do it! Harry could repressurize his cabin from in there! Evan scrambled desperately to the viewing window and beat on it with his fists. "Harry! Harry! Please hear me! Wake up!"

Harry stirred only slightly and turned his face away. Evan beat desperately against the inch-thick glass with the flat of his hand until it seemed that every bone in it would break, calling continually until his voice also began to break with the strain. There must have been a fair amount of noise inside the cabin, but Bennet showed no sign of response at all.

Evan slumped weakly, then rested his forehead against the glass and wept tears of rage and frustration. There was no time to go back and start again; it would take almost half an hour for the depressurization to take place even after he got back to his cabin.

He spun decisively away from the window and shuffled through the tunnel, intending to visit Kurt's chamber also, but as he arrived under the spoke he paused, realizing that the situation would be no different there. He sat on the floor, tortured by indecision. It was his fault, and he owed it to Kurt to go and try!

Then he shook his head; that wasn't even logical. The problem was that he lacked the courage to make a repugnant decision. He climbed slowly through the hatch and, although the action was superfluous, secured it again with meticulous care. It took him a long time to reach the entrance to his cabin, not only because of his slower reflexes but also because he was losing his ability to comprehend the seriousness of his position; it no longer seemed particularly necessary to hurry.

With what amounted to an almost superhuman effort, he clambered back into his cabin and strapped himself to the couch for what seemed to be the hundredth time. The suit umbilical cables were drifting across the cabin, obviously damaged, so he didn't bother to connect them; such trivialities no longer seemed to carry any importance.

Actually, nothing seemed very important any more. He had not even bothered to look out at the advancing booster, although he knew that it must surely be right upon him.

The Mission Control people were no doubt still trying to contact him, but there was nothing left now to be said. If they didn't know what he had been doing, he certainly was not going to bother explaining it all to them. He had taken matters into his own hands, and it was now his ship; he alone would decide what should be done!

He gazed unsteadily at the instrument panel and realized that it was not entirely his ship, because Mission Control had restarted the main engine, and the attitude had changed again.

But of course! It was an attempt to move the entire ship out of the booster's path. He could see it now from his position on the couch, and the immense shadow flashing across his cabin windows told him that the attempt was quite futile.

The answer was clear; he would carry out the separation himself. He reached above his head and began trying to remove the thumbscrews securing a small red plate. His fingers were too numb for the job, so he removed his gloves, flicking them across the cabin before trying again.

Eventually it was free, and the cover pivoted

around to reveal a small turnkey. With a grunt of satisfaction he grasped the key clumsily and turned it.

Nothing happened.

He remained in the same position, hand on key, for several seconds, frowning oafishly in an attempt to understand what was wrong. Then he gave a slightly hysterical chuckle as he caught sight of the open hatch. It was indeed fortunate in this instance that the controls were interlocked, because he would otherwise have just signed his own death warrant.

He released his harness yet again and closed the hatch, then looked out at the booster. It was so close as to seem to occupy the whole sky. As he looked, the huge, grotesquely distorted bell of the rocket engine swooped up toward him, and he instinctively jerked his head back in anticipation of a collision. Miraculously it missed, and he found himself suddenly propelled by the brute strength of panic as he flung himself back across the cabin. He ignored the safety harness and made directly for the turnkey, turning it so violently that his body pirouetted suddenly in the opposite direction.

There was a sharp crackle of exploding bolts, and the panel before him leaped into his face with such stunning force as to produce a shower of brilliant white lights before his eyes. He remained crammed against the wall of the cabin, held there by the sheer acceleration of the separation rockets as they punched the command module clear of the mother ship. There had been no battening down for separation, and it seemed at once as if every component within the cabin had broken loose. The camera dashed itself against the panel behind his head, hurled there by the sudden, short thrust of the solid-fueled rockets. The main engine was still in operation, but its relatively mild thrust was of little consequence.

The acceleration ceased, but before Evan could recover himself there was yet another shuddering impact which spun him across the cabin again and into the opposite wall. He caught a brief glimpse of dark globules trailing behind him and then splattering against the window—his own blood!

The cabin was spinning rapidly now, thrown wildly out of kilter by some secondary impact, and the centrifugal force held him spreadeagled with his face pressed hard to the blood-reddened window. An awful scene careered repetitively across his line of vision like a series of bizarre lantern slides. He saw the great wheel of the Magellan fold suddenly and silently over and upon itself, engulfing the booster in a violent, splintering embrace. He saw further brief glimpses as they sped away from him, turning over and over like a pair of weird dancers spinning into the blackness.

A gigantic blue and orange carnation bloomed silently in space, and next time round there was nothing but thousands of glittering stars which gradually spread out and dispersed as the shattered fragments of the ship diluted themselves into the emptiness. His craft lurched again, hit by a sudden hail of fragments, and then it was all finished. The silence returned, and it was as if the Magellan had never been. He was alone.

He strained to lift his head from the window, then allowed it to slump back again. His nose was bleeding profusely, and the blood was spreading over the glass, creating a weird effect as the sun passed behind it with each spin of the craft—a flashing red light which blinked on and off with mechanical regularity. In a curious way it reminded him of something—that flashing red neon sign outside the motel room; the one that had kept him awake for so long—on and off, on and off, tirelessly repeating its senseless message... whatever it was.

He shut his eyes in an effort to block it out, but it continued to show clearly through his eyelids. How could he sleep with that going on all night? What a ridiculous place to put a neon sign!

He tried to lift his head again, but some gigantic weight was pressing down on the back of his neck. It was growing gradually heavier, pressing harder and harder until he thought he could stand it no longer. He dropped his head back, but the force continued mercilessly, crushing the very consciousness from his brain. The light began to flash brighter with every second, and the noise of the traffic increased, too, rising to a volume that produced pain in his ears.

And then suddenly, inexplicably, it ceased. The pain and the sound were gone, and his body was flooded with glorious peace. The light still flashed, but it was fainter and less aggressive.

This was what he had waited for—the chance to sleep! He needed it so much, and now he had his chance! As he began to slip away he thought for an instant about the argument at home.... It wasn't all that important really, certainly no reason for him to miss out on sleep! Still he would have to ring his

mother in the morning, even if only to tell her he was
sorry.

He had lain for almost an hour in that dreadful
motel room, waiting for the adrenalin to wear off. The
sounds of the afternoon were still in his ears—his
father's incessant preaching, his mother's pathetic
attempts at mediation, and his own foolish words.
Then there was the slamming of the screen door as he
stomped out of the house, his mother calling after him,
innocent and uncomprehending victim of their
warfare. He could still hear her as he threw his
luggage into the trunk. "Evan! Please don't go. Don't
be silly; please. . .not on your last night at home!" He
heard her come to the door. "George! Please go after
him, . . .tell him to stay! Please stop him!"

The sounds stopped abruptly as he slammed the car
door. Of course his father would not come after him!
He was every bit as intransigent as Evan himself.

He had no desire to lie to people about his early
arrival back at the base, so he settled for the motel. He
had been far too stirred up to notice what kind of place
it was until he began trying to sleep. It was then that
the traffic noise and the neon sign had begun adding
their burden to his angry mind.

In a way characteristic of motel curtains, being
pulled across one end simply produced a shaft of light
at the other, and a high window had no curtain at all.
He tried unsuccessfully to hang his suit off the top
window frame as an additional cover and succeeded

only in arousing the interest of people outside.

So he sat back in the bed and glared belligerently at the opposite wall. His annoyance was becoming much harder to maintain now, and he was no longer enjoying it. He *had* been a little childish, he conceded to himself, but it would be quite useless to go back, for childish or not he knew that it would happen all over again. It was a perplexing thought. He could reason the problem rationally from here, and yet he knew that he could not count on behaving rationally once he was home again.

It was primarily a matter of perception—not that he was unperceptive, or that he simply misunderstood his father, but rather that his perception was too acute. To understand a fellow human is good only to a certain degree; beyond this point the other party finds himself revealed, a position no man will tolerate, least of all someone like Evan or his father.

Added to this was the fact that the personalities of the two men were so similar as to give them each a cruel insight into the other. Being so heavily armed with the truth, they were able to inflict grievous wounds.

The argument about the Kingdom was simply the chosen field of battle for that day, a vehicle for the continuing conflict, and it had provided rich source material. They suffered the dilemma of all men in that they carried a dual standard, serving both as a guide to life and, incredibly, a justification for the life lived. This was a contradiction, one standard reaching for the stars and the other grasping for the sweet balm of security. Whatever the final life position of either of the two men, it was to be defended at all costs, for to acknowledge any truth under an attack was to be confronted by the specter of the true self.

In a day beset by more problems than ever before, professing Christians were beginning to claw desperately at their previously ignored eschatological concepts, and the weaknesses were becoming painfully apparent. Evan's father was past middle age—beyond the days of fervent hopes and already into the growing twilight of the acceptance of dreams not realized. It was reasonable, then, that the Kingdom would be obliged to confirm to him that he had not *really* been commissioned to change the world, however much he may first have thought so. After all, he was supposed to be *in* the world, not of it, and who could stand in judgment of him in this respect? The answer, of course, was he himself and any other who knew him accurately enough.

On the other hand, Evan was a young man—active, confident, and capable within the fields he understood. He lived in a world which he could manipulate with his own hands, and he looked with great disfavor on those who would excuse themselves from the task. This was the point of collision. Yet in his own way Evan was equally unprepared to face the truth. It was a relatively simple task to pontificate on a society as it ought to be—an excellent source of instant satisfaction in fact—but to maintain such an attitude required ignoring many harsh realities.

It meant first that one had to pretend to have the answers—answers wrapped up in convenient phrases to be aired at every possible opportunity. It meant also that the blame for things not being as they should be had to be placed at the door of another generation.

In spite of all the ostensible friction, there was not that much difference between the positions of the two men. George Westering explained away the state of the world by saying that he had no power to save it, while Evan simply argued that he had not yet had the opportunity.

This was typical of the arguments of the day, and there were strong reasons why the dialogue, however unfruitful, should continue. The latter part of the seventies had seen an escalation of the world's problems to a point where no one could choose to be a casual observer, and everyone was at war. While the awful prospect of nuclear annihilation was ever present, the immediate problem was one of urban strife, and most of the developed countries were in fact if not officially in a state of civil war. The urban guerrilla activities at the inner core of most major cities made them effectively a no-man's land over which the forces of law and order exercised no more control than a degree of containment. Pollution and environmental tampering had stretched the ecosystems of the earth to a point where it was becoming obvious that it could not recover.

It was not just a matter of national difficulty; the world itself was terminally ill, and mankind had become paralyzed by a kind of future shock from which no power seemed able to shake it. Herein, perhaps, was the greatest difficulty—the mere absence of hope. Historically it had been shown that mankind was capable of surmounting any adversity—as long as there remained a light at the end of the tunnel, as long as there remained another day. Such a hope had, for most inhabitants of the world, sputtered and died. There had been a time, not long before, when the earth had resounded with the cries of groups espousing this cause or that. Now, suddenly, they were all gone.

The reason for their demise was simple. The day of dialogue was long past, and as each movement had risen to the task only to falter and fall, it was simply discarded. No second opportunity was afforded to anyone. The greatest single casualty was clearly conventional religion. Unable to produce even a partial solution, it had strangled on its own words.

Such was the problem for Evan and his parents. Certainly, they were among the fortunate few who at least sustained a hope, but that hope was centered around concepts to which insufficient thought had been given. The pressure was becoming unbearable. As unwilling as they were to accept it, they were developing the notion that the plans God may have had for the world would be far removed from any scheme which they themselves had imagined. It was something which had to be thought out all over again!

Evan had begun thinking about this. Maybe they were both wrong; maybe everybody was wrong! If so, it was surely too late for rectification.

Weariness began to overtake him at this point, and he lay down in his bed. He closed his eyes and could still see that flashing light, but now it troubled him little. There was a problem to be thought out here, but he was tired. It would have to wait until morning.

Mission Control was in a state of shock, and the waves of that shock traveled swiftly around the world. There had been an accident, and all the spacemen were dead! A specialist organization consisting of thousands of people had become in one instant an incredible white elephant. Its entire resources, its eyes, its ears, its very purpose had been directed solely onto a receding speck in space—and now it was gone!

It was not just the end of the mission; it was the end of the space program, the final death of a dream. It was as Harry Bennet had said; there were some five billion people on board, and they were all lost too!

There was no doubt on Earth as to what had happened. There had been good telemetry in spite of Evan's silence, right up to only a few minutes before the collision when the booster had begun to obstruct transmission. There was no way of knowing, therefore, that one of the crew escaped the disaster. Not that it would have been of any help to know, for the small surviving portion of the ship was quite out of control, with no hope of establishing antenna alignment and consequently no hope of recovery. Had the separation been carried out under control from Earth it would have been at least feasible to have kept Evan in hibernation and used the plasma engine to effect a relatively early return. Freed from the great bulk of the mother ship, the engine would have been much more flexible.

As it was, the engine would simply continue to operate aimlessly until it either ran out of fuel or suffered an operational failure, and that could extend into many years. The tumbling motion of the ship

84

would eventually be slowed by the continuous thrust of the engine, and where it would go from there no one could even hope to predict.

Evan had been somewhat prophetic himself, because as time passed, the three astronauts were indeed forgotten in almost the way he had said. It was not that the people of earth were necessarily short on memory, but rather that they were long on problems.

Man had failed on his last desperate bid for the stars, and he would never look up at them again. The very foundations of his being were beginning to crumble beneath him.

Far away from Earth, the small spacecraft traveled an unplanned path toward a never conceived destination. It was no longer tumbling, but had settled down to an even and almost purposeful course. A long, thin shaft of blue light stretched behind it as the coldly efficient engine, no longer encumbered by the dead mass of the main craft, continued to accelerate it along its self-chosen way.

The sun was far distant now, and it illuminated the ship with something equivalent only to bright moonlight. To an outside observer, it would have appeared that the ship was suspended motionless in space, although it was traveling at almost five hundred kilometers per second and would continue to accelerate for as long as the plasma engine was operative.

Its internal systems were functioning perfectly, and

it was quite untroubled by the unscheduled change to the program. It had been designed to operate if necessary quite independent from the mother ship, and it seemed now to almost relish the opportunity. With great dedication the onboard computer went about the task of monitoring the life-support systems, metering out oxygen and carefully adjusting the temperature within the cabin, like a brooding mother tending the needs of her sleeping child. In the cold reaches of space, Evan was protected only by his fragile cocoon from the hostile void around him.

Time and distance meant nothing to the craft, for such concepts were well outside the compass of the machine intelligence which now served as captain. The computer would attend to its duties for many years if permitted, but one day, without alarm or regret, it would simply stop, and the last shred of Magellan would be gone.

Inside Evan slept—a sleep as deep and dark as the space which cradled him.

Chapter four

Evan opened his eyes and shut them again quickly. A searing white light burned into his brain; then a purple triangle appeared before him as his retinas responded belatedly to what they had seen. He kept his eyes shut for a little longer; the sight meant absolutely nothing to him, but he felt far too sick to care about that. He was a disembodied being floating in a sea of pain, and he wished only to escape back into the peace of sleep.

The purple triangle began slowly to grow fainter and less clearly defined. As it did so, the pain faded too, leaving behind only a sense of weakness so great that it seemed to be crushing him. He waited patiently, expecting it to pass, and as it did he began again to be aware of the light through his closed lids.

He risked peeping again, and had another brief glimpse of a harsh white triangle. It wasn't pure white—more of a bone color—and seemed to have a strange, lumpy texture to it. The triangle meant something to him this time—he wasn't sure what—but he felt somehow that it would come to him soon!

A wave of the tiredness swept toward him, and he consciously relaxed, allowing it to pass. Then he went back to the problem. He had been asleep or sick or something which he just couldn't recall. He would remember though...it was just a matter of working on it.

The motel...he was in the motel! It was morning, and he had slept much later than he had planned! His head pained again as the details of the argument the night before crowded into his mind. The neon sign was gone, and there was not even a sound of traffic. Actually, he thought with some relief, he wasn't due back at the base until evening, and he could probably afford a little more time in bed.

But that wasn't right! He'd been back to the base sometime; he could remember it clearly now. He wasn't in the motel, he was somewhere else. He struggled inwardly to resolve the contradictions, and the agonizing tiredness swept over him again as he did so.

He opened his eyes once more and found that he could now tolerate the light. The triangle was still there—a white triangle of quilted upholstery, familiar upholstery; he had seen it before often...but where? His body was without feeling; he had arms, hands, legs, and feet somewhere, but he could neither feel them or determine where they were.

He swiveled his eyes painfully to find that there was much more to the scene. Then it all suddenly erupted into his understanding! The triangle was the harsh light of the sun on the padded interior of his spaceship cabin shaped by the small triangular window through which it came.

He remembered the accident now, and a feeling of cold shock caused the weakness to sweep him again.

Where was he? What was happening to him now? The collision! Was it minutes ago? Hours ago? Perhaps years? It seemed at best to be some not quite remembered experience embedded in a past which he would be happy to forget.

But he *had* to remember! He could see that he was not lying on his couch and he was not pressed to the window as he could last recall. He was lying at the front of the cabin near the entrance to the access conduit and looking back toward the three couches. The severed umbilicals from his own couch stretched out straight across the cabin toward him, as if he were lying on the floor and they were hanging down from the ceiling. There was something rather odd about that, but he felt too ill to ponder it for the moment.

His faculties crawled tenuously back toward him, and he was able to begin mentally exploring the possibilities. They were all terrifying! Maybe his neck had been broken on that second impact; that would explain his apparent loss of feeling! He looked instinctively toward the window where he had last been pinned and, to his surprise, his head moved.

The movement was accompanied by excruciating pain in the back of his neck, but that was of little consequence; the important thing was that he had done something which a short time ago he could not have done—and that was encouraging.

He tried again and found that he could lift his head a little. When he relaxed it bumped back gently to the floor. Well, he thought with relief, it looked as if the paralysis was due to the hibernation drug and would eventually wear off!

He looked at the window again and could see the bloodstains still spattered on the wall and around the window. It was dark brown, almost black, and some of it had flaked off. There was none at all remaining on the glass.

He moved his fingers a little. This produced an unpleasant sensation of quivering numbness, but he continued to work at it until he could lift his entire forearm from the floor. He swung his right arm up and looked at his chronometer, but he did not seem to have sufficient concentration to allow him to make anything out of the information it gave to him.

He stared at it steadfastly and eventually succeeded in ascertaining simply that it had stopped. It was a solid-state type, and the digital readout was dark, so even the date on which it had stopped remained a mystery. The rechargeable cell that powered it, however, had a service life in excess of two years, and since it was unlikely that the extremely robust timepiece had been damaged in the accident he must have been unconscious for at least that period of time. He looked again at the bloodstains; they also seemed to confirm that conclusion.

This meant, then, that the hibernation systems had remained operative. Now, either through failure or design, they had shut down and permitted him to revive. He allowed his forearm to drop back above his head, and it struck some hard object with a sharp crack. It was then that he realized what was strange about his position. He was quite definitely lying on his back when he should have by rights been floating freely in the cabin. He lifted his arm and allowed it to fall again; there was no doubt about it, he was subject to a mild acceleration, less than half a G he thought.

But that didn't make sense! It was not due to the plasma engine for the elementary reason that he was lying against the front of the cabin and facing the engine. The force was in the wrong direction.

Another awful possibility presented itself. His long aimless journey was going to terminate in the sun! The light through the window was bright, not at all consistent with what would be expected had he continued in the planned orbit. The heat had caused a failure of the power supply systems, and this had thawed him out! He was being revived only to experience death in an inferno! He couldn't see the data logger from his position, but it was probably showing a general systems failure.

But then there was still that strange gravity to explain. Would the beckoning of the sun's gravity cause such an effect? He thought about that for a while and concluded that it would not. It would still be a free-fall condition, and the sun was obviously not directly behind him in any case.

He quickly ruled out the attitude thrusters, because even if they were capable of such sustained operation—and they were not—he would still be able to hear them quite clearly. But there was no sound other than the quiet hiss of the air conditioning.

Well, he thought, at least *that* was still operating, although if his theory was correct it would be of little lasting comfort.

He was beginning to feel cold now, and this tended to contradict his suspicions. He realized that he was going to have to assume a better position before he could begin making many more assumptions about what was happening.

An attempt to reach a sitting position proved most unsuccessful, serving only to inform him of the painful immobility of most of his joints. He succeeded, however, in rolling over onto his face, and from this position he began to take stock again. The area around him was littered with the debris of equipment damaged during separation. He had cause to marvel that the craft had continued to function as well as it had, considering the obvious severity of the damage.

The object his chronometer had struck turned out to be the camera, and as he looked into its gold-coated lens he saw reflected in it a dreadful apparition. It was even a little funny, and he picked the camera up in order to see himself more clearly. A yellowed, wildly bewhiskered face glared back at him, and he could not restrain a smile.

His lips formed a silent exclamation, for he had no voice. This was something of a surprise also, and after a few more attempts he resigned himself to the fact that he would probably be speechless for some time yet.

He put the camera down and drew himself laboriously toward one of the windows. He looked at the sun first, and it turned out to be located at a surprisingly ordinary distance away. This effectively scotched his heat-death theory, and he felt profoundly relieved.

He rolled over onto one shoulder, placing his back to the window, intending to look at the data-logger, but the view through the opposite window completely redirected his attention. It was entirely unexpected; it was unbelievable! He ignored the tortured protest of every muscle to scramble across the cabin and press his nose again to the glass. It hurt terribly, but he ignored the pain. Stretching before him and occupying almost his entire field of vision was Earth!

A hoarse gasp escaped his lips and fogged the glass. Had he the voice for it, it would have been a whoop of joy! He furiously scrubbed the glass with his clenched fist and gazed almost hungrily upon it again, savoring its familiar beauty.

Then his brow furrowed....It *looked* like Earth, but on a second examination he was no longer sure. To start with, there was no contrail layer; the rich colors of the continents showed clearly through the swirling skein of cloud, and the sun reflected sharply from a black expanse of water.

Yet he could recognize landmarks! In spite of the cloud cover, he could see what appeared to be the west coast of North Africa passing beneath him. He was moving discernibly in an easterly direction. But then this was an impression which he could not fully substantiate, because looking out into what should have been the Atlantic revealed glimpses of green land masses which just did not fit into the geography of the earth as he knew it.

But it was beautiful...radiantly beautiful!...Evan pressed his forehead even closer to the glass and wept in pure worship of it.

There were still further glimpses of both familiar and unfamiliar looking territory, and there came a point where his euphoria suddenly subsided. It had occurred to him that all this might not be real! Could not the hibernation drug be hallucinogenic, creating for him a cruel wish fulfillment? The very thought was appalling! He tried to shrug the idea off, yet there were definite contradictions in what he saw which called his reason into question.

He knew perfectly well, even though it pained him to accept it, that the chances in favor of his moving into a close orbit such as this with any planet were so remote as to be considered impossible, but to return so precisely to Earth...and if it wasn't Earth, what planet could it be? Certainly no other planet in the solar system fitted its description!

Evan wriggled himself into a more comfortable position and regarded the huge expanse below him through narrowed lids. It was surely an earthlike planet; it boasted seas, major continents, obvious vegetation, and atmosphere.

Could he have wandered into the planetary system of a neighboring star? The idea was preposterous! The very closest star was around four and a half light-years from the sun, and even making the incredible assumption that a random shot into space would find its way there, the life-support and fuel systems of the Magellan had less chance of making the distance than would a garden snail setting out to circumnavigate the earth on a mouthful of grass!

He just had to be totally in leave of his senses, however real and welcoming the sight was. All of his experience and training counseled him that it was impossible!

He turned away from the window and glared disconsolately back into the cabin. There was more to it than that! If he really was in the grip of hallucination, why would he trouble to question it? Surely he would also have taken leave of his ability to summarize the facts! From what he had seen of people in such a condition, however much they may have feared their delusions they still accepted them as real!

And then there was that matter of the acceleration he could feel. Surely that was real. He flipped a small piece of broken equipment across the cabin and watched it find its way to the "floor." It was clearly apparent from the direction of the force that it was guiding the ship toward a reentry.

Evan stretched himself slowly and began cleaning his resting place of broken fragments, piling them neatly in one place. When he could stand up, he'd stow them somewhere a little tidier! If it *was* hallucination, it could certainly be much worse, so for the moment at least he would just accept it as a wonderful if inexplicable reality.

In spite of his considerable bodily discomfort, he felt curiously dissatisfied with just sitting. To be in a spacecraft without being at the one time subject to a rigidly preplanned program was a disconcerting experience with which he had never previously been obliged to cope. He just had to occupy himself!

He resolved to clean up! If he was in fact due for a fiery plunge into the atmosphere of this enigmatic planet he might as well go in style!

He shaved, using an aerosol can of shave cream and a safety razor, idly watching the view as he did so. A lot of money had been spent in an attempt to design an electric shaver which would operate successfully without filling a spacecraft with weightless bristles, but this rather mundane method proved the best. It was a strange experience, because his skin had for some reason adopted the texture of dry parchment. This made him look much older than his years, and he wondered with some little concern whether the effect would be permanent.

He grinned suddenly as he caught himself wondering in such a way about the future, and he realized that whatever his present circumstance, he did not really think he was about to die. True, there were things happening for which he could provide no logical explanation, but in spite of this he was aware also of a kind of silent assurance that he was somehow still in Good Hands.

He could get to his feet, now, even though the acceleration seemed to be increasing. It was a feeling not unlike the lowering of the flaps of an aircraft, and it confirmed to him that whatever force was controlling him was positive and sure.

He washed, using the damp towel provided for the purpose. His toilet facilities were located in a locker far enough down the wall for him to gain access to them in this unusual upside-down position. He would have fitted his helmet, but that was located alongside his couch, too far above his head. He could just reach the hanging seat harness but was quite unable to hoist even his feet from the floor, either due to his physical weakness or the steadily increasing gravitational force.

He detected a slight purple haze through the

window and realized that he was actually entering the outer limits of the atmosphere. He felt a slight tinge of alarm until he glanced at the data-logger and saw that the service module had already been jettisoned, probably before he had awakened. It was obvious now that his entry into the atmosphere was going to be almost vertical—an approach which would have meant almost instant death in normal circumstances.

He watched from the window in fascination as the noise of rushing air began to intrude into the ship. The resistance of the air added rapidly to the braking effect, and he was obliged to lie on the floor again as it continued. The ship had apparently been decelerated even more than he had realized prior to reentry, and his speed was no more than a few hundred kilometers per hour.

The acceleration suddenly faded and he was again in free fall, drifting across the cabin surrounded by the heap of debris which had begun again to distribute itself around him. He groped desperately for the floating straps of his seat belt, and had just taken hold of one when the entire craft suddenly whirled itself around him and he was dumped none too gently on his back across the couch. There was no mistaking the soft, bouncing motion which followed. Through the windows above him he saw bright patches of orange and white as the main parachutes blossomed out to fill the sky.

He scrambled into the correct position and fastened his seat belt. The craft was now hanging the other way up, and he was denied any further view of the ground. He knew that the descent would take some fifteen or twenty minutes yet, so some patience was going to be required. He thought to put on his helmet, but the situation was already quite impossible. Having been so curiously spared up to this point, it seemed almost a lack of faith to take such a precaution; and in any case, he was managing quite well without it.

He decided to just wait and see.

* * *

David Cohen walked slowly through the immense foyer of the biological studies building and contemplated the view outside. To say that the building was a striking one would be a gross understatement. The furnishings and appointments were both luxurious and beautiful, and the enormous unobstructed transparent walls on two adjacent sides commanded a panoramic view of idyllic gardens. The young receptionist smiled and rose from her desk, moving silently across the plush carpet to greet him.

"Hello, Mr. Cohen. Are you going now?"

"Yes, . . . I'm afraid I must."

Her face fell in genuine disappointment. "Oh, that's a pity. I thought you would be here all day. I had wanted to talk to you. . . ."

"In that case," he smiled, "we are each the poorer." He placed an immense hand at the back of her head as they walked toward the door. "Could it wait until later tonight?"

"Oh, it's not as urgent as all that." She laughed. "I'll wait until it suits you; I know how busy you are." She tripped on ahead and opened the door for him.

"How's your new charge coming along?" she asked after him as he passed through the door.

He turned back to her and stooped close as if to convey a confidence. "I have it that he is quite well...and very, very confused." He laughed as he swung out into the sunlight, and his face conveyed an almost childlike merriment. "We will have to break it all to him slowly of course."

He strode down the wide flight of steps and, shunning the smooth, marble-like pathway, walked alongside on the grass. As he continued, the lush, green setting could be seen to occupy not just the immediate environs of the biological studies building but extended for as far as the eye could see. In the distance, other equally imposing buildings could be soon, each blending into its surroundings in the same unique way.

He soon approached the bank of a quiet lake. The view around it was mirrored in a looking-glass surface disturbed only by the activities of numerous birds of many varieties.

He paused and contemplated the surface of the water thoughtfully, his brow furrowed; then he raised his eyes to the sky. He did not appear to be looking at the azure canopy itself but regarded the heavens as if he could somehow see beyond.

He was an imposing figure, unusually large of stature and conveying the impression of considerable vitality and strength. His age would be all but impossible to estimate. At first glance one would place it at around forty, but his smooth, clear skin and sparkling blue eyes suggested less than half that age.

The sun reflected from a shock of wiry gray-white hair, and his features exhibited the bold lines and coppery color of one of Middle Eastern descent.

He stood there with just the slightest suggestion of a stoop, as if unconsciously trying to offset his height. The effect was minimal. The merest trace of a smile flickered around his face as some pleasant thought passed through his mind. Then he nodded to himself, as if coming to a satisfying decision.

When he looked down he was surrounded by birds, both on the water and on the ground around his feet. He reached into the folds of his loose clothing and pulled out a handful of crumbs—which brought an excited response from his audience. He stooped to spread them in a wide arc on the ground, stepped carefully over the happily occupied crowd, and continued his walk beside the water. Still smiling to himself, he began to quicken his pace.

A few moments later he walked up the wide, fine gravel drive toward his home, a low graceful dwelling which blended into the incredibly beautiful landscape. He pushed open the gate and stepped into a small courtyard. There was good clearance above his head in the gateway, but some inbuilt sense of self-preservation bade him lower his head still further as he passed through it.

He straightened up and stood smiling with arms outspread as an adolescent girl streaked across the courtyard to greet him. She said nothing but clung to his arm as they continued across the courtyard and entered the house. He was then greeted as he entered by his wife—a tall, dark, attractive woman. She too

100

carried the unmistakable signs of her race, sharing the clear skin and eyes which suggested an extraordinary degree of health and youthfulness, even though at first glance she was a mature woman.

"Hello, David, you're earlier than I thought you'd be!" Her manner was relatively reserved and quiet.

The girl on his arm bobbed up and down in undisguised glee. "I *knew* he would be early! I knew it when he left this morning." She swung around to look into her father's face. "I know why you came, don't I?"

He feigned ignorance. "You do?"

"Yes, I do," she explained to her mother. "He won't admit it, but I know that he is excited about his new charge...he can't wait to meet him."

"I have many charges," he protested. "What is just one more?"

"Because you get worked up over all of them, doesn't he, Mother? And this one's special, isn't he?" She directed the last question back to her father, studying his face closely, trying to detect the flickering at the corners of his eyes which would signal the end of his mock-seriousness.

His face creased into a smile. "You have more of the gift than is good for you, my child."

"May I come with you?" Her voice changed to one of pleading. "You said I could."

"Now, as I recall the facts of the conversation, I said you just might."

"Please...may I?"

"Of course...if you'll promise not to talk the poor man to death." She began to lead him away by the arm, but her mother motioned her to stop.

"Don't be too anxious, Lyddia. It's only the fourth hour, and you have not eaten yet."

The bright, young face lit up triumphantly. "You've already prepared my lunch to take with me, haven't you?"

Her mother's tone remained serious. "That depends on your father."

She spun to face her father, but he had already raised an admonishing finger. "We will eat; then we shall go."

Lyddia did not reply but sped to the kitchen; immediately there was the sound of furious table-setting.

"Were you planning to leave so early, David?"

"No, but it doesn't matter—we will take the boat and make a day of it. We won't call for our friend until he's had time to acclimatize a little." He chuckled to himself. "If I let Lyddia talk to me first for a couple of hours she may go a bit easier on our charge later." He placed a large arm around his wife's shoulders, and she permitted a faint smile to pass across her otherwise serious features.

They ate a leisurely meal in spite of Lyddia's exuberant prodding. Soon afterward David and Lyddia set off down the narrow path leading away from the back of the house. They walked side by side, carrying between them a large wicker basket.

Ahead of them the path stretched away into a green valley, lush and overgrown in its depth but with its flanks crisscrossed by a patchwork of small farming plots. Beyond the end of the valley could be seen the shimmering reflection of the sun on quiet water.

Miriam Cohen smiled quietly as she watched them disappear into the distance, gradually dissolving into the cool, flickering shadows. The large figure was stooping more than usual to keep the basket at a manageable height for the other. Lyddia, hanging on to the basket rather than carrying it, tripped alongside, her hair flashing from side to side as she went. A gentle breeze wafted up from the valley, and with it came small snatches of Lyddia's animated chatter, growing gradually fainter until it was indistinguishable from the murmurs of the forest.

David's pace was a long one, and the girl was noticeably hurrying just to keep up. Miriam noticed this and understood. For all of his feigned indifference, David Cohen had business which he was simply bursting to commence.

Evan did something which he normally would never have so much as thought of. Tortured with curiosity, he unfastened his seat harness and stood up in the cabin to see out of the window. In the absence of his suit umbilicals and telemetry he felt oddly free and unobserved, like a schoolboy misbehaving while the teacher is out of the room. He just *had* to see where he was going, and he had convinced himself that he could belt up again quickly enough when the time came.

He was handsomely rewarded for doing so, because the view was fantastic. The clarity of the atmosphere was such that, in spite of the cloud cover, he could see to the horizon in every direction. The seas that he had spotted earlier turned out to be relatively small, looking instead like a number of unusually large lakes, many of them joined together. Evan had an impression that they were seas in the process of being filled in.

The planet was obviously not the earth, in spite of the many similarities he had noted earlier. There were, as far as he could tell, few desert regions of any great size, nor could he see any of the telltale brown smudges which would indicate the presence of large cities.

He had resigned himself to the fact that the planet defied explanation and concentrated instead on simply observing as many of its features as possible.

Even the cloud patterns suggested a different weather picture than normal. The veil of clouds swirled almost evenly in all directions, and there was no evidence of hurricane activity or large holes in the cloud cover to indicate a perpetually rainless region.

The same even covering stretched both north and south, suggesting even the absence of polar weather extremes.

The ground was moving rapidly closer now, and he observed that he was coming down on the morning side of the terminator. It was impossible to determine with any accuracy where he would actually set down, and he was quite unsure whether it would be on water or on land. The latter possibility disturbed him greatly in spite of the obvious external controlling forces on his ship; it was not designed to put down on land!

When eventually he estimated his height to be around twelve thousand meters he returned to his couch and belted up, resolving that, having come this far, he was not going to concern himself unduly over such a minor detail as the landing.

He did not have long to wait, and after passing through a remarkably ordinary-looking layer of cloud, he was almost startled to see, of all things, a swirling mass of birds around and above him. A dark shadow fell over the interior of the capsule and he found himself descending rapidly alongside an extremely high and precipitous cliff face. He was falling into a deep valley, and the air around him seemed to be darkening into a soft, blue haze as he continued endlessly lower and lower.

His progress was suddenly arrested by a crackling but cushioned impact as he plunged into dense, yielding, foliage. The capsule stopped, and he saw the bright orange and white canopy of the main chutes collapsing gracefully down toward him. A moment later he felt the craft slowly tilt and begin to slide off the branch that supported him. For a terrifying moment he descended in a free fall that promised to dash him to pieces on the ground.

Mercifully, he was stopped for a second time, and he felt the torturous strain on the chute lines as they stretched and bounced him to a halt. He was dangling in a slightly tilted position now, swinging like a great pendulum and bouncing against the enormous trunk of the tree which now trapped his parachutes in its upper branches. He saw a long sliver of bark fall down toward him and drape itself across a window, and as he looked back up the trunk he could see the shining wound which he had inflicted upon it.

Evan lay still, hardly daring to move lest he become dislodged again. His heart was pounding wildly from the sheer fright of that first fall, and in his weakened condition he feared this might be more than it could stand.

The swinging gradually slowed, and he became more assured of the fact that he was held securely, although in a most fortuitous way. Even through the heavily insulated walls of the cabin he could hear snatches of the cacophony of hysterical birdcalls which attended his ungainly arrival. Then he could see them beginning to settle back into the trees around him.

Hanging by his seat harness, he could look down and see the ground below him—no more than about four or five meters away. He was surprised that the stretching of the chute lines had not allowed him to hit the ground.

Inexplicably, as if by an unseen hand, the main access hatch opposite him fell away, letting in first a torrent of forest noises and then following up quickly with the sweet, moist smell of a luxuriant rain forest. After his long experience of the hospital-ward type atmosphere of the Magellan, it was the most exciting and exhilarating perfume he had ever known, and he permitted himself a few moments simply to breathe it in.

He was apprehensive about unfastening his harness because he was now aware of the full, crushing force of the planet's gravity. The torturous strain of the harness against his fragile body told him that he was not yet ready for it, even if it was an entirely Earth-like force. Also, to lower himself from this position would necessitate standing on the instrument panel, and although it would certainly be of no further use to him, his ingrained respect for the equipment forbade him to do so.

He succeeded eventually in letting out the slack in the harness to the extent that he was much closer to a stepping-off point. He tripped the catch and fell into a crumpled heap against the lower wall, then simply lay there giving his body every opportunity to adjust to the radically changed condition.

He did not rest for long but made his way laboriously to the now open hatch, turning around so as to slide out feet-first. He had intended to move carefully, but he was quite unable to arrest his progress once he had begun to slide, and he permitted himself to fall limply to the ground. The drop was longer than he had anticipated, for the grassy surface sloped steeply away from the base of the tree.

He fell pell-mell down the slope like a rag doll, filling the wide round collar of his pressure suit with forest mulch as he went. When he halted he was supported relatively comfortably on a cushion of dense ferns, and he elected to remain there for a time, taking stock of his surroundings and removing the debris from his mouth and suit.

Considering the length of the drop, he suffered little from this ungainly landing. Lacking the strength to correct his tumbling, he had remained relaxed, and this had undoubtedly saved him from injury.

The scene was all the more incredibly beautiful for his being out in it. He lay on the soft floor of what appeared to be a luxuriant rain forest. The foliage was very high above, and offered several openings through which the direct rays of the sun streaked through a blue-white mist to the forest floor. The air was cool and scented with the heady perfume of moist foliage and forest wildflowers.

A light wind stirred the upper reaches of the trees, but where he lay the air was perfectly calm. It was alive though, with many sounds, and he lay still, separating and savoring each one of them. There was the incessant chatter of the birds and of what may have been monkeys, although he was unable to see any. Above the murmur of the high foliage there was a distant but more powerful sound—surf, perhaps, or a waterfall; he could not discern which.

The transition from life in a spacecraft to this was a little more than he could fully accommodate, and he felt both strangely elated and unreal—as if taking part in a beautiful dream, yet knowing also that it was indeed but a dream. If this was only a temporary illusion, he thought contentedly, it was just the type of balm that his ravaged soul needed at this time, and he was not going to allow it to go to waste!

The traumatic events that had led to this enigmatic situation were beginning to recede from him, and he could even persuade himself that they were simply bad dreams of another time—dreams that would, like all dreams, fade and die as the day wore on.

He had no desire whatsoever to do anything but stay where he was. He was warm and comfortable and overpoweringly tired. He felt safe and protected in this congenial place, and it seemed perfectly in order to just close his eyes and sleep. On the other hand, there were many things he yet wanted to know about this place, and he was a little afraid of sleep, lest when he awoke he might find the vision ended.

He knew without even trying that he would not yet be able to walk, although he was also aware that he was gradually recovering, and given a bit more time he would be able to move around normally.

He began again to mentally traverse the events that had brought him here, and although he could not produce any workable answers, there were many things about his situation that were demonstrably real and tangible. He saw no real reason why he should further doubt his sanity.

He was in the midst of persuading himself about this question when he dropped off into a deep and welcome sleep.

As he slept, the forest around him began to stir. The animal sounds fell strangely quiet, as if to avoid disturbing him. Birds came silently closer to observe this strange visitor. They were followed also by forest animals of many kinds, even great cats which moved close enough to sniff at an outflung hand. They held no threat, but simply displayed a cautious and even courteous animal curiosity, examining him in turn, and then padding away silently into the blue-green curtain of mist and shadow from whence they came.

Other eyes watched Evan also—eyes which he could have no comprehension of at this time. The watchers wished him to rest, and he had no power to resist, nor would he have desired to had he known their intent.

Hours passed, and the scene changed little, except that Evan's breathing was no longer the hoarse gasp of an exhausted man but of one who was now at peace. Some of his facial color had returned, and it was as if this kindly planet were breathing new life into his frame.

The shadows began to lengthen, and the mist became more dense, rising out of the ground and moving silently around and among the tall trees, caressing the foliage and forming droplets of clear water on the leaves.

Evan's fertile mind would have delighted in speculating about this, but that was yet to come.

For the moment he knew nothing.

Chapter five

Evan awoke suddenly and was immensely relieved to find that the vision remained. He sat up rather abruptly and discovered that he could do so without any great discomfort. His nose was rather sore though, and he felt it gently, wondering if perhaps it had been broken. It was strange that his nose should still be sensitive since he had hurt it so long ago in the accident. It could have been that the self-repairing ability of his body had been inhibited during the hibernation; if this was the case, the bruising might only now be coming out.

He had no idea how long he had slept, except that he seemed to have landed about midmorning, and it was now drawing toward evening, presumably on the same day. He did not even know how long a day was on this planet, but it was so unexpectedly Earth-like in many respects that it seemed a safe guess it would be somewhere the same as Earth.

He was rapidly beginning to form the conclusion that he was in fact back on earth. That theory produced a myriad of other questions, but at least there were fewer of them than any alternative would have produced. He could even have returned to earth at some other time—a thought that was both exciting and alarming!

He looked up again, and for the first time became aware of the huge bulk of his craft hanging above him. It seemed suddenly inopportune that he remain any longer where he was, so he got cautiously to his feet. It was a delightfully strange experience to stand again in such a setting, and he managed much better than he had anticipated. He walked a little way along the slope so as to be out of the path of the module should it choose to disengage itself from the tree.

Apart from his sore face, there was one other factor which bothered him. He was hungry, and it occurred to him for the first time that there was plenty of food in the ship. This was of little use to him, because the ship was quite out of reach. A slow walk around the base of the tree confirmed what little chance he had of scaling it, even if he were physically fit.

He shook his head slowly in exasperation at his own thoughtlessness; it would probably be dark soon, and he had effectively denied himself both food and shelter for the night. The mist was thicker, too, and he realized that he would have to leave the area and look for a more suitable camping spot.

He set off with an ungainly shuffling gait, down the gentle slope away from the cliff face and toward the distant rushing sound. As he moved farther out of the shadow of the cliff it became noticeably brighter, even though the color of the sky clearly indicated the approach of a sunset.

The forest was less dense here and seemed to consist of a series of wide, interconnected clearings, still sheltered by the canopy of high trees and deeply carpeted with a fragrant layer of freshly fallen leaves. It was extremely beautiful, and the place even seemed to possess a kind of benevolent spirit—something he could not quite put his finger on.

He had walked for about five minutes through scenery such as this before a sudden movement caught his eye. He looked and froze to the spot.

Not more than twelve meters away stood a magnificent lion, and he felt his blood turn to ice. A furtive glance around him confirmed that there was nothing to be achieved by running; he was in the center of a clearing, and even if he could cover the distance to the trees he would be unable to scale the tall trunks.

The lion stood stiffly, regarding him with a kind of pompous air. Another head broke through the ferns, and a beautifully proportioned lioness pushed in front of her mate to scrutinize him also. Then others appeared—lions, lionesses, and tiny cubs. Evan had walked unwittingly into a whole pride of lions, and he was more alarmed by this than by anything which had happened up to this time.

They stood looking at each other for some time—for Evan, an eternity. He made no attempt to escape, and the lions showed no inclination to attack.

He began gradually to relax, because he sensed that they were regarding him with no more malevolence than would a herd of cows.

The head lion snorted loudly and shook his head. Then, as if to write finis to the engagement, he turned suddenly and disappeared into the undergrowth. One by one the remaining members of the group turned away with similar terminating gestures, and Evan soon stood alone.

He took a deep shaking breath and exhaled slowly. He had not even considered the possibility that there could be wild animals; they seemed so completely out of place in this idyllic setting. But these creatures were not wild animals in that sense, for they fitted this scene perfectly, and he was counseled by some inner voice that they would not have harmed him, either now or at any other time.

He began to walk again, and soon he had little doubt about the noise he could hear. It was the muffled, rushing sounds of a seashore, and he began to detect the salty tang of an inshore breeze. The foliage was thinning out and the glades becoming much wider, revealing still more animals—all of them familiar earth creatures. Without exception, they afforded him a kind of inquisitive but friendly reception, and he felt himself becoming curiously drawn to them.

He lengthened his strides, anxious to reach the shore before it should become much darker. Then, suddenly, he was upon it—climbing over a low grassy dune and stumbling awkwardly down the other side into the cool white sand. The beach was wide and clean, and he walked across it and stood where the water broke over his feet.

It was not a large body of water, because he could see distant hills on the horizon. Most likely it was one of those large, lake-like areas he had observed on the way down. He tasted the water off the tips of his fingers and confirmed that it was salty. It was unusually clear, though, and impressed him somehow as being water unmolested by man.

He straightened up and squinted into the sunset as he surveyed the horizon, panning the scene completely from the steeply rising forest behind him to the long ribbon of clear white sand which bounded the crystal sea. Looking back along the beach in the opposite direction, he could see a low, rocky headland which stretched out into the sea for about one hundred and fifty meters before disappearing below the water. There was no surf but a gentle swell, and its breaking over this bouldered surface was responsible for the sounds he had heard.

He began to walk slowly along the beach toward the headland for no other reason than that it seemed to be a feature worth exploring. The beach broadened considerably at this point and the broad expanse of open space seemed to accentuate his vague feelings of being terribly alone. Indeed, it was quite possible that he was entirely alone on this planet, never again to meet another human being! That thought should have been alarming, but for the moment at least it was somewhat refreshing.

There was something strangely disturbing about this rocky outcrop, and he stood upon it, hands on hips, for several minutes before he realized what it was. The rocks were rough and irregular, and even at the waterline they lacked evidence of the prolonged weathering of the sea; they had not been dumped there by an act of nature—someone had put them there!

He selected a comfortable-looking boulder and sat down to consider more carefully this new possibility. He perched with his knees up under his chin, and as he did so felt a slight pang as it momentarily brought to mind the last occasion when he had sat like this beside his friend.

But there were pangs of hunger also; and it was then that he remembered he was not as entirely without food as he had thought; there was the suit supply which he had forgotten entirely! It consisted only of a couple of fruit chew-bars, intended originally to provide supplementary sustenance for the astronauts while they were engaged in long periods of astronomical observation and were not free to partake of normal meals.

He felt clumsily around inside the collar of his pressure suit and retrieved a small bar wrapped tightly in plastic. He brushed only a token amount of the forest soil from it before peeling the paper back and tasting it. It was very stale and dry, and the interior had almost disappeared, but it was delicious!

He chewed his meal slowly and with great deliberation as he returned again to the problem of deciding where he was. The stones around him had a random appearance, yet he could not escape the feeling that they had somehow been "placed" to give just that effect.

He screwed up his sore nose incredulously. That was just plain contradictory! But then much the same observation could be made about the whole scene, and he turned to look again in the direction from which he had come. Sure, it was a wilderness, but a curiously

116

perfect one, as if each tree and fern had been planted to achieve the best effect. In whatever direction he looked, he saw a wilderness that carried also an artistic sense of order, like a series of Thomas Cole paintings.

He thought back to his walk. The same feeling had been there, then; he had been aware of it as he passed into each new clearing—as if every scene was a kind of project on its own. It was not a forest; it was a garden!

A garden? He shook his head. The mere size of the project made it unthinkable! Every mountain, valley, and plain would have to be engineered to fit this kind of environment; and yet. . .

He had finished his mouthful, and his attention went back to the precious delicacy in his hand. He carefully peeled back a little more wrapping ready for the next bite. The bar was up into his mouth when he saw the sail, and the effect was to freeze him so suddenly that it was as if he were pictured on a single frame of a movie film. He gazed at it stonily, determined to convince himself entirely that what he saw was real before risking movement.

It *was* real! Directly in front of him, and almost at the horizon, was a tiny sail. It must have appeared quickly, because he was certain that it was not there when he had looked only a few moments before. He dared not take his eyes from it, and slowly but quite unconsciously he rewrapped his fruit bar and returned it to the suit recess. Then he rose slowly to his feet and began to make his way carefully toward the tip of the headland.

His progress was a dangerous compromise between keeping the boat in sight on the one hand, and

watching where he was walking on the other. When
he could go no farther, the sail had drawn closer, and
he could now make out a small sailboat, barely four
meters long, he thought.

There were two figures on board. The one at the
rear was large and heavyset—obvious even at some
distance—while the other was a much smaller figure.

Evan stood as close to the breaking swell as he dared
and semaphored wildly with both arms. They must
have seen him, for the smaller figure waved gaily. The
other gave little more than a perfunctory salute.

As they drew much closer he could see that the
larger figure was a man dressed in what appeared to
be a white robe—curiously unexpected attire! The
other was a young girl with long dark hair. She was
dressed in a bright red loosely fitting smock.

A deep, resonant voice boomed out at him across the
water. "You'll have to go back to the beach. We can't
get you from there."

Evan realized that he was right—in fact it was quite
obvious. He had no voice with which to reply, so he
simply obeyed the instruction as best he could, making
slow and ungainly progress back along the headland,
looking back over his shoulder at intervals as if to
guard against the possibility that his visitors could
vanish. By the time he had reached the shoreline, the
boat was coming in some eighty or ninety meters
farther down the beach.

As he walked along the firm damp sand he became
suddenly aware of his hairnet and removed it,
allowing his long hair to fall down around his
shoulders.

The boat was close into shore by the time he reached it, and the man had climbed out into the water to greet him. His garment was not a robe as it had first appeared but a loose fitting suit with the legs rolled up to allow him to stand in the water. He strode enthusiastically onto the sand, hand extended. It was an enormous hand that seemed to engulf Evan's completely.

"I'm David, and that's Lyddia." He dispatched the greetings with such brevity that Evan barely had time to look from one to the other before a strong hand took his elbow and began guiding him toward the boat. He found himself unexpectedly lifted bodily over the side and set down on his feet in the boat. He stood there stupidly, tottering weakly and clinging to a loose edge of the lowered sail.

David pushed the boat back firmly into deeper water and leapt over the other side with a light agility that quite belied his size.

Evan turned to face the small figure crouched in the bow, and he realized for the first time that the wide, dark eyes held traces of fear. David's voice came from behind him. "Don't mind Lyddia; she didn't realize that you had long hair."

Evan glanced quickly back to the stern at this strange remark, but the big man hastened to explain. "She has a fear of men with long hair—it's not your fault."

The girl instantly regained her composure. "I'm not afraid of you at all. How do you do, Mr. Westering."

Evan's jaw dropped visibly—they even knew his name! She spoke again, this time more authoritatively.

"If you don't sit down, you'll tip us all out, and I'll get my dress wet."

Evan sat slowly.

Her voice became more motherly. "You must be terribly hungry. Would you like a piece of chicken?" She didn't wait for his reply but dived her hands into the giant basket beside her and produced a small roasted chicken wrapped in a piece of cloth. Evan sat and watched her numbly as she proceeded to break off a leg and then hold it out to him.

For some reason he was unable to respond; his hands had become glued to his sides. This just wasn't happening! It was all completely unreal! She shook the leg in front of him and cajoled him softly. "Come on, take it. It's quite all right."

He managed somehow to lift his hand and take it from her, but he continued to stare at her dumbly. Then he lowered his head to his knees and began to laugh—or cry—voicelessly; whatever it was, something had welled up inside him over which he no longer had control, nor did he care! It wasn't as if he was just anybody! He was a returning astronaut, a station normally attended by helicopters, aircraft carriers, top brass, and the media. Instead he was but a lost child, picked up in nothing much more than a rowboat—and told by a little girl to sit down. The great bulk of his spacesuit in this setting served only to make him seem all the more ridiculous!

Eventually he was quite spent, and he lifted his face slowly to find Lyddia's face close to his own, her dark eyes filled with concern. "Do you want your chicken now?"

He smiled at her rather foolishly and then began to eat. It was extraordinarily tasty, and he attacked it hungrily, to Lyddia's obvious approval. He tried to signal to her the fact that he could not speak, but she waved his efforts aside. "That's all right; we know about your voice, Mr. Westering." She continued to prepare food for him as she talked. "We know quite a lot about you actually. Daddy is a Chief Judge, and he has charge of you." A slightly superior tone entered her voice as she added, "I'm helping." She glanced over his shoulder and a mischievous look crossed her face. "I can't say any more," she added quickly. "Daddy's glaring at me."

Evan looked behind him in time to intercept the beetle-browed expression from the stern. He smiled as David spoke.

"You will find Lyddia to be an eternal source of information on all things, Mr. Westering—whether you want it or not." He raised his chin and addressed his daughter. "For the moment our guest is in need of both food and rest. We have time sufficient for everything else—later."

Evan winked slyly at Lyddia and returned to his chicken.

It was almost dark as they moved quietly up a small tidal stream and moored the boat. David motioned ahead, indicating a steep valley up which they were presumably about to walk. Evan viewed it a bit apprehensively, unsure as to whether the feat was really within his capability, but Lyddia shooed him on confidently.

The shadows continued to deepen as they traveled up the valley, and Evan witnessed for the first time the phenomenon of the rising mist. No one spoke—not even Lyddia, and Evan was pleasantly surprised at the ease with which he was handling the relatively long trek. It was as if there were something in the air which lifted and fortified him—just another of those things he was going to ask about when the opportunity presented itself. He was reasonably content to wait for the moment, but when he regained his voice . . . !

With the onset of darkness, the place seemed to become even more beautiful, for the twilight drew itself out as if unwilling to leave, and the western sky remained decorated for a long while with a fascinating array of changing and blending shafts of light.

As it grew darker he realized that there were many more dwellings on the face of the land than he had first thought, for he could see the yellow lights winking through the trees and scattered on a distant hillside. They were widely spread, and never grouped together in even the hint of a town or village. Looking back across the water from a point farther up the valley he could see, of all things, a single multistory building of about fifteen or twenty floors standing beside the shore, its lights reflecting on the water.

The valley eventually began to widen, and Evan could see ahead the long low line of a magnificent house. He knew almost instinctively that this was David's home. When they reached it, he had even more reason for astonishment, for it was an architectural masterpiece, fusing almost into a work of art a rustic charm and a kind of subdued technological excellence.

His introduction to Miriam was carried out quickly and quietly, almost as briefly as his first meeting. This did not concern him though, for he had the distinct impression that he was both already known and expected. Miriam hardly needed introduction, because she was simply an older and more serious edition of Lyddia. Evan even thought he detected for an instant that same fearful look which he had earlier seen in Lyddia's eyes, but before he could be sure, it was gone.

The home, both comfortable and inviting, was softly lit by what he first took to be oil or gas lights. Later, when he was left in the bathroom to clean up, he investigated the light and found it to be quite cold to the touch—probably electric, but if so it was far more efficient than anything he had known before.

The luxurious hot bath surpassed anything he could remember, and he lay in it for a long time, idly contemplating the obvious quality and workmanship that surrounded him. No one hurried him, and when he finally emerged both Lyddia and Miriam had retired for the night. David sat alone in the spacious drawing room, reading. With Evan's entry he arose quickly to greet him.

"Ah, my boy, you look greatly refreshed. Are the nightclothes comfortable?"

Evan nodded, although he was conscious that this amounted to an understatement. He was wearing pajamas and a lounge coat of far grander quality than he had ever seen, let alone worn!

123

"I'll take you to your room right now," said David. "A good night's sleep and you will be fully restored, I promise you."

In the quiet of the house it seemed safe to try to talk, and Evan spoke for the first time in a hoarse whisper. "I seem to have done nothing but sleep lately."

David put a hand across his shoulder and guided him firmly across the room. "Believe me, my boy, you need every bit of it. You have not as yet even begun to learn of what has happened to you. Your arrival here has been planned with your good health in mind. Tomorrow we can talk, but tonight you must rest."

Evan needed no further telling, for tiredness was indeed beginning to sweep over him again, and he allowed his guide to steer him through the house and out onto a long, covered balcony, from which they had an elevated view of moonlit gardens. The balustrade was alive with a profusion of climbing flowers, and although their colors were but dimly discernible under the soft lighting, their perfume hung in the air like a cool mist.

They had walked almost to the end of the balcony before David stopped at a door and opened it inward to reveal an attractively furnished bedroom.

"Here we are. I hope you will find it comfortable, Mr. Westering."

Evan hung back. Farther along, the balcony widened out into a spacious sundeck, and he motioned to David that he would like first to go there.

"But of course." David extended a broad hand in invitation, but he did not follow.

Evan walked to the sundeck. It was roofed over

124

with a pergola from which hung masses of wisteria. He moved to a position where he could clearly see the sky. His first interest was the moon, and with almost exhilarating relief he recognized it as the familiar moon of Earth. The stars also exhibited the patterns he was seeking, and he was finally convinced that he was indeed back on Earth.

He stood there for some time, momentarily forgetting his waiting host, drinking in the warm security of a friendly sight. Nevertheless, as familiar as they were to him, they had never looked quite the same from Earth—even before the contrail layer had clouded out all but the brightest stars. Now they stood out as clear white lights against a jet-black sky, and it gave them a curious kind of presence, almost as if he could reach out and touch them.

He returned suddenly to the present, and walked back to the room where David waited for him inside the doorway.

"You will find everything you need here, Mr. Westering. If you should need me there is a paging cord beside the bed. Would you like me to leave the door open?"

Evan nodded, then signaled that he wished to speak. He managed only a hoarse whisper. "Will you answer just two questions?"

"That is a reasonable request."

"Well, first, will you please call me Evan?"

David laughed heartily and slapped Evan's shoulder so firmly as to almost unbalance him. "Yes, of course, Evan. I was not really trying to be all that formal. What is the other question?"

Evan thought for a moment, choosing his words as economically as possible. "I know I'm on Earth—but when?"

David's hand was still on his shoulder, and he felt the firm grasp soften. "It is after your time, Evan, although not very much after. In fact we are just nine years into the seventh dispensation."

Evan did not know fully what this meant, but he had some strong suspicions. "Are you telling me that this is the...the..." He waited for his host to finish the sentence.

David smiled patiently. "Your suspicions are correct, although I would counsel you not to try to take in too much at this point." He dropped his hand from Evan's shoulder. "You have returned to Earth during the period of the millennial reign."

The answer was quite as he had expected, but he was no less stunned in spite of this foreknowledge. David seemed to understand, and he patted Evan's shoulder gently again before turning and walking quietly from the room, leaving his guest with the remaining hours of the night in which to digest this startling revelation.

Paul Bernard stabbed at the canvas with such unnecessary force that the easel moved along the floor. He was annoyed, and he was venting his anger through the only channel immediately available to one of his station.

Paul was a prisoner, and the reeducation program

left few openings for the display of uncontained emotions. An angry painting was allowable though, and he carried a chip large enough for a massive painting at this particular time.

His status in the community was not immediately apparent; indeed, the apartment in which he worked was anything but cell-like and could well be judged luxurious. The medium-sized room was decorated in a manner consistent with that of an artist, its elegance marred only by the scattered profusion of art equipment and unfinished works.

He stepped back to survey the results for a few seconds, and then reacted impetuously by simply dropping the palette and brushes on the floor. Stepping heedlessly over the resulting mess on the carpet, he walked out through the open French doors onto a small, ground-level terrace.

The cool darkness placated him a little, but he still leaned indolently against the awning post and glared into the blackness in the direction of David Cohen's home. It was concealed from him by the ridge at the edge of the valley, but he had a perfect knowledge of its direction.

It was enough, he thought, to bear all the indignities of his position, but now he was required again to be nursemaid to yet another of David's charges.

David had done this before. He was mentor to many people, including Paul himself—more people than Paul cared to know or even count!

At least on this occasion he knew in advance. Usually David would turn up suddenly and unannounced with some such disciple in tow, and with the usual perfunctory introductions attended to, Paul would find himself conducting an impromptu lecture tour of the grains project.

The thing that most irritated him was incommunicable—an accusation he could never bring himself to level at David. It was not the grains project but he himself that was on show! He was the prized first exhibit in the kind of before-and-after sales pitch which David delivered to all new pupils. But to accuse David of such a purpose would be to make inadmissable admissions about himself, and he was never going to do that!

The apartment was comfortably adequate for one person, and was part of an orderly layout of some thirty-odd similar dwellings dotted along the hillside. They would have appeared to be quite independent units were it not for the long, covered walkway which joined them all along one side.

There were no locks or bars, for Paul was not a prisoner in that sense. He was, in fact, free to move around as much as he wished. There were far more subtle chains which bound him.

He was up late tonight, well past the time at which he would normally have retired, but his anger refreshed him. He had plenty of cause to be tired, because David ran a tight ship. Paul's main chores were involved with the grain ecological recovery project—hard work, which he nevertheless secretly enjoyed. Then there was the tuition; reeducation they called it, and that was singly his greatest burden. The painting was his hobby, his release, and perhaps even his future profession, although it was far too soon to make predictions like that!

Paul was French—or at least he had been before the tribulation. There were no nationalities in any geographical sense now, although ethnic differences remained and were accepted and even encouraged. He was a man of quite dark complexion with black, closely cropped hair, rather tall, and just a little thin for his height. His sharp, angular features were concealed partly by a squarely trimmed beard which he tended by habit to stroke nervously when disturbed as he was now.

He had given up one important facet of his nationality though, and that was his language. Along with every other person to come under the new order, he had been obliged to learn the new language. Superior teaching techniques had made this task relatively easy, but in spite of the new eloquence that this perfect tongue gave him, he nevertheless resented the intrusion. The ability which he now had, to converse equally lucidly with a Russian or an Eskimo, seemed to serve no purpose which could be of interest to him.

David's protégés were of no interest to him either, and sooner or later he was going to spell it out! He would have done so a lot earlier had he not begun to acquire, somewhat against his will, a degree of the gift. The gift was quite free, and it was not thrust upon anyone who did not wish it, but it had a way of entering in by a kind of osmosis which Paul had desperately tried to avoid. Interactions with other people, especially the kinds of relationships that David kept guiding him into, were partly responsible for this phenomenon, and Paul was therefore justifiably afraid of them.

As he gazed into the darkness he felt more than usually afraid. He had sensed in David's manner that there was something rather strange about his new charge, and he was uncomfortable at the prospect of meeting him on the morrow.

His mouth formed into a firm, thin line; he was not going to let it show! It was useless, of course, to try to fool David, but he would shrug off this new arrival with ease!

He turned swiftly on his heel and walked back inside. Then, skirting the mess on the floor, he went to bed.

Evan woke quickly and easily to find his room awash with light and the sounds of birds. The door was still ajar as David had left it, and through it he could see the massed color of the climbing flowers on the balcony.

He did not arise immediately, but lay comfortably drinking in the unspared luxury of his surroundings. He had no idea of the time, but he sensed that there were no demands on him to hurry.

It was curiosity which eventually compelled him to rise. He did so slowly, feeling his way as one barely recovered from a long illness.

The room was a marvel of workmanship, and he

spent some time running his hands over the finely finished paneling and soft furnishings just to confirm to himself that they were real. On closer examination he began to realize what the fascination here was—it was the way in which an almost rustic simplicity concealed an awesome technical excellence. There were the cold lights he had noted earlier. Then there was the immense windowpane—so invisible that he was obliged to touch it before he was sure it was there. It yielded pliably to his touch.

There were the incredibly fine textile materials of the bed coverings, and the curtains were smooth and soft to the touch with not so much as a trace of seam or a stray thread. The materials did not appear to be synthetics but rather natural materials which had been subject to processes and craftmanship far surpassing anything he had seen. The carpet was of similar quality also, and he dropped to his knees to examine it more closely. The view from the window was glorious, fully in keeping with the natural splendor which he was now beginning to expect.

He felt more restored by his rest than he could have thought possible, and to his frank amazement, even his nose seemed to have healed.

A doorway in one wall led him into a small washroom where his toilet requirements had already been carefully laid out for him. He moved close to the large mirror and examined his face carefully. Yes, it was returning to a normal color and the injury to his nose had disappeared entirely!

Then his eye fell on the long, bedraggled hair flowing over his shoulders, and for a moment he saw again the flash of fear that had come to him through Lyddia's eyes.

It was an impulsive, even a childish act, but he opened the drawer beneath the washbowl and felt about quickly till he found the pair of scissors which he knew would be there. A few short snips were all that were needed, and he stood before the mirror with the excess hair around his feet. It left him looking like a slightly deranged page boy, but he stood back and admired the effect with satisfaction.

When he arrived back in the bedroom he found clothing laid out on the bed for him. It was a simple, bone-colored outfit not unlike the one worn by David at their meeting. He regarded the garment with reservation, but having noted that his body suit was nowhere in sight, he condescended to try it on.

Standing in front of the mirror, he was obliged— almost with some misgiving—to acknowledge that the style suited him well, certainly much better than he would have expected. In fact it was unexpectedly comfortable, affording him a bodily freedom which seemed to quite compliment his renewed vigor.

Stepping out into the sunshine on the balcony was like rebirth. He had been a small child when last he could remember seeing the sun shining out of such a clear sky. The view from this position took in the valley up which they had walked the evening before, and he could see the narrow pathway leading from the rear of the house into the deep shadow of the trees.

He wandered unhurriedly along the balcony, pausing at intervals to admire the scenery or to tug idly at the hanging blooms which adorned the railing. He arrived eventually at the door through which he assumed they had come the night before. He had pushed it open and stepped through before he realized his mistake.

He began to leave, but something about the room intrigued him, and curiosity prompted him to investigate further instead. He glanced self-consciously out through the doorway, then closed the door carefully behind him.

He found himself in a large and softly furnished study. It was a long and relatively narrow room, the most distinctive item of furniture being a large wooden desk at the far end underneath the windows. The desk was obviously in frequent use, its top strewn with papers and writing materials. Also on top of the desk, lying across everything else, was a gnarled wooden walking stick—a strange sight indeed in such a place as this.

But it was one of the long side walls which fascinated him most, for it was hung along its entire length with portraits, oil paintings—four rows high. He walked softly across the deep carpet to look at them more closely. None of the faces that gazed coldly back at him were familiar. They could not be family portraits, for they showed no similarity to anyone else in the household; in fact they obviously represented many different nationalities.

He walked slowly along the line, hands behind his back, looking very much like any curious visitor to an art gallery. The line did not continue completely to the end of the room but tapered off to only a single row, as if the collection were still being added to. Some of the end frames were blank, as if the portraits had, for some reason, been removed. It seemed strange that someone should leave only a blank frame still hanging, and it struck him that the canvases had been removed hurriedly, being easier to store elsewhere on their own than with the heavy frame attached.

He became suddenly aware that he really had no right to be snooping around in here, and he felt guilty at being so quick to abuse the hospitality of his genial host. He was just about to leave when he saw the small pile of rectangular panels stacked neatly on the seat of the chair behind the desk. He knew immediately what they were, because of their size; they were the paintings from the empty frames.

He stood in frustrated indecision; his curiosity was sheer agony. He wiped his hands self-consciously on his hips and stole a furtive glance at the door before walking quickly behind the desk and transferring the pile of small canvases, stacked facedown, to the desk. His heart quickened as he turned the first canvas over—it was another unfamiliar face. The next couple were the same, and he had begun to think that he was wrong in believing that there was something strange about them, but when he turned the next one he felt his face freeze with shock. He gazed into the belligerent face of a grizzled old man—a familiar old man, although not the face of the man as he had last remembered him; he was much older!

He replaced the painting with trembling hands. There was only one left now, and he knew that this one would be familiar too. He did not really wish to see it, but he no longer had a choice—he had to go on!

134

He turned this one over much more slowly, and it stunned him in spite of his anticipation: the face was his own! It would have been more bearable had it been a painting of him as he now was, but it was not. Instead the face that regarded him stonily was different in some most disturbing ways: it was older, stranger, maybe even wiser, but the eyes...they had seen something, a secret thing, but something which had burned into them and remained!

It was not a portrait for which he had ever posed, for the face was the face of a man of forty or more. He stood gazing at it in horrified fascination, his mind reeling crazily as he sought desperately for some reasonable explanation. There was none.

He replaced the paintings carefully as he had found them on the seat and backed away slowly round the desk. Then he turned and fled the room.

Out in the sunlight again, he stood for a long time against the balustrade, staring unseeingly into the garden and nervously destroying a leaf in his fingers. The experience had quite unsettled him, and he was not ready now to rejoin the others. Why would David have paintings of Evan and his father? It would have been strange enough for him to have even contemporary portraits, but the nature of the ones he had seen truly frightened him.

Of course he had had no business being in there, and for this reason he was unable to tell anyone what he had seen. It was going to be a difficult secret to keep, but keep it he must until such time as someone saw fit to explain it to him.

His attention was drawn by distant sounds of

laughter coming from somewhere inside the house. It tended to offset somewhat his own anxious feelings, and he allowed the sounds to guide him, this time to the correct door.

The laughter subsided as he passed through the sitting room, and as he walked into the dining room where the others were gathered it stopped abruptly. David stood at the far end of the room, an enormous silhouette against the open windows. Miriam was in the midst of serving a meal to Lyddia, sitting at the head of the table. Also at the table sat a young man in about his mid-teens. They all stared at him in obvious surprise.

It suddenly occurred to Evan that they had reason for surprise, and he involuntarily raised a hand to tug sheepishly at the ragged ends of his once-long hair. It was David who came to his rescue, walking down the room to welcome him.

"Good morning, Evan, my boy. Come in and sit down."

He obeyed with a flush of embarrassment showing in his cheeks.

Lyddia was still regarding him with a kind of wide-eyed amusement, and he carefully avoided her gaze. But she was not going to let him off that easily. She cleared her throat in scant warning before she spoke. "What happened to your hair?"

"I cut it." His voice, albeit a little hoarse, had returned.

"Oh."

Evan squirmed inwardly; this child had a way of making him feel infantile before her.

"Did you sleep well?" David asked, apparently unaware of his discomfort.

"Yes, thank you," Evan said, smiling, "although what you told me last night kept me awake for quite a while. I thought of so many more questions to ask you that I should have written them all down."

"This is my brother, Matthew." Lyddia interrupted, waving toward the young man, who now smiled at him also. Evan nodded acknowledgment.

"I suppose you know who I am, too; everyone else seems to know all about me here." The remark was made lightly, but the rueful tone was detectable nevertheless. Matthew continued to smile pleasantly.

"I can appreciate how you feel, Evan. The transition that you have made in the last twenty-four hours is unique—no one else has ever done it before. You have good reason for feeling out of step."

"Out of step!" Evan retorted. "I feel just about out of mind! My greatest problem at the moment is in convincing myself that this is really happening—that it's all true!"

David moved across and sat beside him, beaming a kind of fatherly benevolence that Evan found just a little irritating.

"That's why we don't want you to rush things. You have as much time as you need to come to terms with life here in the Kingdom, and our purpose is to see that you receive all the help you may require."

Evan's eye fell on an object on the table; it was the remains of the chew-bar which he had so carefully retained. It looked most unappetizing, and he realized what had been the source of the amusement before he entered the room. He grinned self-consciously.

"I hope you aren't going to make me finish it."

David laughed. "If there is one thing you will never have to endure here, it is poor food. Of course you will have to relearn what is worth eating and what is not."

Evan raised his eyebrows. "Relearn?"

Everyone laughed—a joke that they passed among them over his head. "Believe me," said Matthew, "that is the correct word. You will hear it many more times."

Evan protested. "You speak as if I were some strangely twisted individual who needs to be straightened out."

Miriam placed a bowl in front of him, containing a cereal of some kind. "Don't let them laugh at you, Evan." Her usually serious expression relaxed a little. "Everyone in this room is in the process of being 'straightened out' as you say. That's what this place is all about."

"Now you make it sound as if I'm in prison," said Evan, "although I must say you don't look at all like prisoners." He looked at the circle of bright, fresh faces around him, and it struck him that these people also blended fittingly into the atmosphere of this beautiful place.

Matthew finished his meal and rose from the table apologetically, explaining his need to leave. "I'll be seeing you quite a bit soon, Evan," he added, "because you will eventually be working with me."

"What do you do?"

Matthew fenced the question. "We'll explain that later on, but you might say that I'm a biologist."

"That's not exactly my field."

Matthew laughed again as he departed. "Don't you believe it!"

Evan sat, brow furrowed, staring at the door through which Matthew had gone until he caught Lyddia still looking at him.

"Don't do that; you'll get wrinkles," she teased.

"What did he mean—'don't believe it'?"

Lyddia put on her superior expression, but David answered first.

"He just meant that you have not necessarily been working in the field to which you are best suited, that's all."

"How would you know that?"

"We know everything about you—you said that yourself."

"Even more than I do?"

"Yes," said David simply. Evan was inclined to argue, but it was difficult to know how to challenge David's blatantly authoritative attitude. He redirected his annoyance into the eating of his meal.

David arose quietly, patted his shoulder reconcilingly, and departed. Only Lyddia remained with him at the table now, and it began slowly to dawn upon him, much to his chagrin, that he had been left in Lyddia's charge for the day. She made her role clearly known to him, fussing over him like a mother hen.

"David will not be back till this evening," Miriam explained, "but Lyddia has a few things to show you. She will take you across to see Paul Bernard at the grains project."

139

"You'll like meeting Paul," said Lyddia, just a little too lightly. "He's a mortal."

Evan stopped abruptly with the spoon partway to his mouth at this strange remark. He would have asked for an explanation except that Lyddia's eyebrows had lifted sharply in sheer impish enjoyment at his surprise.

He ignored her and went back to his meal.

Chapter Six

They walked together down a cool forest trail and—somewhat to Evan's surprise—in silence, Lyddia speaking only when he questioned her. He stole a clandestine glance at the small figure beside him. It was foolish to be afraid of her—she was only a child, yet there was something else there too. . . something he could not quite fathom. She was different; the young face carried a seriousness far beyond her years, especially now when she didn't know he was watching her. That could be inherited from her mother, of course, but there was definitely a side to her personality which he was yet to uncover.

Noisy and vivacious some of the time, she could suddenly slip into another role altogether, providing thoughtful and serious answers to his questions in a way that left him feeling strangely inferior to her.

That could be said of all the people he had met so far, he mused, and it hurt a little, because he was not accustomed to this particular posture. They knew so much about him. . . and in a strange way too! It was not the kind of knowledge that could be obtained simply by reading a dossier on him before he came, but a kind of immediate thing, a presence in which it was impossible to erect any facade. He quickly discovered that if he asked her anything other than a direct and simple question, Lyddia would fix him with an amused gaze that left him feeling as if he were made of glass. From one so young it was embarrassing.

He was yet a stranger here, and he realized that this was a fact to be kept in mind. The discomfort was his alone, and he simply had no cause to blame them. In fact, when he considered it, he had to admit they had showered on him an affection which was not his due. Maybe this bothered him more than he fully realized!

They were little more than a kilometer from the house before Lyddia guided him abruptly from the trail and they began a fairly stiff climb up the wall of the valley. At the top the forest opened out to reveal rich fields of waving grain which, on closer examination, were actually made up of many smaller plots of various varieties. There were people at work here also, and he found himself constantly obliged to acknowledge friendly greetings which he would have considered to be quite unnecessary. Such effusiveness he found to be embarrassing, and he tried to walk as close to Lyddia as possible.

She began to slow her pace, and eventually she stopped and pointed ahead. "That's where you are going." Evan squinted and shaded his eyes; it looked like a small village—a strange sight in this place where everything seemed to be spaced out with such obvious care. The dwellings were pleasant enough, but there was a certain sameness about them which gave the impression of a common project. He had moved a small distance toward it before he realized that Lyddia had dropped back.

142

"Aren't you coming with me?"

"No, I don't need to come any farther. You will find Paul Bernard in unit seventeen. He knows that you are coming."

"But that's silly; surely you aren't just going to make me walk in cold like that?" He spread his hands inquiringly. "If you can walk this far, why not a bit farther?"

She stood rigidly in the one spot as if to further underline her position. "No. . . I don't choose to come any farther."

Evan shrugged and began walking away, but his pace slowed again before he had gone very far. He turned back to face her, still standing stiffly in the one spot.

"Lyddia."

"Yes?" She did not move.

"Do I really have to go there right away?"

"Why do you ask?"

"Well, couldn't I talk to you for just a little while?" She hesitated, clearly undecided about her answer.

"I guess so." He walked back and sat down on the cool grass beside her. She sat also, slowly and uncomfortably. Something was making her uncomfortable in his presence, her face betraying even something of the hollow fear he had seen before. For the first time he began to feel at an advantage, and that was a good opportunity to ask her a few more questions. Her behavior now and the silence that had preceded it was a mystery to him, but he perceived that it would be unwise to ask her too directly about that.

"You said something rather strange back at the house—about Paul being a 'mortal.' What did you mean?"

"There are two kinds of people here—those who were either resurrected or made immortal after the tribulation and those who continued as mortals—that's all."

"That's *all*?"

"Yes." She was trying to play down the matter now that they were alone, but he was determined to make her explain.

"When will I meet one of these 'resurrected' people?" His sarcasm was only thinly veiled.

Lyddia's eyes widened in genuine surprise. "But you already have!"

"I have? Who?"

"*Everybody*, that's who—my parents, Matthew..."

"And you too?"

She lowered her eyes suddenly and tugged at the grass. "No." Evan shook his head incredulously. "I just can't believe it!"

"Do you think I'm lying to you?"

His manner softened. "I'm sorry, I didn't mean it that way. I just meant that I can't grasp...all these people...well, they don't *look* like immortals."

"What would you expect?"

Evan thought for a moment. He didn't really have the slightest idea...then he laughed. "I don't know...perhaps they should be floating around with their feet off the ground or something. I would have recognized it easier if they had looked maybe a little more angelic I guess."

144

"They're not poltergeist, you know," Lyddia cut in. "They're human beings like we are." She was beginning to get on top again and reasserting a superior manner. "There's nothing at all taken away from resurrected people; in fact it would be more correct to say that something has been added."

Evan sat in silence, mentally studying the people he had met. They had indeed exhibited a certain glowing health and vitality, but it had not occurred to him that they might have been immortal.

"Does that mean that these people are sort of...sort of perfect physical specimens?"

"Of course."

"Are they perfect in *every* way?"

"I don't think you should even ask me that. You would do better to ask Daddy or Matthew."

Evan switched the line of questioning. "How about you...why aren't you immortal too?"

She did not look up. "I survived the tribulation. They didn't."

"What happened to them?" He asked the question quickly and instantly regretted it, but it was too late to retract it. She sat for a very long time, tugging aimlessly at the grass alongside her before she answered. Her voice had become harsher and firmer. "We don't talk about that...not ever!"

She looked up into his face and set her jaw in a way that underlined her words. It was Evan's turn to look away now, and he bit his tongue as he did so. Had he thought about it a little more he would not have asked that question. Now the conversation was finished.

He climbed to his feet slowly. "You're still not

coming with me?" She shook her head vigorously. "Okay," he said, "I'll see you later."

He strode toward the complex with a determined tread. There was only one entrance that he could see, and it was at the end of a long, covered walkway. The gate was heavy and ornate, but other than a light catch it had no lock, and it floated open easily.

He looked back and saw the small white figure still standing where he had left her. She waved to him and he returned it, strangely conscious as he did so that she was concerned for him, but the reason escaped him. She turned away then, and he stood watching her until she was completely out of sight before entering.

It was cool and pleasant inside. The sides of the walkway appeared at first glance to open directly into the gardens, but they proved to be closed off with the same invisible glass that he had seen in David's house. At this moment he was rather glad of its plastic qualities, because it arrested him only gently when he tried to walk through it.

He found unit seventeen without difficulty and knocked gently on the solid paneled door.

"Come in." The voice answered from somewhere deep inside. He pushed the unlatched door open and stepped into a softly furnished entrance hall.

"Come in, spaceman," the voice repeated from another room. "We don't have locks here, we're all too..." The voice stopped abruptly as Evan stepped into the sitting room. Paul was sitting on the opposite side in a large easy chair, his face a picture of unguarded surprise.

"What's the matter?" said Evan, aware that this was a strange way to greet his host.

"Oh,...oh, nothing...nothing at all." Paul regained his composure instantly and rose quickly. "I thought you were...I mean, you reminded me of someone else...just for a moment that is."

"I thought it might have been my haircut." Evan grinned. "It seems to have been a knockout with everyone else."

Paul extended a hand in greeting, and Evan took it. They stood like this for a few moments, each sizing the other up. It was a curious, silent greeting.

"What *did* happen to your hair?" said Paul.

"It seemed to bother David's little girl so I cut it off."

"Oh, I see." Paul fingered his beard as he turned away. "Find yourself a seat," he called back over his shoulder. "I'll get you a drink." Evan glanced about the room quickly before sitting in another of the chairs. It was magnificently appointed, although perhaps a little untidy. The walls were hung with many paintings, mostly watercolor landscapes except for a couple which were done in oils. There were even one or two impressionistic works, although they were obviously not completed. Paul returned, carrying two glasses.

"Did you paint all these?" Evan asked.

"Yes, it's a hobby of mine."

"They're very good," said Evan, although he was not at all sure of his competence to pass judgment upon them. Paul shrugged.

"Is that a pop-art creation on the floor?"

"Sorry about the mess," said Paul unconvincingly,

"but I haven't got around to cleaning it up yet." He seated himself on a small stool directly in front of Evan. "Well, well, well. . .so you are David's latest protégé."

Evan was not entirely sure that the remark was a kindly one, but he avoided a rush to judgment. "I don't really know what I am. To be quite honest I feel that I'm regarded as someone under instruction."

"Welcome to the club," Paul sniffed. "I hear you came in the back way."

"Well, I didn't intend to be here, if that's what you mean. As you probably know, I was involved in an accident that somehow short-circuited a fair lump of time."

"Yes, yes. . .I know all about that. You were very lucky."

Evan gazed morosely into his drink. "There were others who weren't."

"As a matter of fact, I didn't mean that you were lucky to survive the accident. I meant that you were lucky to miss out on that 'lump of time' as you call it and still survive as a mortal in the Kingdom. You got off very lightly!"

"Was it as bad as all that?"

Paul continued to gaze intently into Evan's face and shook his head slowly. "They really haven't told you anything, have they?"

"I'm supposed to be finding out slowly, but at the rate the data is coming in, well, I'm afraid even to ask!"

Paul laughed, but with no trace of mirth. "I can provide for you all the data of doom that you may need. David may not have said so, you see, but my job is simply to show you what happens to the nasties. This place is not as peachy-pie as you may be led to think."

Evan ran his fingers through his tousled hair, visibly irritated. "Look...before you go making too many assumptions about me, I don't have any preconceptions about this place at all. You don't have anything to sell me, you know." He slumped back into his chair. "But why you? Why should David send me here to you?"

Paul grinned somewhat awkwardly. "He's just sparing you from having to ask him. David is one of the resurrected ones—I suppose you know that. People like you and me find him a bit difficult to talk to; he upsets us."

Evan was surprised at the accuracy of the statement. "You're right, I know just exactly what you mean. Even Lyddia is a bit the same for me, and she's just a mortal."

"That's because they both have the gift. It's a matter of degree with Lyddia, but it's there just the same."

"The gift? What is that?"

Paul stroked his chin carefully and looked at the ceiling for some time before he answered. "It's not an easy thing to explain, but it's something which has been added to the otherwise normal faculties of these people; it allows them to go considerably beyond what would usually be their human limitations. You might say it's an additional knowledge—a knowledge that is untouched and unimpaired by anything that happens around them; it sort of trancends everything that they may see or be told." He stood up and paced quickly to

149

the other end of the room, hands behind his back, before continuing. "When David speaks to you, he knows exactly how you feel about it. It's even more than that; he knows of every last consequence that his words will have—even before he says them."

"Can he read my mind?" Evan asked cautiously.

"I really don't know. I don't think so—at least I don't think he chooses to. But he just *knows* so much, do you see? He knows so much that any kind of an untruth, even an indirect question, is quite wasted on him. It just never comes off."

"Does that mean you cannot even differ with him?"

Paul laughed again, with genuine amusement this time. "If that's the truth, then I've been bucking the system for nine years at least. Yes, you may differ with him—but let me tell you one more thing." He walked back close to Evan again. "You will always, but *always*, be wrong!"

"Is he really as infallible as all that?"

"Yes, he is." Paul resumed his perch on the stool and looked at Evan directly as he spoke. "Try looking back over your own life and imagine that the eventual consequences of every thought, word, or action were somehow known to you in advance. How many things do you think you would have done...or not done?"

Evan gave a long, low whistle. "I would have kept my mouth shut on a few occasions, that's for sure! I'm beginning to see the kind of advantage that David must have over us. But why should I feel the same thing with Lyddia too? Isn't she just a mortal?"

"The gift is not the exclusive property of the resurrected, although to receive it fully does qualify a

150

person for immortal status. When it's all said and done, the acquisition of the gift is the reason for the millennial reign—to give everyone a reasonable chance."

Evan was becoming interested. "What do we have to do to get this so-called gift? The test must be pretty severe."

"You're overlooking the fact that it *is* a gift. It's there for the having...for anyone who wants it."

"You just ask?"

"It's not much more than that. It's sufficient to say that it's there for the choosing."

Evan, determined to be tactful, thought for a few moments before phrasing the next question. "Do you have this gift?"

Paul did not answer immediately, and Evan sensed his slight discomfort if not annoyance. "I have a little of it, but the correct answer to that question would really be 'no'!"

"But if it's a gift, and it's there for the asking, why don't you have it also?"

Paul's discomfort was more obvious. He arose again and walked slowly to the other end of the room. When he spoke, his voice carried almost a small hint of triumph which Evan could not understand. "I don't have it because I do not *choose* to possess it. That's all."

Evan frowned incredulously. "But that's contradictory. I can only say that in the light of what you have already told me, it just doesn't...."

"I know what you are going to say," Paul cut in sharply, "and you can forget it. When you come to try for the gift, you can start advising me on how it is done if you like, but until such a time as that, you could not possibly understand. And it's none of your business either."

Evan ducked his head and raised a hand. "Okay, okay...I didn't mean to offend you."

Paul collected himself with some visible effort. "You aren't offending me; I'm only warning you not to try solving everyone else's problems here. You have quite enough of your own."

Evan flushed. "So everybody here keeps telling me!" He stood and walked to the window. "But let me just remind you that I haven't necessarily accepted that situation. After all, I didn't ask to come here. I didn't choose to live while the others died. That was forced upon me. I didn't ask David or the others to 'take charge' of me here. I might owe them something I guess, but they don't own my life. I am my own man, you know, and if this didactic attitude continues to crop up with every person I meet I might just have to prove it!"

When he turned back he found Paul looking at him curiously and not without amusement. "You know what, spaceman? I had decided before ever you came here that I wasn't going to like you. But despite myself I think that maybe I do."

"That's very charitable of you." Evan felt somewhat disarmed. Paul ignored the sarcasm. "I like you because you have so little of the gift. You talk like what you are—a naïve tourist in a strange country."

"And you like me because I'm dumb?"

Paul laughed genuinely this time. "It's just so long

since I've heard any upstart speeches like that that I had forgotten they ever existed." He extended his arm toward Evan, sizing him up across the room using the long handle of a paintbrush, as if preparing to sketch him. "Stay just as you are, will you? Never change!"

Paul turned and left the room suddenly, carrying his laughter with him to some other part of the house, leaving Evan standing in enraged bewilderment. He sat abruptly back in his chair and sulked.

Paul eventually reentered, carrying two pairs of overshoes. Evan had had time to cool a little. "Before you ask any more questions," said Paul, "put these on and we'll go outside for a look around."

Evan obeyed in subdued silence. In spite of his little speech he sensed that he had much to learn from Paul, and he would be simply doing himself a disservice if he allowed his irritation to interfere.

Paul led him back into the fields through which he had walked previously. It was apparent from the acknowledgments paid him by the field workers that Paul was of senior status in the small colony. Not only that, he was obviously well qualified to be, because Evan could detect that apart from being extremely knowledgeable on matters of agriculture he displayed also an animated and energetic interest.

Paul left his side to discuss some problem with one of the workers, and Evan regarded him from a distance. Why was it that people had to be enigmatic here? As far as he could tell, life in the Kingdom was treating Paul extremely well. He was comfortably housed and provided for, and he was employed in a field in which he was obviously competent and at ease. Yet there was underlying belligerence...and that sardonic humor which left Evan feeling curiously uncomfortable. Something was wrong here, and he could not help feeling it was closely allied to the discomfort that had attended him ever since he had arrived.

Paul's contrived amusement at his "speech" was somehow significant, and he found himself thinking about it, searching for a clue. He had taken the words out of Paul's own mouth! That's what he had done! Paul was not likely to admit it, of course, but the humor was simply a front hiding an unconfessed accord.

Paul came back toward him, trailed by a group of field workers whom he began to introduce to Evan. The succession of names passed over his head, and he realized later that he could not recall even one of them...there were too many other things occupying his mind.

The people were friendly, but this was tempered with an almost strained politeness. They carried with them simple garden utensils, and wore work clothes which appeared to be made from the same fine material as his own outfit.

When they were again walking alone, Evan began to explore the reasons behind the grain project. "All these people...they seem to be equipped with rather rudimentary tools. Don't you have machines?"

Paul grinned. "Don't judge our farming methods too much by this project. We aren't actually involved in producing crops; this is an environmental recovery project, and all the grains you see here are essentially hand-nursed."

154

"Those other workers...?"

"Those 'workers' are all experts—experts with access to a technology far beyond anything you would have known in your time."

"If you're not growing crops, what are you doing?"

Paul kicked at the ground with a kind of contempt. "Basically we are trying to put the earth back more or less as it was before man—particularly your generation—got to it."

"I don't understand what you mean," Evan replied. "My generation brought intensified technology to bear on agricultural problems and made tremendous strides in feeding the world's hungry. I mean, there was the green revolution—wasn't there?"

Paul put a hand to his head, feigning pain. "The green revolution in the long run was a scorched earth policy. You took from nature her greatest defense, her greatest resilience; you took away her diversity. You covered great areas with vast monocultures of genetically inferior grains. They had little resistance to blight and predator, so you just doused them with pesticides and fungicides. You literally poisoned the earth with those! Crops wouldn't grow in ordinary soil, so you heaped artificially produced fertilizers on them as well. The environmental impact of these was no better. Then you started to run out of energy, and that was the finish. You set about killing each other in order to lay hold on the last fossil fuels remaining on the planet."

Paul gesticulated as if laying before them a vast canvas. "Can't you see it? You had two tigers by their tails—to continue the green revolution was either to

155

pollute yourselves out of existence or exhaust your last remaining natural resources, but to discontinue it would be to produce famine and national animosities that would be unthinkable."

"I can't say that we didn't know about that," Evan admitted, "but what was eventually decided?"

"The disputes over energy supplies had the effect eventually of just turning people off. They were denied energy to manufacture fertilizers and pesticides, energy to work crops, energy to transport them. The whole thing just...just came down...." He gesticulated again as if to wipe the canvas clean.

They walked slowly back toward the home units, Evan deep in thought. "You say they ran out of energy, but what about the other sources besides fossil fuels?"

Paul stopped walking abruptly. "What other sources?"

"Nuclear energy and solar energy and so on...."

"Oh, yes." Paul nodded knowingly. "You mean all those fantasies that your generation invented so as to avoid changing its life-style."

"I don't understand!"

"It's simple; people in your day knew well enough that Earth's resources were being depleted—you just admitted that—but to act on the truth would have cost you too much. You invented a great list of excuses, not the least of which was the vague notion that some other alternative source of energy would 'turn up' some day. As for the fossil fuels, your little affluent corner of the world was set to use them all up in the meantime."

156

Evan found himself moving to the defensive. "But those sources were there. I mean they were already in use, weren't they?"

"Yes, they were already in use, and the eventual consequences were always there for you to anticipate—had you cared to, that is."

Evan nodded. "There were a lot of people opposed to it—nuclear power I mean."

They began to walk again, and Paul continued. "Opposition wasn't enough. You see, when the crunch came, the real power rested where the money was, with the wealthy nations and their big corporations, that is, and in spite of the fact that everyone *knew* what was happening, you all went your own econocentric way. No one was willing to make the decision which at all jeopardized what he considered to be his fair share of the 'good life.'" He thought for a moment before going on. "Just imagine for one moment, spaceman, politicians in your country operating from a platform designed to avert the catastrophe. Imagine a policy of reducing economic growth or creature comforts. Imagine winding down the motor industry as an environmental hazard, walking instead of riding. Imagine doors opened to other nations regardless of the economic or cultural impact upon your own society." Paul grinned with obvious satisfaction at the weight of his argument. "Would they have got your vote?"

Evan did not answer but continued to look at the ground passing slowly beneath his feet. He could have answered immediately, but Paul possessed sufficient of the gift to place him considerably at risk; he knew that the question was too well placed to sidestep easily. He needed time to think! He eventually answered thoughtfully, "I don't think that question is entirely fair...I mean it sort of doesn't let me answer without incriminating myself by inference—as apathetic on one hand or hypocritical on the other. It's true enough that we knew of these things, but then again, it was a world that we were obliged to live in. I mean we couldn't just step off, could we?"

"That argument is a bit convenient, don't you think? You didn't exactly rail against things as they were, did you?"

Evan smiled ruefully. "You sound as if you are trying to hold me individually responsible for the sins of the world. I don't see that I really have to answer for them; I genuinely believed that the answers would come up."

"That's what you all thought...and you were all wrong."

"Why should we pay for an honest mistake?"

Paul stopped walking again. He was serious now. "Because it was not a mistake—it was a lie! You claim that your inaction was due to your faith in technology, but it wasn't. You had faith only in the notion that someone else would be around to pick up the tab for you. Isn't that true?"

"What makes you so sure?" asked Evan, avoiding the question.

"Because, spaceman, it doesn't even make sense. Let's look at the things that you knew." He began to mark off points on his fingers. "First, you knew that you were depleting vital natural resources; second, you knew that your meager portion of the world's population was responsible for the depletion. You knew that fossil fuels were needed for things other than mere energy—things like drugs, fertilizers, pesticides and industrial chemicals, raw materials for paints and plastics and so on. You *knew* that technology would never be able to put oil back in the ground; it only promised alternative energy. What did you expect the rest of the world to use for these requirements after you had thrown them all away? Even if you didn't really care for these people, as indeed you didn't, did it ever occur to you that there would be generations following after you in your own land? And what about that nuclear energy of yours? It turned out to be a veritable Pandora's box. You ended up eventually devoting more effort to trying to put the lid back on than you did to exploiting it—except as weaponry that is."

Evan scratched at his tousled hair thoughtfully. "I still think we had no other choice. For the most part, our society was already constructed for us. Our bridges were already burned."

"Come with me!" Paul placed a firm hand on his shoulder. They were back at the entrance now, but Evan found himself being guided onto the pathway running parallel to the wall. They walked quickly and in silence for some minutes until they were at the opposite side of the complex. It was an elevated position, commanding a panoramic view across a huge plain far below them. Paul held out his hand, inviting Evan to look.

The scene was breathtaking. Evan had not realized

just how elevated this position was. The plain was heavily forested, similar to the area where he had landed. A cool breeze swept up the mountainside toward them, and he could smell the same rain-forest perfume which had so impressed him on his arrival. "It's beautiful," he said simply.

Paul just grunted. "Look farther...toward the horizon." Evan looked. A range of mountains was visible at the other side of the plain, a long way off, at a distance of about fifty kilometers. Then suddenly he realized what Paul was referring to. The plain was not uniform but was perceptibly less fertile looking as the distance from where they were standing increased. At a distant point the forest dissolved into what appeared to be a desert. The air was clear enough for them to discern that the distant hills were bare and rugged.

"This garden doesn't cover the whole earth?" Evan inquired.

"No, but it will some day. What you see out there is but one of its many growing edges."

"And beyond that?"

Paul selected a smooth stone with some care and sat down. "You said a few minutes ago that the people in your day couldn't go back because they had burned their bridges, right?"

"Yes."

"Did the thought ever occur to you that man would eventually have to walk back over the ashes?" Evan felt a strange chill pass over him.

"Is that what people are doing out there?"

Paul nodded. "In a sentence they are putting it back as it was...with their bare hands."

Evan decided that it was time to sit also. He sat on a patch of soft, slightly damp grass in front of Paul and tucked his knees up under his chin. He recalled his landing on the previous day, and the first wonder of gazing upon the magnificent garden-like setting. "It's strange" he said. "I sensed that when I arrived...that it was done by hand, I mean. But the scope of it! How could men do so much with their bare hands?"

"They aren't doing it entirely on their own. You need to remember that the technology available to them is vastly superior to anything you would know of...if they choose to use it, of course."

"They have a choice?"

"Oh, yes! In fact the choice goes right on down the line—from the cooperative ones who choose to work things out hand-in-glove with God down to the people who insist on living with the consequences of their former ways. When the Kingdom was established it simply became the dominant government of the world; all the others were disbanded. But on an individual level people weren't dragged screaming and kicking into it if they didn't want to come. Some people, even some nations, fought it physically for a time."

"So people still do as they please?"

Paul grimaced and tugged at his beard. "In a way I suppose the answer has to be yes, but only insofar as they accept all its consequences. That's the difference here, you see—no one is able to sidestep the consequences."

"What category do you fall into?" said Evan, cautiously.

Paul grimaced again. "I was hoping you wouldn't ask. You see, it's not the kind of question that can be readily answered." He gazed thoughtfully into the distance, carefully choosing his words before uttering them. "I guess I could say that I cooperate as much as I am able. As you can see, I fare pretty well here."

Evan cut in. "What I can't understand is why so many things seem to be available here but they aren't wanted by everyone. I mean, you talk about the gift, and about technology, even access to the Kingdom itself as if all these things are free for the taking. Why don't you just take?"

Paul's face darkened visibly, and Evan realized that he was treading forbidden ground again. "You have a lot to learn yet about the Kingdom, spaceman." He spoke with a strange kind of finality, as if to end this line of discussion.

Evan looked away to the horizon again. Some of the work being done was visible, because he could see the clouds of dust and the patterns of vast earthworks etched onto the wilderness.

"In a way," he said quietly, "you're doing the same thing, aren't you?"

"The same what?"

"You're putting it back—with your hands. I mean, those hand tools and everything?"

Paul's expression was an admission in itself. "Yes, I guess so. . . ."

"Are you a prisoner here?"

Paul's head jerked up suddenly. The question had been most unexpected. "Yes, I guess so." The answer was soft but guarded.

Evan waved toward the plain. "Were you out there?"

"Yes. Not out there, exactly, but on a project similar to it."

"And now you're sort of 'promoted' to here?"

Paul winced. "You might call it that...but I wouldn't."

"You can't deny that you are more favored here though, can you?"

"I am more favored now, in some ways—but you see...well, there *is* a price."

"You said it was all free."

Paul stood up abruptly. "You're moving too fast, spaceman." He began to walk back along the path. "Would you like to try your hand at some painting?" he called back over his shoulder.

Evan masked his feelings of rejection with some effort. "All right," he said, getting to his feet, "but I'll need quite a bit of instruction."

As they walked back to the entrance, Paul explained his work at the grains project in more detail. Primarily, he was concerned with the reestablishment of diversity in the grains, not only of the grains themselves but their blights and predators also. To Evan this seemed at first to be a strange kind of planned devolution. The notion persisted, however, only until he had begun to appreciate the vast and intensified technology involved, and at this point Paul could move comfortably over his head. He not only was obviously competent in every branch of science associated with his work but also appeared to possess some kind of total recall, as if every fact were somehow constantly at his fingertips. Evan did not ask the question, but it was clear to him that this was a manifestation of the gift, even if Paul was disinclined to acknowledge it.

His host was equally ebullient about his art, and Evan suddenly discovered that he was under quite high-pressure instruction. Paul lectured him continually during the midday meal and later escorted him back to the point at the rear of the complex, heavily laden with the necessary materials for his initiation into landscape painting.

Paul elected to sit on the same stone again and sketch, but Evan, eternally unsatisfied, continued to carry his easel laboriously along the ridge in an effort to find an aspect more to his liking. When finally he had settled on a location, he was near the next corner of the complex, almost out of earshot. Although the panorama was not as wide at this point, the view back down the valley was particularly beautiful, and it included David Cohen's home.

"Why don't you come up here?" He motioned to Paul to follow him. Paul simply shook his head and became more engrossed in his sketching. Not wishing to retrace his steps, Evan chose to work alone without assistance. The results were not just disappointing but disastrous!

In spite of the futility of his attempts, he welcomed the opportunity to be on his own for a while. He could see the wisdom in David's warning about going too fast. Paul was saying the same thing, although in a far more belligerent manner, but he knew that they were right. When he thought about it, there was wisdom even in David's decision to send him here to Paul, for Paul was just the kind of person to put him firmly in his place. The realization was a little painful, but it was a truth to be faced!

The afternoon was well advanced when he finally admitted defeat. He was relieved that Paul had not come to look his work over. Glancing frequently over his shoulder to look at the other man, he could see that he was not even particularly interested in his own work, but seemed to be spending most of his time sitting motionless, staring out over the plain as if completely preoccupied with some other problem.

Evan amused himself for a short while just tearing his painting into long soggy strips before he considered it sufficiently disfigured to risk going back to Paul with the remains. He was within about thirty meters of him before he realized that David was there too.

This was a little startling, simply because only a few seconds before Paul had been quite alone and David was nowhere in sight. The two men were speaking softly as he approached, and it was David who broke off to greet him.

"Hello, Evan. Have you had a good day?"

"Well, yes and no." Evan grinned. "Would you accept that as an answer?"

"Under the circumstances, it is the answer I would have expected," David beamed back. Even out in the open, he was of spectacular build, and the expansive gestures of his hands made him appear still larger.

"Lyddia is coming over to walk back with you. I wish to spend some time here alone with Paul now. Do you mind?"

165

"No, of course not." He glanced at Paul, but the other was not looking at him, perhaps even avoiding his gaze. He snapped his sketchbook shut with a kind of resigned finality which suggested that he was not entirely in agreement with David's suggestion.

Evan felt embarrassed. "I'll take these things back to the house if you like, Paul. I suppose I'll see you later?" Paul neither replied or looked at him, but David passed a secret nod, gesturing him to leave.

Once back near the gate, he looked behind him to see David sit gently beside the other man and place a hand on his shoulder. He was speaking as he did so, but the words were lost over the distance.

He took the opportunity, once inside, to explore Paul's house a little more closely, not without a sense of guilt, but he was driven by an almost insatiable curiosity to find out more about this man.

His investigations revealed little. The home unit was somewhat smaller than he had first thought, and it was obvious that Paul lived quite alone. The workmanship in its construction was of the same incredible quality as he had seen at David's house, and it would certainly have been a most expensive dwelling back in his own time.

And yet, in spite of all this, there *was* something of a prisonlike quality about it, revealed perhaps a little more in Paul's attitude than the building itself. He spent a few moments picking up the pallet and brushes from the floor, and as he did so he found himself wondering again about the thinly veiled belligerence in Paul's manner.

He wandered thoughtfully through the house for a

little while before he suddenly remembered Lyddia's unwillingness to come there. David had said that she was coming! He left the house hurriedly and returned to the main entrance. People were coming in from the fields now, and they acknowledged him politely as they passed, a little more quietly than they had previously. He was conscious as he walked through the covered way that people were watching him from their doorways, regarding him with a kind of reserved silence—perhaps even hostility. It made him feel curiously uncomfortable, and as he emerged into the late afternoon sun he was even quite relieved to see the small white figure standing beside the path —not a step closer than she had come that morning. He wondered how long she had been waiting there!

He broke into a clumsy run and was somewhat out of breath by the time he reached her.

"I'm sorry, Lyddia. I forgot that you wouldn't be coming up to the house."

"Oh, that's all right." She flicked her hair quickly to one side as if to emphasize the unimportance of his lateness. "Did you have a good day?"

"That's just what your father asked," Evan commented as he fell into step beside her.

"Well, did you?"

"Yes, I guess so. I'm starting to learn a bit more about the place now, or at least I'm beginning to realize how much I didn't know."

"Did Paul like you?" she asked casually.

Evan scratched his head awkwardly. "Well, as a matter of fact, he told me specifically that he did. He's a rather odd fellow to work out though." He arched

167

his eyebrows inquiringly. "Is there some reason why he shouldn't like me?"

"Oh, no," she said hastily. "I knew he would like you...in fact we *all* like you." She made the remark quite unaffectedly, without the usual condescension, and Evan was flattered.

They had walked in silence back to the floor of the valley before he had summoned the courage to mention what was troubling him. "I'm sorry if I asked you too many questions back there...I didn't mean to be too inquisitive...they just sort of came out."

She flashed him a conciliatory smile. "You don't have to worry about things like that here, Evan. I can't be hurt by anything you say—and that's the truth. On the other hand, we *do* care for you, and that's why we don't tell you everything you ask."

"You can be afraid though. I've seen you looking afraid."

She nodded. "Yes, I do recall fears; but they are only memories. They will all fade completely in time. But there is nothing that I need to fear—or that you need to fear for that matter."

"I don't know about that...." He paused and cleared his throat. He was beginning to confess more than he had intended, but it seemed not to matter very much now. "I think I *am* afraid—after being with Paul, that is. I had the feeling that he is being hurt or punished somehow. It's as if this place, however beautiful, is a veneer over a kind of suffering that I can't quite put my finger on." He watched her face closely. "Your father has something to do with it."

She took the remark well, smiling as she replied.

"No, Evan, you are quite wrong if you think my father could hurt anyone. He is a ruler, of course, but his sole interest is in serving and ministering to people. You'll find that out for yourself. But you are right when you say that Paul suffers, because he does. That suffering originates with him —it doesn't come from anywhere else."

"Does it have anything to do with consequences?"

She registered slight surprise. "It has *everything* to do with consequences, but I wouldn't advise that you ask him about that. . .not for the present anyway."

He waited for a little while before he spoke again. "And what about me?"

"I don't know what you mean."

"Well, if everyone is tied up with consequences like this, why is it that I don't seem to be?"

"Oh," she said, laughing, "I wouldn't be so sure about that. No living soul really sidesteps the results of the way he chooses to live. Of course. . ." she became slightly superior again, "there have been a few concessions made in your case."

"Like what?"

"For one thing, the gift has been withheld from you, and then of course there is the language."

"The language?"

She looked sideways at him rather coyly. "I have a feeling you're not going to believe this when I tell you, but you have a new language and you are using it right now. Others have had to learn it, but to you it was given."

He stared back at her incredulously, although he was disinclined to argue; he was learning already to be

169

accustomed to the incredible. "Do they speak this language everywhere—I mean, throughout the earth?"

"Not quite. There are still some areas where people have not accepted it, but that will be corrected soon. We are fairly close to the Eastern center place here, and there are little of the old ways left. It isn't the same everywhere yet."

He frowned in an effort to encompass this concept of a changing world. He had assumed from the first that there had been a dramatic and spontaneous change with the coming of the Kingdom, but had never thought of such a life-style growing and spilling out gradually over the old.

"Do you know what?" he confided. "I'm still afraid."

"Why should you be?"

"It's just something that keeps chewing away at a corner of my mind. I seem to have short-circuited the system somewhere in more ways than one. I'm getting some kind of preferential treatment...I know it...and I think other people know it too."

She became suddenly serious. "Evan, you are a very special visitor here—you need to remember that—and it does make you somewhat different. I can't explain it to you any better, except to say one more thing...."

"What's that?"

"By virtue of a higher law than Earth has ever acknowledged, it is not possible for anything here to prevail which is unjust. Can you believe that?"

"Yes...I guess so."

"Well, then"—she grinned—"You don't have a problem, do you?"

Chapter Seven

Evan did not see Paul again for some weeks. The first several days he spent at the house, sometimes alone, as everyone seemed to be occupied, and sometimes in the presence of other members of the family. As David had promised, there were few demands made upon him, and he found it very easy to slip into the style of life which the Kingdom offered. What had seemed at first to be a somewhat Spartan existence, lacking many of the more obvious mechanical conveniences of his former days, was in fact a rural paradise. Without the fierce pressures of the old urban society, he found himself beginning to appreciate again the simple pleasures that were to be found in such things as reading a good book, walking in the beautiful countryside, or even sitting in silence with another person.

Such idyllic days could not last, of course, but it was not until well after the desire for action had begun to tug at him that David permitted him to begin working. Matthew told him little about his vocation other than what was necessary to keep his curiosity at fever pitch, preferring to leave explanations until he could show him at first hand. It was an astute course of action, because Evan's curiosity grew day by day to the point where his inactivity became pure agony.

Lyddia was his greatest companion. Once his own facade of superiority was lowered, hers seemed never to have existed. There were things they left undiscussed, but these were understood, and she became to him a confidante in whom he knew he could trust.

Communication with the others became, if anything, even more difficult, particularly as he began to appreciate the awesome nature of the gulf between them. The problem was his—not theirs; this he knew well, and yet there was a vast unexplored area between understanding the problem on the one hand and knowing how to handle it on the other.

In a way, it was very frustrating, because these people had obvious access to knowledge and understanding beyond his comprehension, yet he could not begin to tap this resource without somehow contracting to lay his soul bare to their piercing discernment, and that was just not possible!

Lyddia was perceptive also, but as long as she pretended not to be he was happy to go along with the deception—a luxury he could not afford with the others. He even managed to extract from her some of the delicate details about family life in the Kingdom. The idea of resurrected married couples was a difficult one to handle, but he dared not ask the others about it for fear of appearing morbidly curious.

The sole reason for a nuclear family in this case, it turned out, was Lyddia herself, for it was now forbidden that any mortal child should be denied that privilege.

172

But what would happen later? Would the family simply disband because this one immediate goal was accomplished? Lyddia proved somewhat less than equal to this problem, explaining rather unconvincingly that the satisfactions of resurrected people went beyond what would normally be considered classic satisfactions.

Such questions as these were to remain a problem for him, but there were some compensations in the discovery that even Lyddia's overflowing well of knowledge ran dry at some points.

In spite of all her assurances, his apparent status in the community still worried him considerably, and he began to look forward to working with Matthew Cohen, even if only to partly justify his presence among them. His old vocation as an astronaut was quickly slipping away from him, almost unnoticed, being so foreign to his new way of life as to seem distant and unreal. He had not even asked whether space exploration was still being carried out.

There was certainly no end to research, and this realization was dealt out to him very heavily on his first visit with Matthew to the biological studies building. Lyddia had arisen earlier that morning to prepare his breakfast and had dispatched him on his way with all the ceremony and trappings of a mother sending her child off for a first day at school. The others had watched this with unconcealed amusement to which Lyddia seemed quite oblivious. Evan was embarrassed, refusing even a parting wave as he set off self-consciously at Matthew's side to walk to the biological studies building.

Once there, he entered a world which he previously could never have conceived. The magnificence of the building alone was breathtaking, but the sheer scope of the work being done there was an even more stunning revelation. He followed Matthew through the gloriously furnished structure, looking apprehensively out through the immense transparent walls which, at the higher levels, gave the whole building a disturbing illusion of soaring flight.

Matthew ushered him into a small, attractive office and bade him be seated; then he sat behind the untidy, cluttered desk and grinned at him with almost childlike enthusiasm. "Well, what do you think of the place?"

Evan gestured helplessly. "It's fantastic! I just never thought that it would be anything like this. Whatever do you *do* here?"

"Research...just pure research."

"Into what?"

"Our particular interest is biological studies—living things. This whole place is a complex of nurseries, laboratories, computor rooms....We have just about unlimited access to any tools needed for the furthering of our understanding."

Evan regarded the other man quizzically. "Don't misunderstand me when I say this, but I sort of thought that...well, I thought that you people already knew everything...being resurrected, I mean."

Matthew laughed. "If you mean the gift, then I suppose that is partly true. Along with other insights it does bring us the advantage of total recall. One could not really operate in a field such as this without that faculty. But the gift is something which is *added* to our knowledge; it doesn't replace it."

"Then every knowledge is not given to you?"

Matthew looked at him carefully for a while before he answered. "I think you may have the wrong idea about the real purpose of knowledge, Evan." He rose from his chair and moved around to sit on the front of the desk. "If you think about it for a while, you'll realize that the quest for knowledge is of greater importance to people than the knowledge itself. Surely there is no greater experience for a man than the pure thrill of discovery!" He grinned down at Evan. "You were an astronaut. You should know all about that."

Evan nodded.

Matthew continued, "If this were not so, what kind of madness could you think of to explain why the Earth of your time—being so beset with problems, many of them financial—would expend so much of itself to simply shoot three men out into space just to have another look at it?"

"I had wondered about that myself."

"Then you didn't need to. You need only to look into your own mind—the thoughts that led you into that crazy escapade—and find the answers there. Man *needs* to discover new areas, new insights, new concepts; it's basic to his nature."

Evan thought for a while. "But if there is such satisfaction to be gained from adding to knowledge... and I realize that there is... would not a knowledge of all things simply provide this, but without the wear and tear?"

"The 'wear and tear' as you put it is the satisfaction in itself. There *is* a thrill of discovery, but it is always transitory. The mysteriously unexplored one day can be terribly mundane the next. I'm sure you realize this."

"Is there ever any end to it?" Evan asked, almost appealingly.

Matthew laughed again. "I'm afraid that has to be included on the list of things we don't really know. For the moment I like to think that there is not. Quite frankly, Evan, it doesn't really concern me at this time. You can probably understand that, being freed from the limitations of mortality, I can follow the things that interest me for as long as I care to. The work we are doing now should be good for the remainder of the millennium at least."

"Can you explain to me what you actually *are* doing. . .simply, I mean?"

Matthew dropped his chin to his chest and thought carefully. "I'm involved in the study of the animal brain. My particular task is recording and commenting on our findings, then writing them in reports in a language that everyone can understand. You see, not everyone who is interested in this field is necessarily free to work in it. There are many other specialists, for instance, in this very building who would rely on my department to keep them informed on any developments that could be useful to them."

"Do you carry out research on animals?"

"Yes. I'll take you to the nursery very soon and you can see them for yourself."

Evan shifted in his seat. "What do they think about all this...the animals, I mean."

"If you're thinking about vivisection you're on the wrong track entirely. As I said, every item of knowledge may not be available to us, but we do have access to techniques for which many of your scientists would have given their eyes."

"The animals aren't harmed?"

"Our methods are quite nondestructive, and the advantages in this are enormous. In times past, for many types of investigation, the biologist would take some hapless animal, carve it up, and then examine it. That's a most extraordinary way to find out about living creatures, isn't it? It provides a certain amount of information, but it quite forbids the investigator to observe the functions of a normal, healthy animal."

Evan's interest was aroused. "May I see you do some of these things?"

"Yes, but you can't expect to be able to understand too much all at once." Matthew stood and walked to the window. "As a matter of fact, we are already well beyond the point that would have previously required vivisection. We have had the physiological parameters of the animal brain quite well defined for some time now. The really interesting study is why it does what it does."

"Are you examining the human brain also?"

"Not as a specific project; we have too far to go in other areas yet I'm afraid. There are related fields, though, in which other people are hard at work. The thought processes involved in the recognition and use of language, for instance, is a study that will occupy many years."

The conversation was beginning to get too far ahead of Evan. "Could we go back to the business of knowledge again?" he asked.

"Certainly."

"As I understand it, a resurrected person like you has been re-created . . . well . . . perfect. Is that the word?"

Matthew nodded carefully.

"Well, if you are perfect, why is your knowledge not perfect? I mean, if you have to bow to some higher source for a continuing growth in your understanding, surely that makes you somewhat less than that source. If you were perfect, then you would have to be like God, would you not?" Evan concluded with a deep breath.

Matthew turned from the window, smiling patiently. "Come with me, Evan. I have something I would like to show you."

"Where are we going?" Evan asked as they made their way down the thickly carpeted corridor.

"Up on the roof—that's where the nursery is."

Evan followed in silence, completely absorbed by the profusion of interesting-looking departments through which they passed. Behind vast, transparent walls he saw fantastic sights—elaborate laboratories and magnificent rooms housing computors and other scientific equipment. He found himself beginning to feel rather small and insignificant in this setting. Up until only a short time ago he was one of the privileged few—an astronaut, a man who rode on the very bow-wave of advancing technology. Now he was just a raw recruit, worthy of nothing more than a

178

stamp-licking job in this awesome enterprise. But he was flattered, also, because he sensed nothing of the supercilious facade which often surrounded such competent people. On the contrary, he was conscious of an outgoing regard for him evidenced in the friendly face of each person that they passed.

They entered the breathtaking spiral stairwell and walked effortlessly to the roof, sixteen stories higher, and some thirty or so floors from the ground. When they emerged on the roof, Evan had the curious feeling that he was stepping out onto ground-level again, for the entire roof was planted as a garden. They appeared at first to be under the open sky, but Matthew pointed out that they were in fact under a huge transparent dome.

The whole area was literally alive with the sights and sounds of animal life, the noise from the myriads of birds that about masked off everything else. Evan just stood, savoring the sheer wonder of it—an indoor zoo, in effect, which somehow afforded the animals almost complete freedom. He laughed. "You seem to have happy enough research animals."

"Yes," said Matthew, "I think you can sense how unthinkable it would be for us to harm them."

Evan ducked as some of the birds dived playfully at his head, and walked slowly down a path that was heavily overhung with lush, green foliage. Monkeys of various sizes and hues cavorted noisily over his head, following him with impish curiosity.

He realized, with sudden involuntary dread, that even the big cats were here, too, for a leopard appeared on the path ahead and stopped to fix him with its baleful stare.

Evan returned hastily to Matthew's side. "I know they are harmless, but that doesn't stop me from *feeling* that he's regarding me as a possible breakfast."

"Don't worry, we all had that problem for a short while. They are actually quite affectionate you know."

"You brought me up here to show me something?"

"Yes, it's nothing much—just a little object lesson you might say. Come over here." He led the way, and Evan followed, skirting apprehensively around the cat. The path widened out to form a beautiful bower, over which there hung masses of extraordinary blooms.

"What do you think of this?"

"It's very . . . beautiful!" said Evan, quite at a loss for sufficient superlatives.

"Pick yourself one of them."

Evan moved to select a rose from one of the bushes and returned awkwardly to Matthew's side with it.

"What do you think of it?" Matthew asked again.

"As I said, it's beautiful."

"Would you say it was perfect?"

Evan arched his eyebrows and viewed the bloom at arm's length. "I'm not any sort of horticulturist, so I wouldn't know. It *looks* perfect . . . I guess."

"So does that make it God?"

Evan grinned wryly. "I get your point. If a perfect rose isn't God, then a perfect man isn't either."

"That's right," said Matthew, "but I haven't finished yet. Would you permit me to pluck a perfect rose also?"

"Be my guest," said Evan, a little bemused. Matthew walked to the shrubbery, and shunning the roses that hung there, stooped instead to reach below the foliage. He returned carrying the limp remains of a fallen bloom which had been lying partly decayed on the ground.

"That's a perfect rose?"

"Ah!" said Matthew, "it seems that we have to get right down to deciding what we mean when we say perfection."

"Are you calling that a perfect rose?"

"Yes, I am. Why should I not do so?"

Evan scratched his head warily. "I'd like to see you face the judges with it."

"But what would your judges be looking for, Evan? Would they not be looking for a rose that was at some particular peak in its life?"

"Yes, that's right."

"Then here is your problem; you are viewing perfection as a state when, in fact, it is a process."

Evan shook his head. "Come again?"

"This rose. . .I know it may not look very attractive at this stage, but it is still perfect. You see, it would only cease to be perfect if it should somehow depart from the purpose of its creation. Part of that purpose is that after a time it should return to the earth from whence it came so that the cycle may continue. It is perfect because it has done everything that was expected of it."

Evan nodded. "So the merest twig of that bush there could be considered perfect!"

"Yes, that's it! Just as long as it continues to fulfill its purpose. We talk of a perfect rose, when what we mean is a rose that has reached a particular point in its life which is pleasing to us—but perfection is much more than that transitory moment!"

"Are you trying to say that man can be regarded in exactly the same way?"

"But of course!" Matthew spread his hands and beamed at him, looking for a moment surprisingly like his father. "We talk of a 'perfect' man, and usually we are thinking of some kind of final state; the fact is, though, that man cannot be 'perfect' without continued growth. It's part of his nature and purpose to grow; that's why that thrill of discovery that we spoke of goads him on the way it does!"

"Does that mean, then," Evan spoke slowly, "that a person can be perfect at *any* time?"

"Yes, Evan, it does. Consider, for example, the little child who does some act for no other reason than that mother says it is 'good.' Then consider, perhaps, the man who lays his life down for others. Is one greater than the other?" Matthew answered his own question. "Of course not! Each one of them, in his own way, is doing the very most that can be expected of him at that particular time, and *that* is perfection!"

Evan threw his rose back into the garden. "That's all very well, but the fact remains that man consistently does less than is expected of him. He *knows* what he should do, but he rarely does it without some kind of pressure. The kind of perfection you are talking about seems to me to be possible but still highly improbable."

Matthew replaced his rose also, carefully putting it back precisely where it had fallen. His reply was

182

kindly. "What you say is quite true, Evan, to a point. Don't forget . . .," he waved a cautionary finger in front of Evan's nose, "one of the things that is expected of you continually is repentance, and that presupposes all these failings that you speak of. It's part of this business of walking in the way just as much as 'doing good' is, so it's not as if no allowance has been made, is it?" He sat down on a rustic bench and bade Evan sit also. "True . . . there are way-stations of life through which we pass, often long behind our schedule . . . but no one is waiting there to say 'You're late!' We are only asked to stay on the tracks!"

"That doesn't sound quite fair."

"Maybe it doesn't, but it's also quite beyond judgment. You'll recall, no doubt, that parable about the workers in the vineyard—the one where those who had worked all day were paid the same as the others who came later. Some of them objected, saying that the owner of the vineyard was unfair. What they failed to recognize was that as far as their employer was concerned, only their agreed service was important . . . the time was not!"

Evan scowled and shook his head slowly. "I still think that it's somehow unjust. . . ."

Matthew laughed. "You are still worrying about your own position, aren't you?"

Evan nodded; he had forgotten the gift.

"Well, you shouldn't, because I can assure you that it will all be equitably resolved. You just don't understand it yet."

"Thanks," Evan said quite genuinely.

"It's funny, you know," Matthew continued, "but

man, however grudgingly, can quickly understand such concepts as judgment and justice...yet grace, the gift he stands most in need of, is difficult for him to accept."

"How does it affect you? I mean do you have to rely on the grace that you speak of to feel right with yourself?"

Matthew considered the question for a short while before answering. "No, actually I don't, because you see, Evan, this touches on one of the basic differences between you and me. Those who receive of eternal life are those who, having demonstrated at least a consistent desire to walk in the way, are then permitted to so continue but without the encumbrances of mortality. It amounts to nothing less than being truly alive!"

Appreciation of Matthew's position seemed to sweep over Evan like a flood, and he was enthralled by the possibilities of the liberty he sensed in the other man. "Then why don't people *choose* this? I mean, people like Paul. If all these things are gifts, why don't they join you?"

"You speak of these gifts as if they were something entirely new, but they aren't! Man has always known that if he would walk hand in hand with God, then all things would be to his profit. Even you—you know it—but it doesn't follow automatically that you will act on what you know. I'm not answering your question, Evan, because you must find the answer for yourself!"

Evan gazed at the ground without reply. He felt cheated, because for a moment he believed that a nagging problem was about to be resolved; instead, he was again confronted with himself. Matthew was trying to make him answer questions about himself first—he could feel it! The line of investigation was therefore ended.

"What about physical perfection, though...are you freed from all those imperfections also?"

"That's partly a subjective judgment, but generally speaking, yes!"

"Then you don't suffer illness or physical infirmities?"

"No, not at all. You have some reason for asking that, don't you?"

Evan grinned he had forgotten the gift again. "Yes, I do...I hope you don't mind my asking the question, but why is it that your father seems to walk with a stoop?"

"I was expecting that," said Matthew, "and it's not a particularly easy one to answer."

"Does it actually mean that he has some infirmity?"

"No, he doesn't. In fact the rather robust build that he has now is a kind of compensation for how poorly he fared before. That defect you noticed is more of a psychological one."

"How is that?"

"You need to understand the brain a little, Evan. Usually when we think of it, we tend to perceive it as merely that grey area inside of our skull—but it is much more. The brain extends to our eyes, our ears, to the very tips of our fingers and toes. It shares a relationship with them that actually makes them not so much separate parts of the body as actual extensions of the brain itself. Your brain is curiously harnessed to your body; it is sensitive to every detail from the length of your fingers to the distance between your eyes. Your brain without your body would be a hopelessly incomplete machine."

"I don't quite get your point."

"Let me give you an illustration. Imagine that during your lifetime you had been say—a violinist, a very good violinist. It could perhaps be said that all of your knowledge and training was somehow locked up inside your brain—as indeed it would be—but there would be more to it than that. You would play the violin in a way that would be quite peculiar to you, and this would be due not only to the particular characteristics of your brain but also such things as the length of your arm, the shape of your fingers, even your tonal acuity or the shape of your ear, and so on. *All* of you would be involved in that activity, not just your brain."

"And so?"

"Imagine that you were then resurrected with a body that was dramatically different to the one you had in mortal life—so much so that it even interfered seriously with your previous ability." He spread his hands again in a questioning gesture. "Could it not be said that something had been lost? Even if the new body was in fact a better one?" He grinned at Evan's deepening frown. "Can you see what would have happened? Your 'musical' mind would now be linked to a body which had yet to relearn your art!"

Evan shook his head. "I still can't see what this has to do with your father's being stooped."

"Well, it works in the other direction as well. You see, a person with a crippled physical frame in mortal life who then receives a new body in the resurrection will still, to a degree, be a cripple in mind, at least until it has time to pass."

"Your father was a cripple?"

"He was a hunchback!"

"Oh!" said Evan softly, trying to visualize David Cohen as a hunchback. A small recollection suddenly clicked into place in his mind. "Did he use a walking stick—an old, gnarled looking one?"

"Yes, he did. How did you know?"

"I saw it...I saw it in..."

"In his study?"

Evan was suddenly embarrassed. "Yes...I went into...at least I took the wrong door...on that first morning...." He finished the sentence as matter-of-factly as possible, wishing again that he had thought before speaking.

"He treasures that old piece of wood very much." Matthew gave no hint of curiosity, although he must surely have been aware of Evan's discomfort.

Evan's mind was racing. Could it be that Matthew was the person he could ask? Surely he would know about the portraits. The answer could well be a quite simple one! It took him only a split second to decide: he *would* ask him, straight out, no hedging or indirect questions!

He glanced up to ask the question, and Matthew's eyes met his—calm, friendly, understanding eyes, but eyes which nevertheless stopped him suddenly. Something curious happened. The very words he was about to frame suddenly froze on his tongue and he was powerless to mouth them. A strange dread swept over him, unexpectedly and yet for some reason without surprise. It was as if some power from without was speaking wordlessly to him.

It was not Matthew! He knew it was not Matthew, even though it had been Matthew's glance that had stopped him. There were reasons—reasons that he knew not of—but they were there nevertheless. He simply could not ask the question.

"Am I keeping you from your work?" he asked lamely, trying to ride out the strange emotion which had taken him.

"Not at all!" said Matthew gently, betraying only a slight awareness of Evan's plight. He rose, lifting Evan's arm with him. "Would you like to return to the office? It's almost time for lunch."

They dined in the biological studies building cafeteria. It was a magnificent place, located on a series of massive cantilevers so as to provide an almost unobstructed view of the panorama below.

In keeping with the rest of the building, it was both strikingly and luxuriously furnished. It could well have passed as an exclusive resort hotel in times past, Evan thought, except that for all of its beauty it also had a kind of classlessness which allowed him to feel quite at ease. It occurred to him that it was not the appointments and furnishings which lent a snobbish quality to a building but the people who were in it. That was a major difference; in the midst of this bustling crowd of people he seemed to be unusually aware of it.

188

It required little of his powers of observation to determine that he was the only mortal present—a fact that was mildly disturbing, awaking again the old doubts as to whether he should be there.

If he *was* at all out of place, then no one conveyed any indication of it to him. The cafeteria staff in particular treated him to a degree of courteous service that was little short of embarrassing.

The food was delicious, but Evan paid relatively little heed to it. Not only was he continually distracted by the sights around him but he remained also a little shaken by the experience on the roof. As if in deference to his feelings, Matthew did not speak any more than was necessary to attend to his needs.

After their meal, Matthew outlined his program for the rest of the day. It would place Evan under little pressure, giving him time to assimilate his surroundings. He suggested that he spend most of the remainder of the afternoon looking over the center; he had already arranged for a couple of technical assistants to escort him.

There were wonders to be witnessed indeed...so many of them that Evan's mind rapidly reached the point where the unbelievable was continually overlaid with the unbelievable! The tools in use were almost beyond credibility! He stood in numbed fascination in a darkened circular room while a technician demonstrated such a tool.

In a small compartment somewhere out of sight to him a rat was contentedly feeding, totally unaware of the awesome machine it was serving. The room appeared to be quite deserted apart from the technician and Evan, its dome-like ceiling and smooth walls composed apparently of a pink, slightly translucent material.

Before his astounded eyes a giant figure of the animal suddenly materialized in the room, and he realized that he was looking at an enormously sophisticated hologram so clear and detailed as to persuade him that the animal was actually present. The image could be increased or decreased in size at will, even to the point where the smallest detail could be magnified to fill his whole field of vision.

But that was not all! At a spoken command from the technician, the figure suddenly turned entirely transparent, as if made of glass. On further instruction, individual organs and systems within the animal became sharply visible, even identified with different colors if it was desired. The circulatory system, nervous system, digestive or lymphatic systems could be selected either singly or in unison. Trace colors could be added to plot the movements of fluids or the paths of individual neurons. Instrumentation and recording of any desired function were instantly available if the examiner required them, along with real time access to any computations required for the study.

Evan followed his guide humbly, for the most part not really comprehending the things that he saw. Wherever he looked, open corridors of research stretched away into areas he could never have even imagined.

He was well beyond the point of being amazed by the time his escorts returned him to Matthew. Only one burning fact seemed to have embedded itself into his overstretched mind—these things were being done by surprisingly ordinary people!

He sat limply in his chair while Matthew regarded him with satisfaction. "Have you seen enough for one day?"

"Is there much more?"

"But of course! You have looked at only a relatively small corner of one particular field of research. Not everyone is interested in biology you know! Most of the things you saw today are concerned with a phase of research through which we have already passed; we keep those devices mostly for training people new to the field."

"Are there other research centers similar to this?"

"Oh, yes, there are hundreds more, both here and on the Western continent also. There are sufficient facilities for any person who chooses to be interested in this field."

"Are there many other fields to choose from?"

Matthew smiled at him gently. "There are as many fields, Evan, as you could ever conceive of, and they are all being worked at with the same degree of intensity that you see here. There are centers devoted to all of the sciences and all of the arts. Can you imagine the field of music, for instance, being explored to the same extent?"

"No," Evan said truthfully.

"That's why we have to take things a little at a time, because the Kingdom is a little like an explosion— starting from one point but with its outer edges traveling continually faster. There is no visible end to it!"

"It must end somewhere, mustn't it?"

Matthew shrugged. "I don't know. We live in a whole universe that's something like that. It's exploding outward continually. There are whole galaxies racing away from us right now at thousands of miles every second. But we don't sit around wringing our hands about where it's all going to end—because we know it's going to be happening for a very long time yet. Perhaps one day it *will* end...and if it does we may understand it by then."

Evan sat silently, trying to put all these things in their eternal perspective. He knew what the problem was; his human mind simply boggled quickly, while a resurrected being like Matthew was untroubled by it. Not only were his faculties expanding continually but he was unbound by the chains of time. It would not be necessary for an immortal to flit grasshopper-like between all the fields that might interest him; he merely had to store them away as something to do in the future...when he was ready.

"I am at least beginning to appreciate what you meant, Matthew, when you spoke about the tools being provided but not the knowledge. I mean, the work still has to be done, doesn't it? But you are spared all the mistakes—that's what the difference is here, isn't it?"

Matthew thought before he replied. "No, that's not quite right. God has always worked with man in exactly the same way. He's always offered to give him all the help that he needed, but it had to be a two-way deal. Look back at all those people at Horeb; they made a deal with God—a deal they didn't altogether keep, of course, but look at the things that were promised to them. Do you remember?"

Evan squirmed in his seat. "No, not really."

"Ah, then you should have studied it a little, shouldn't you? They were promised all the help they needed, even to such things as weather to suit their crops. They were promised peace, and if perchance some aggressor was to come against them, they were promised that five of them would put a hundred of the enemy to flight. They were given healing from any infirmity, guidance and direction, water from a stone—anything they needed but could not of themselves supply. We saw only a small part of these blessings fulfilled, of course, but that doesn't mean the offer wasn't always there. God didn't just pick people up and carry them to wherever they wanted to go, but he did work with them as long as they chose to keep their part of the arrangement."

"And you have taken up that offer?"

"Exactly—and that is the difference between this time and yours. We have made a new contract, as it were, but we walk a road that has always existed. Until now it has never been walked by man with any great determination. Now we walk in harmony with creation, and all of the necessary assistance is guaranteed."

Evan slid down in his chair, brow still furrowed. "When I hear you tell it, it sounds like the greatest thing ever. But then I think of all the people who don't yet seem to feel this way...people like Paul

Bernard for instance. He seems to contradict your view altogether. He supports many of the things you say, but he acts differently; he even claims not to have the gift, although I can see very well that he does. If the Kingdom way is all that much better, why aren't people in it up to their eyeballs?"

Matthew smiled almost coyly. "That is one of the things you have yet to work out for yourself, Evan. The problem is that although man is capable of profound logic, he is rarely actually motivated by it; his feelings have far more to do with the way he acts. We were talking a short time ago about areas of research—how even such studies as music and the arts are available to anyone who desires them. When you think about it, would you not expect that, among the mortal population, we would have an overabundance of musical virtuosos and the like?"

"I guess that figures."

"Well, we don't have very many at all as yet!"

"Surely people would be lined up in droves for that kind of opportunity?"

"This is just my point, Evan; they don't do it here for exactly the same reasons that they didn't do it in your time. You see, availability of opportunity is nowhere near the influencing factor that you would imagine it to be. If you can understand that problem, you will be on the way toward answering your own questions."

Evan still did not understand, but he was not inclined to demonstrate his ignorance any further. "How free am I, then? I mean, am I free to do whatever interests me?"

"Not quite, Evan. Mind you, no one is going to try forcing you at all, but your situation is a little different. I know you understand that...and my father is responsible for you."

"I *have* to do as he wishes?"

Matthew nodded. "Believe me, that would be the far wisest course." Evan searched the other man's face for the threat that he felt surely must be present, but it was not to be found.

"Okay then, I'll go along with that."

"But how am I different?" Evan directed the question back over his shoulder. Paul was painting behind him, a little farther up the slope. "Why am I different? Why am I permitted to live and work among a class of people with whom I have almost nothing in common while others are shut out? I mean, I've been at the biological studies building for some weeks now. I *ought* to know whether I just imagine the feeling or not!"

Paul walked slowly down to him and looked over his shoulder. "If you finish the wash there, you're going to get a line across the work."

"Why should I be allowed to stay there when others are not?" Evan persisted.

Paul took the brush from his hand and carried the wash quickly to the bottom of the sheet; then he stood back to view the effect. "Who isn't allowed to do what?" he asked without looking at his companion.

"You know what I mean—all those opportunities

that everyone tells me about here; I still don't see anyone really taking them."

"There's a line across it even now—you let it dry too much. You'll have to start it again." He turned to look at Evan. "I thought we covered all that before, spaceman; no one is prevented from doing anything!"

Evan shook his head in frustration. "I'm sure you know very well what I mean, Paul. You're just being difficult. You say that you are free, yet I know perfectly well that you are not! Say you were to decide right now that you wished to change from the grains project and move into the arts; I mean, you *are* artistic, aren't you?"

"So?"

"So you would have to move to one of the arts centers, wouldn't you? Would you do it?"

"No, I wouldn't choose to."

"That isn't what I asked. I said *assume* that you wanted the change."

"That's right. I wouldn't choose to even if I wanted the change."

Evan sighed with satisfaction; he was making headway. "You would be free to, but you still wouldn't choose to go?"

"That's right."

"Why?"

Paul handed back the paintbrush. He unpinned Evan's sheet and painstakingly replaced it with a new one. It was almost as if he had not heard the question. "You keep harping on this one question, don't you, spaceman? Why is it so important to you?"

"I think you know the reason. You know that I'm

uncomfortable here. In fact I feel that you already know more about me—and what is to happen to me—than I've been told."

Paul's expression changed to one of pained innocence, and Evan felt his hackles begin to rise. "I know that I'm not free, and I know that you are not either. A few weeks ago I wanted to ask Matthew a question, and I couldn't. I've wanted to ask you, because I feel that you know about it, too. Yet I know that I cannot. I'm not free, am I?"

Paul continued to look at the blank sheet of paper, and Evan waited only long enough to be sure that no comment was forthcoming.

"Is it the gift, Paul?"

"I guess so." Paul tugged at his beard as he turned and walked back to his own easel.

"Then I'm not free, am I?"

"It sounds as if you were warned, not prevented."

Evan stopped short. That could just be true, because he had not persisted with his intention. "Does the gift do that?"

"Yes."

"Does it also have something to do with the way you don't get on with immortals?"

Paul gave a short, humorless laugh. "Spaceman, you're beginning to catch on." The conversation was finished, and Evan returned thoughtfully to his painting.

Chapter Eight

Evan moved to the cafeteria servery and caught the eye of one of the assistants. Her face lit up as she saw him. "Oh, yes, Mr. Westering, you're taking lunch away with you today, aren't you?"

Evan nodded quickly, wishing that she would speak a little quieter. She disappeared from view and then returned with a large basket which she placed on the counter before him with all the ceremony of an unveiling. "There you are."

Evan cleared his throat awkwardly. "It looks a bit large. I wanted to take only my own lunch with me."

"It's best that you take it, Mr. Westering. When you eat out there it pays to be prepared, you know!"

Evan would have liked to ask "Prepared for what?" because the basket obviously contained sufficient for a family picnic. On the other hand, he was attracting attention, so he simply muttered his thanks and moved on, carrying his basket so as to play down its size as much as possible. He felt more comfortable as he left the main entrance, except for the receptionist's holding the door open for him.

Matthew was away for a few days, somewhere with David, and Evan had elected to eat his lunch out of doors rather than go to the cafeteria alone. It was not as if he did not know many people now, for he had many working acquaintances, but he found the continual presence of immortals a little taxing. It was a relief to have an excuse to avoid them.

He walked on a marbled pathway, scanning the scene around him for a likely place to eat. The whole landscape was so beautiful that the decision was a difficult one. It would have sufficed simply to sit in the middle of the path! The lake was especially attractive, though, and he decided to sit alongside it. He chose a spot on the side opposite the building and spent several minutes walking around to it, pursued with great enthusiasm by noisy birds. The bank rose more steeply at this point, as the lake nestled against a small, heavily foliaged hill.

He had not been aware of the fact before he arrived, but there was a small path beside the lake, slightly above the bank. It was a path used by many travelers, and it showed evidence of the passage of many feet—an interesting path, he thought, one which he must some day explore. He could not see where it went, because within a hundred meters or so in each direction it was lost among the trees.

He stepped down from the pathway and seated himself with his feet almost in the water, his basket beside him. He also noticed for the first time that the lake abounded with fish, and they hovered in the clear water in front of him, obviously begging morsels. The birds no doubt had the same idea, and he was suddenly wary about removing the cover from the basket for it seemed possible that the food could well be distributed contrary to his wishes.

He removed it with great care, shielding the contents covetously with his arm, and to his surprise the birds demonstrated great restraint, settling quietly to the grass around him. Most of the food consisted of fruit, to which he was not particularly partial—or at least had not been in times past. The Kingdom was changing his mind about this though, for the fruit that was available was delicious.

He selected an apple for himself and broke up one of the small loaves of bread between the birds and the fish, wondering idly whether he had perhaps been given the extra food simply to hold off the wild life. The view was breathtaking. The biological studies building rose majestically before him, its image mirrored perfectly in the crystal waters of the lake. He marveled at the way in which this great building harmonized so serenely with its surroundings. If he could only take a photograph of it back to his own time—no one would believe it! It was something to do with the shape, for the easy flow of its cantilevers rather curiously mimicked the spreading foliage of the gardens below. It was a masterpiece!

But would people believe anything? He tried to imagine himself as being back in his own world and possessing even the meager knowledge of the Kingdom that he now had. It was true—no one would believe any of it! What a tragedy—that such a world had always been offered, but man had declined to accept it! There was something of the answer to his questions in this, and he found himself thinking about Matthew's words on the matter of walking in harmony with one's purpose. From this new standpoint it was easy to see what the problem was back there. It was that man, in spite of his protests to the contrary, did not really believe in any kind of eternal purpose. Shuttered and blinkered down within the confines of his own mortality, he treated only his immediate circumstance as reality, forbidding his imagination to explore a fuller and greater purpose.

If he went back, what would he tell people? It seemed that everything he thought of was something they already knew—things he knew himself. He just hadn't believed them enough!

He watched the rippling line of a gentle breeze move across the water away from him, and his attention was once more brought back to the beauty of his surroundings. It was one of those scenes which people used to like to paint—beautiful and idyllic, but not real. Where did men get those insights? How could they take a mundane landscape and breathe into it this dreamlike quality? Was it some divine glimpse of the future—a subliminal hunger for a land as yet unseen but still recognized as being home?

Evan could recall almost forgotten dreams which for some reason seemed to be coming back to him—dreams from which he had awakened to find himself pondering their meaning. They were dreams in which he was exploring an unknown house, or garden, or pathway. As he continued, the object of his exploration would become continually larger or longer, as if it were without end. Then when he awoke the unknown would seem oddly familiar—as if he had dreamed that same dream before...and could expect it to visit him again!

Experiences of his life fluttered before him like the birds hovering around him. Something was tugging at a corner of his mind—the beauty surrounding him was like that; it was familiar—as if it had always been there and he had always known about it. He stopped eating and gazed with narrowed lids across the shimmering water. Was it because he remembered this place from some such dream—or was there a barren place within him—within every man—which awaited its arrival?

His mind traveled back to the Magellan, and to other times when he had looked down on the Earth and felt a great sadness. Why should not such a thing of beauty invoke feelings of joy instead? Was it possible that beauty belonged somewhere else—somewhere just outside of man's memory and recalled only in mourning at its loss?

A faint shiver of excitement ran through him as he realized something that was important. Not only did this place lead into such channels of thought but it also promised the answers! They were here—the answers to all the questions that a perplexed or adventuresome man had ever asked, answers available for the seeking, undimmed by doubts, errors, falsehoods, or conjecture. There was nothing to fear here—only the truth! But he would have to think a little more about it.

Rufus was happy. In fact he was ecstatic! He demonstrated this to himself by raising his arms above his head and executing a little dance in the middle of the pathway. Had onlookers observed him they might have concluded that he was quite ridiculous—possibly mad. But there were no observers, and he danced happily in his own private little world, the long Hessian bag in his hand fluttering behind him like a cape. Of course, madness was not to be found in the Kingdom, but release from inhibition was. To Rufus a dance was a shout of delight, and he hummed to himself a staccato, breathless rhythm as he danced.

Bearded, thin, and brown, he was a quaint little old man who in spite of his obvious great age was both light and nimble on his feet. He concluded his dance with an appropriate flourish of his bag and peered shortsightedly at his surroundings. It was the same kind of country through which he had been walking for the past week, although his feeble eyes would have permitted him to discern little difference anyway. He was beginning to feel hungry, and his bag was now quite empty. This caused him no real anxiety, for he was quite sure that he would be provided for—after all, that was the law; a pilgrim had the right of demand—although it had not been necessary for him to do so.

He pushed his chin forward and continued in his determined, swaggering walk along the path, the dappled sunlight flashing intermittently on his large crown of unruly silver hair. He had come a long way in this manner, and he had yet a considerable distance to go.

Rufus was not his real name because by nationality he was a Pakistani. It was just a title he had acquired somehow down at the work project; it had something to do with his incessant, tuneless whistling on the job, although the exact reason still escaped him. He answered to that name now, and his old one was almost forgotten, along with many other things which he had been only too happy to forget. But now all of those things were truly past. The days at the work project had been happy, even though his labor had been long and hard. He appreciated the value of the new start, the chance to begin his life over again—even in his twilight years.

Now he was free; the bad experiences were behind him. He would not be obliged to recall them if he did not wish to. His only care was for the future. He didn't understand the future well, but it was sufficient for him to know that it would make him happy, hence the childlike joy which lifted his aging feet and carried him effortlessly over the miles.

He began to feel quite hungry, and he knew that he must soon stop to eat. He peered intently from side to side as he walked, wondering how his needs would be met.

He came suddenly upon a beautiful lake, and despite the limitations of his eyesight quickly discerned the figure sitting at its bank. He quickened his pace again and soon stood behind what turned out to be a young man. The young man showed no sign of having observed his approach but continued to gaze across the water as if totally lost in thought—a half-eaten apple hanging limply in the hand that rested over his knees.

Rufus cleared his throat noisily, and the man started so violently that he almost slid into the water. The apple did, and the surrounding birds pursued it noisily. Quickly he arose to his feet.

"I am so sorry to disturb you, my good friend," said Rufus, "but do you have food?"

"Yes, I do...in the basket."

Rufus required no further encouragement, and slid down the bank to sit cross-legged by the basket. Then he lifted the cover and began hunting around inside, making various exploratory noises as he did so.

His provider regarded him with puzzled amusement. He had hardly begun to recover from being distracted from his reverie, and this fellow was already raiding his basket! Rufus was eating hungrily by the time he looked up again.

"Don't stand on my account, friend; pray sit down with me and eat also." The young man shrugged and sat down slowly.

"Would you like another apple?" Rufus thrust the fruit in front of him.

"Thanks."

"Who is it that provides for me?" Rufus asked with his mouth full.

"What do you mean?"

Rufus gesticulated toward the basket and raised his eyebrows questioningly. Somewhere in Evan's head a penny dropped. "Oh," he waved his hand toward the building, "they did—the people in the biological studies building."

Rufus raised his chin and peered myopically across the lake. "Is that it—the building over there?"

"Yes."

Rufus turned and suddenly extended a thin brown

arm toward him. "May I shake your hand?"

Evan obliged.

"You must be a very good man—to work over there." Evan began to protest, but Rufus was not listening. "When I am changed I hope one day to be able to do something like that—but I will go back to the work project first. I know more about that kind of work, you see."

"What work project is that?"

Rufus raised a gnarled finger to point back down the path in the direction from which he had come; then he frowned and altered the direction a little, obviously unsure of his position. "I've come from the upper regions; there are a lot of projects up there. I was on one on the White Nile, you know."

"That's a long way from here, isn't it? What were you doing there?"

Rufus looked embarrassed. "Well, to be quite honest, my friend, I don't really know what we were supposed to be doing. I just worked hard, you see...."

"If you don't know exactly where you've come from or what you were doing, how do you know where you are going now?"

The old man shrugged. "I just walk. I know I will be guided...and provided for."

Evan thought about the unnecessarily large basket. "You must have been walking for a very long time," he said.

Rufus scratched his head vaguely. "Yes—a few months I think; I don't remember very well these days; my old head lets me down a bit. I'll be glad when I'm changed."

206

"What do you mean, 'changed'?"

Rufus regarded the young man curiously. "Surely someone so well advanced in the Kingdom as you would know what it means—changed, made new! I am an old man; my body is beginning to fail me, and I must soon die. But . . ." he raised a finger to heaven, "I have, heaven be praised, been permitted to make the pilgrimage to the center place that I may request full measure of the gift."

"You'll be immortal?"

"Yes—God willing."

Evan was a little shaken at this revelation, and Rufus began to wonder if there was not something rather strange about him.

"Do all old men do this?"

Rufus stopped eating in order to peer more closely at the young man. He *was* strange! While he seemed to hold the status of a privileged mortal, he seemed at the same time to be incredibly naïve.

"Anyone can do this, lad. You don't have to be an old man. Most people don't take the opportunity, of course, until they are old like me."

"Why?"

"Well, I suppose because they have nothing to lose then. In my case I have done what I could to offset my poor beginnings. I have worked hard, and I have been obedient."

"Are you a 'good' man?"

Rufus threw his head back and laughed merrily. "Oh no, no, no! No one is good—but I have tried to make restitution—and I have faith. There remains only grace for me now."

"And that is what you are seeking?"

Rufus spread his hands. "Of course!"

"Do you know," Evan said slowly, "you are the first person I have met here who makes any real sense about this business of the gift? You are actually going to ask for what is offered, aren't you?"

Rufus frowned curiously. "Yes, but why is it so strange to you? I go because I am free and unafraid."

"You said that you would go back to the project after...after your 'change.' Why would you return to such a place of hardship?"

"Oh, it has not been hard, my good friend. I have borne much worse burdens than that. There are some at the project who complain, but to me it is no burden...rather it makes me free." He spread his hands again. "Climbing a steep pathway is always hard work; but if it is from darkness into light..."

"You'll go back there just because you are interested in it?"

"Yes, and I may even help others to be free also. Perhaps I shall be given charge of some if I am worthy of it. Then I may go back to my own land, for there is much to be done there yet."

You're an Indian, aren't you?"

I was a Pakistani, but it could truly be said of me now that I am many races, for I have mingled with many. I have worked with Italians and Turks, Jews and Africans. I can even dance like a Greek!" He leapt to his feet so quickly that Evan almost lost his apple again. "I will show you." He raised his arms and did his dance again for his bemused one-man audience.

"You are good on your feet...for an old man," Evan conceded candidly.

Rufus stopped. "Ah, yes, friend....I have been obedient to the laws of health." He returned just as quickly to his spot beside the basket, "but my eyes are not good, and I don't carry a load as well as I once did." He beamed a brilliant white smile. "But when I am changed...ah, my friend, when I am changed... I shall dance as you have never seen one dance!"

Evan was finding the old man's enthusiasm infectious, and he could not restrain himself from laughing. "Your appetite seems to be okay," he said, viewing the diminishing contents of the basket. Rufus flashed him another smile and continued with the task in hand. Finally he burped loudly and slapped his stomach, which did not appear to have become any larger in spite of the prodigious amount which it must have contained.

"My thanks, young friend...and my thanks to them also." He nodded toward the building. "May I feed my bag too?"

"Certainly."

The bag turned out to be emptier than the man himself, for the basket was quite bare when he had finished. Then he knelt and drank long and noisily from the lake before climbing back up to the path. Evan followed with the empty basket.

"Are you on your way again so soon?"

"Yes, my good friend. I mustn't stop, for I have far to travel yet. Good-bye to you, and thank you again." He shouldered his now bulging bag and strode abruptly away. When he reached the point where he would soon pass out of sight, he stopped, placed his bag on the ground and for a moment performed a quick encore of his "Greek" dance. Then he picked up his bag and was gone.

Evan turned the basket upside down and patted it, donating the remaining crumbs to the birds. Then he stood for a long time, looking up the pathway in the direction which his dinner guest had vanished. Slowly at first, and then with gathering momentum, an idea was forming in his mind—not necessarily a wise or carefully considered one but an idea which flooded him with a great new kind of excitement.

The moonlight bathed the room with long shafts of white light from which all the colors had been bleached out. Evan half sat, half lay in his bed, contemplating the open doorway. Sleep was far from him. The air in the room seemed unusually oppressive, and the silence of the night roared in his ears. It was odd how night could change things and magnify the searchings of a troubled mind.

The idea didn't seem so attractive now, but he had more or less committed himself to it. Paul had been disappointingly unhelpful, and he wished that he had not even told him. It would have been better had he simply slipped away without telling anyone. Perhaps he should have joined the old man on the pathway; then he would not have had to face any of them!

The evening meal had been a chore for him. He had

decided before he came home that he was going to follow that old man to the center place. It was an obvious, positive step that he could decide and execute himself. It was all so simple—until he sat down to the meal table. Being unsure as to what extent Miriam and Lyddia knew his thoughts, he ate in great discomfort. He was thankful that at least David and Matthew were not there, because that would have been intolerable. He had undertaken the extra walk to Paul's place on the way home in order to tell him of his plans. Paul had been very busy, which was bad enough, but he had regarded Evan's idea as extremely unimportant, and that was a deep injury.

When he chose to think objectively about it, he also realized that if David had considered the trip desirable he would almost certainly have suggested it in any case. It was because of this possibility—the possibility that David would not approve—that he had decided to leave before having to face him.

The plan was childlike in its simplicity; he would simply depart during the night and leave a note. That way he removed the possibility of being deprived of his adventure.

Now the heavy blanket of the night made his plan seem fanciful and unreal, and he was beginning to suspect that it was every bit as foolish as Paul had inferred. But nothing would permit him now to lie back on his bed and sleep. It was almost the kind of experience he had had before; the only suffering greater than waiting out the start of a mission was to have it postponed. He stepped decisively out of bed and dressed in the darkness. He made up the bed and taking his carefully prepared note from the bedside drawer placed it on the pillow where someone would be sure to see it.

He did not really need to close the bedroom door as he left, but he did it unconsciously—as if to bar his own return. It made more noise than he had expected, and he stood motionless, straining to hear if he had disturbed the others.

In the darkness of the sitting room he easily found the bowl of fruit he had noted earlier, and he carefully slipped the contents into his bag, feeling as he did so that he was surely the most common of thieves. There was bread on the table also, and this represented an unexpected bonus, as it had not been there earlier in the evening. He knew Miriam had baked some earlier in the day, and he had the odd feeling that it may even have been left out for him intentionally.

The night was unusually quiet, and he seemed to find his way through the house with all the silent grace of an elephant with extra feet. He reemerged onto the balcony and walked back past his room to the sundeck and slid from there to the ground, intending to walk around the house rather than risk being heard leaving by one of the entrances. It became obvious to him as he progressed that it would have been wiser to have first explored his exit route by daylight, because it turned out to be much more hazardous than he had anticipated. He found himself stumbling blindly through the masses of dense foliage around the house and succeeded eventually in wading through one of Lyddia's carefully constructed rock pools. By the time he had emerged near the outer wall of the courtyard, he was already having serious second thoughts about the efficacy of his pilgrimage.

Then he froze to the spot. A tingling chill swept over him—there was a white figure standing in the courtyard gateway—standing motionless, as if waiting for him to come past. He looked back the way he had come, but it was clearly too late; whoever it was must surely have seen him. In any case, he wasn't going back to face that jungle again!

He strode on with an air of condemned resignation, and as he approached the gateway he could see that it was Lyddia, standing barefoot in her long, flowing nightgown. She was standing a couple of steps above him, and it made her appear unusually tall. She addressed him in an urgent stage whisper.

"Why did you go that way? Wouldn't it have been easier to come out the door?"

"I didn't want to be heard."

"I've listened to you ever since you left your room. Did you fall in my rock pool?" He could not see her face in the darkness, but he knew that she was smiling at him.

"No, I just stepped in it," he replied stiffly.

"Where are you going?"

Evan took a deep breath. "I'm going to the center place. . .at least that's what I intended."

Her voice was triumphant. "You know, I thought that's what it was. I knew you had something like that on your mind when you were at the table. It's a rather long walk, you know."

"I realize that." He grinned sheepishly. "Are you going to squeal on me?"

She gave a stifled giggle. "Of course not. You have some funny ways of going about things though." Her tone became more serious. "Will you promise me something, Evan?"

"Are you blackmailing me?"

She ignored the jest. "I want you to promise me something that is very important."

"Okay, what is it?"

"You will pass by Project Delta on your way up. In fact, you will probably be obliged to skirt around it." She paused, seemingly unsure of what to say next.

"So?"

"So I want you to promise me that you won't go there—not even near it I mean."

"Why?"

She hesitated again. "There are things. . .well, there are things that I can't tell you—not now anyway." Her voice became almost pleading. "Please, it is important—for your own sake. Don't ask me too many questions. Just trust me, will you. . .please?"

Evan could hardly refuse. His curiosity was aroused, but he could see that she was genuinely distressed, and it would not be fair to press the matter any further. "Okay," he said lightly, "I won't go near the Delta project, or whatever you call it—not if you don't want me to."

"Do you promise?"

"Yes, I promise."

She seemed greatly relieved. "Then I mustn't delay you. You had better go."

He took his leave and crunched noisily down the graveled driveway, looking back over his shoulder only briefly to wave before vanishing into the forest. He was almost disappointed now that she had not opposed the plan, because he would have appreciated the opportunity to honorably abandon this escapade which no longer seemed particularly attractive. To be waved good-bye on his "secret" departure was something of an indignity.

It took over an hour for him to walk the now-familiar path to the biological studies building, and when he arrived it still had many lights showing. He could see people working inside. He cut across the immaculately tailored gardens in front of the building, his way illumined by the shafts of light emanating from its windows. It was only as he began to walk away from the building, away from the lights, and into the cool shadows surrounding the lake that he began to consider how little thought he had given to his mission. He was totally unfamiliar with the countryside; in fact, he had no idea at all as to how he would find his way to the center place. He had lightly assumed that the pathway beside the lake would be his starting point, but only because he had seen Rufus walk that way. It was even possible, he mused, that the path would take him back in the way he had come.

He climbed briskly up to the path and set off. If he became lost, he would only have to ask someone. Rufus was old, half blind, and living from hand to mouth, so surely he could manage at least as well. He lengthened his pace and even began to enjoy himself. The prospects of a very long walk did not particularly concern him, because he had become quite accustomed to walking over the past few months. With the old pressures of time removed, walking was an enjoyable form of travel.

The nature of his surroundings made it even easier, and although his view was somewhat limited by the darkness, there was still sufficient moonlight to allow him to appreciate its beauty. The path was quite clearly defined, and as he walked he became progressively more confident that he would accomplish his pilgrimage without any great difficulty.

By the time dawn had begun to wash the darkness from the eastern horizon to his right, he figured that he had walked better than twelve kilometers, which was fairly good time. He was still striding through similar countryside which was lightly undulating so as to provide continuous interest. The path continued through valleys, sometimes filled with dense undergrowth, sometimes with a succession of glades shaded by leafy canopies. Each turn seemed to beckon him on . . . to see what lay beyond.

In spite of his enthusiasm, he was becoming tired, and eventually he was compelled to stop and sit down beside the path. He was within a spacious glade, with the tops of the trees so far above his head that he had to tilt it back to see them. The sun was just catching the uppermost foliage, and the soft reflected light was filtering down through the gently dispersing mist, giving him the impression of being within an enormous, vaulted cathedral.

Birdcalls echoed above his head as clearly as if they were enclosed within a great building. He began idly to wonder about the others. Miriam and Lyddia would be waking up now. He thought of the note on his pillow and felt a sudden pang as he realized how unnecessarily melodramatic and downright foolish it would seem.

Then there was David! How would he react? Would he be angry? Did resurrected people get angry? If they did, what did resurrected people do when they were angry? And Matthew—the one who had been so patient with him, tirelessly counseling and instructing him in his work, ever willing to explain slowly and in great detail if required—was it not a slap in the face for him?

He felt suddenly impelled to go on, even though he had not eaten as he had intended. It was the alternative to thinking about all these things. But having started to wonder, his mind continued to churn over now. What did one do at the center place anyway... just walk in, or was it perhaps necessary to make an appointment?

He arrived at the fork in the path unexpectedly. It gave him a choice of three alternatives: right, left, or straight ahead. The side tracks did not go off at right angles, but rather diverged slowly away on either side. It was the first time he had been confronted with such a decision, and he was caught off guard. He had not even concerned himself particularly with the direction in which the path was heading during the night, and he now had no idea whatsoever as to which path he should take.

He looked around him. There was no one he could ask. He had noticed a few dwellings between the trees from time to time earlier in the night, but they would be several kilometers behind him now. He was disinclined to retrace his steps—even for a short distance.

He decided to continue straight ahead, more or less in a northerly direction, figuring that if he should discover the path to be wrong, he could strike out cross-country to pick up the correct one again. He was uncomfortable, now that he was facing his first uncertainties. He began to pay more attention to the position of the sun, and he deduced that he was traveling mostly in a north to northeasterly direction, which he was inclined to think was correct. Part of the problem was that he did not really know from which part of the continent he had set off. It was just one of those things he had never bothered to confirm. On his descent, he had had the impression that he was coming down somewhere near the east coast of North Africa, and he had continued to assume that his observation was correct. Now he was beginning to wish that he had gone into the matter a little more thoroughly.

His worst fears were soon confirmed, for after he had walked about five kilometers with still no signs of habitation, the path veered sharply to the left and headed off into a northwesterly direction. Not only that, but it rose steeply into what appeared to be heavily wooded hill country—not the kind of terrain he would wish to traverse unnecessarily.

He stood in the center of the path somewhat nonplussed. He was suddenly beginning to feel both tired and frustrated. There seemed to be little reason to stay on the path in the vague hope of coming across a dwelling; it was not the sort of country where one would expect to find farming land. In fact he had the distinct impression of being in an entirely uninhabited region.

He decided eventually to leave the path and go east. It seemed reasonable to assume that he would eventually pick up the other track again. The countryside was fairly open here and certainly not inhospitable. He left the path and walked for a few hundred meters before looking back to find that the path was no longer distinguishable. He was not an experienced bushwalker and this loss of contact with the beaten track was somehow disturbing to him, but he pressed on nevertheless.

The traveling was pleasant enough—not quite as smooth as the path, but still varied and interesting. The variety of the scenery was disturbing in another way, in that he was quite sure that he would be unable to retrace his steps should he later decide to do so. Whenever he looked behind him, he saw a scene of totally unfamiliar country, territory seemingly different from that through which he had just passed. He was becoming more lost with every step he took.

After almost three hours of walking, he was beginning to feel afraid. The other path had just not turned up, nor had he seen another living soul. He was reasonably sure that he was still traveling in the same direction, but he had not the remotest idea as to his position. He had allowed panic to encroach upon himself also, for he realized that he was becoming short of breath; his anxiety was spurring him to greater effort than was really necessary.

He emerged into a clearing that housed a deep pool of clear water fed by a tiny stream. There were animals gathered about the pool, but they paid little heed to him, except to move discreetly out of his way as he approached. He took a long drink and felt much better. He ate some of his food, and then, sprawling luxuriously in the cool grass, he slept.

"How's your charge coming?" David lifted his head from the cluttered desk and grinned at Matthew.

"Oh, he's stumbling around in the scrub somewhere at last reports. It didn't take him long to get lost. He's left the track and headed off into sector 05, so he's going to be a bit lonely."

"Do you think he'll come up this far?"

"Yes, almost certainly." David arose and walked to the giant map on the wall. "He will have to come across the monorail eventually, unless he walks in circles. Then he will follow it until he comes to the Aswan project road. I've instructed our drivers to keep a watch out for him, so we should pick him up before he gets himself into too much trouble."

Matthew stood, hands clasped behind his back, looking out of the giant window. Before him lay an unobstructed view of a broad valley, a scene of fierce industry, milling with giant earthworking machines and thousands of people. He was in David Cohen's project office.

"You won't take him onto the site at all, will you?" asked Matthew.

"No . . . and I think he'll see enough of it on the way through to deter him from making his own way there." David chuckled. "My guess is that he will be quite through with walking by the time we pick him up."

"Why are you leaving him out there now?"

David sat back into his chair slowly. "Because, quite frankly, I think he needs the break. After all, we *have* been breathing down his neck a bit. He is suffering from what they would have once called an identity crisis."

Matthew turned from the window. "I guess that explains why he just wandered off. He had to do something that didn't require someone else's permission first."

"Yes, and we shall respect that. He can't come to any harm there, so we might as well leave him to his own devices for a little while."

David gathered up a sheaf of papers from his desk. "Look, Matthew," he was almost impishly apologetic, "I have quite a few things to do here, and I would like to be here when he comes...so would you mind attending to a couple of matters on the site for me today?"

Matthew smiled understandingly. "Certainly."

"It's mainly that disciplinary problem in sector sixteen. I think it will require a rather firm hand. There are a few others though—I have their names recorded here somewhere—who are being adversely influenced by it all, although I don't think they will object to good counsel. It may even be advisable to move some of them, because there has been a demonstrable development among them—and we don't want them influenced by a few unruly and rebellious ones."

Matthew examined the paper work. "Yes, I know all of these quite well, and you are right in what you say. I can handle most of them, but there are others with whom someone else may have better rapport."

David waved an immense hand. "That's all right. You may refer some of them if you wish. I'll leave that entirely up to you."

Matthew grinned wryly as he gathered up the remaining sheets. "I may have to leave the main troublemaker to you. Is that all right too?"

David was examining the map closely and seemed little concerned. "Yes, yes—that's all right."

"Good! I have been told that he's on his way over now."

David was too engrossed to respond, and Matthew left quietly. He made his way down the freshly landscaped area in front of the office, and after politely refusing a truck driver's offer of a lift struck out on foot across the broken, undulating terrain toward some distant portion of the project.

Chapter Nine

Evan awoke with a start, causing momentary panic among the animals at the pool's edge. He had not slept well because his troubled mind had struggled with some unfathomable problem which he could now no longer remember. His body ached, and he was still suffering the consequences of the way in which he had been forcing himself along. He had not slept long—at most a couple of hours—but he knew that he would not easily return to sleep again.

Slowly he stood up and considered his position. He was tired, almost out of food, and lost! He walked slowly in circles for a while, stretching each muscle separately so as to restore circulation. Then he set off again, determined to keep going until he at least found another inhabitant in this seemingly deserted place.

He would not starve, of course, because there was obviously plenty of food around; the main problem was isolation. Being alone in this beautiful place was more difficult to endure than he would ever have thought, and he longed simply for the opportunity to speak to someone.

He walked for another hour, more slowly now, because the terrain was becoming more difficult. He had the impression of traveling slightly downhill most of the time, as if he were descending from a vast plain. The trees were generally lower and more jungle-like.

Suddenly he caught sight of a small show of white through the trees ahead, and he spurred himself on, curious to find out what it was. At a distance of about three kilometers, he could discern, much to his relief, what appeared to be a long, bridge-like structure supported on a succession of graceful arches standing on deceptively thin-looking pylons.

When finally he arrived at the base of one of the pylons, he realized that it was not a bridge as he had first thought. Not only did it appear to be too narrow at the top to support a road but there seemed to be no gap to be bridged; it simply disappeared into the distance in either direction. The top was at least some thirty meters over his head—too high for him to determine with any certainty what purpose it served, but it did remind him of something which he had seen before. Suddenly he knew—it was an elevated railway of some kind, possibly a monorail! It was constructed at that height, no doubt, so that it would safely clear the forest below. He marveled at the pylons—so thin and yet obviously capable of taking the weight. What had appeared first to be concrete was actually a substance which he could not identify.

He leaned against the pylon wondering what his next course of action should be. Because of its height, this discovery was of little immediate benefit to him. Climbing to the top was quite out of the question! It could, however, serve as a guide, and it was even possible that it would lead him all the way to the center place!

He had just begun to move away from the pylon when something happened! He was not sure what it was—maybe a slight change in the behavior of the birds, or even a sound which he could not quite hear, but something was coming on the rail above! Almost instinctively he began to run away from the pylon, shading his eyes with one hand to look upward.

He saw it only briefly, a short flash of metal and glass as it appeared almost from nowhere over his head. He looked quickly farther along the rail in time to catch another sharp reflection of sunlight as it negotiated a slight curve of the track before vanishing from view. It was gone as quickly as it had come, and only the wheeling and crying of the birds above left record of its passing.

Evan was enthralled! It must have been traveling at better than Mach one, yet it passed without so much as a whisper of sound! As he stood gazing into the distance, a soft, quiet rush of cool air passed around him, bearing evidence that the train did at least disturb the air a little. But that was the amazing part! It would be conceivable, he thought, that a linear motor of some kind could be used to achieve such silent power, but the complete absence of the sounds of air resistance made it certain that some as yet unknown technology had been employed in the design of this speeding bullet.

There was not a chance that anyone aboard the train could have seen him, of course, but should the track come to some lower level farther along the way, he could perhaps draw attention there. This hope turned out to be vain, because although he followed the rail until nightfall, it showed no sign of descending any lower, nor did he sight any evidence of other people.

He gathered a small meal of wild fruit before it was dark and sat against one of the ubiquitous pylons while he ate it. More trains passed during the night, but he no longer even looked up at them. He slept fitfully and was on the move again well before dawn. The morning light revealed that he was, in fact, descending from a great elevated plain as he had earlier thought, because he could now see a long way ahead. The monorail continued to stretch into the distance, and his heart sank as he began to appreciate, in the growing light, just how far it went. The foliage here was low, dense, and very green, so that the white ribbon of the rail could be seen stretching away over it until it was simply lost in the distance.

His view was open to the north also, and he could just perceive what appeared to be water at the horizon. He was standing on the side of an enormous valley which presumably drained toward a far-distant sea. The monorail curved slowly, following the gentle slope to take up a more northerly direction also.

The north was interesting for other reasons. As he studied the distant view, he could pick out small changes in the color of the terrain which suggested the presence of earthworks similar to those that Paul had pointed out to him. He decided that since the rail was going in that general direction, it would be safer to stay with it, at least for the time being, although his hopes of finding a lower section or a terminal of any kind had all but completely faded. At the speed at which those things were traveling, it was possible that he could walk a hundred kilometers without finding anything.

Then he discovered the road and changed his mind yet again. He came upon it quite suddenly, for it was concealed within a shallow cutting into which he almost stepped before he realized it was there. It was a most unusual kind of road in that it was cobbled with smooth white stones. They were actually a material not unlike that used for the pylons on the monorail, and although they were of various square and rectangular shapes and sizes, they were fitted tightly together and smoothed off.

There was a junction of some kind farther ahead, and he realized when he got there that he had been walking down an access road which now entered a broad, two-laned highway. The lanes were separated by a median strip, and the whole road was about thirty meters wide. It headed in a direction which he figured to be about north-northwest, which was a bit off course if he was going to the center place, but he welcomed the change, because at least there seemed now to be some better chance of contacting someone who could direct him further.

He walked down the median strip to be sure of being able to intercept travelers in either direction. The grass was low and smooth, even lawn-like, and the area had been planted with many small shrubs and eucalypts—fairly recently, he thought. From time to time there was evidence of careful landscaping along the road, although these projects had the appearance of being only partly completed.

He walked for another few hours without sighting any traffic or sign of life. The road had leveled out somewhat and was probably following the valley floor. This had the effect of considerably reducing his forward vision. Flat as the terrain was, the road still swept in a series of gentle curves which prevented his seeing far ahead. There seemed to be little reason for the curves, other than perhaps to make the road more scenic, but Evan now understood the mind of the Kingdom dweller a little better, and that reason could be considered a valid one.

He became progressively more aware of the changes in the scenery as the day wore on. The forest continued to become lower and more sparse, opening up on occasions to reveal vast, fertile-looking fields which stretched away on either side. To his right they finished against a distant, shimmering line of trees which could perhaps be a river, although he had not noticed one from higher up the valley.

There were more signs of earthworks, too, not only along the road but also at points more distant to him. Occasionally he spotted wheel tracks bearing the ribbed imprint of truck tires leaving the road.

He was looking up one of these tracks to his right when he saw the line of figures in the distance—some seven or eight people standing motionless. He stopped walking to peer at them more intently, wondering for the moment if it was not a trick of distance. Then one of the figures could be seen to move, and he knew that they were for real. Only the upper portion of their bodies was visible, their legs being obscured by a low hedge.

228

He waved and shouted, and although they were too distant for him to see them clearly, he was sure they must be aware of him. There was no reply, though, not even a wave, and this struck him as being curious indeed, for he had begun to presuppose the effusive courtesy of the inhabitants of the Kingdom. It was just possible, of course, that they had not seen him, and he set off up the track at a slow jog toward them.

As he approached it was clearly confirmed that they had seen him, for no one had moved, and they were still looking at him. They were all men, presumably field workers because they bore the tools and attire which he had previously seen at the grains project. He called out and waved again, still without achieving any response except a line of icy stares.

The low hedge still separated them, and Evan stopped when he reached it. The men stood only about five or six meters away. "Hi!" said Evan. "Can you tell me where I am?"

One of the men moved slightly and the others glanced toward him. He was taller than the others and very thin. Evan sensed that he was regarded by the others as being senior in the group. Finally he spoke.

"Where are you from?" The voice was expressionless.

Evan hesitated. He didn't know where he was from actually, but it would sound ridiculous to say so. He waved his hand vaguely to the southwest. "I've come from back there," he said a bit lamely, "but I'm on my way to the center place—I hope."

"You immortal?"

Evan could not avoid a slight double take, but the

question was unexpectedly flattering. He gave a nervous laugh. "Of course not. I wouldn't be lost now if I were."

"You got permission?"

The questioning was becoming a bit of an ordeal, but Evan subdued his annoyance with some conscious effort. "Yes...I mean, I didn't have to ask permission. That is, I have a kind of special permission...." His voice trailed off. The answer sounded apologetic and rather foolish. "Look, are you guys going to help me or not?"

The leader walked toward him with a slow, gangling gait. With great deliberation he pushed his pitchfork into the ground on the other side of the hedge directly opposite Evan and leaned forward on it toward him. Evan was nonplussed by the apparently purposeless action, and he realized the other's intent only when it was too late! He lifted his head suddenly and spat into Evan's face!

He spun away and instinctively wiped his face savagely with his sleeve, then stared back at his attacker in stunned amazement. The man's face was quite expressionless, although a few sardonic grins had appeared on the faces of his companions.

Evan felt himself washed by a white flush of rage. With one great leap he flung himself blindly at the dividing hedge that stood between them. It yielded unexpectedly and his wildly flung punch simply grazed the man's temple as he crashed into the other's chest, knocking him to the ground. Evan's momentum carried him forward over the man's head so that he also dived face-first into the softly plowed ground. By

230

the time he had recovered his footing the other man had also commenced to rise. Evan had carried the pitchfork with him in his headlong plunge, and left the man now unarmed.

He lunged again, this time with much greater precision. The man's face had paled noticeably, and he raised his hands in only a halfhearted attempt to shield himself before Evan's fist smashed into his face, driving him again to the ground. Evan followed up furiously, raining wild punches on every undefended area of the prostrate figure beneath him.

He had successfully landed many more blows before he realized that the man was making no attempt to retaliate, nor were his companions moving to his aid! Suddenly the sensation of his fists striking the yielding flesh of the man's face and head was repugnant to him. He stopped abruptly and scrambled to his feet, curiously shocked by the realization of what he was doing. The man had done little more than insult him, but the violence was entirely Evan's!

There was a smear of blood along the side of his hand, and he wiped it off hurriedly on his tunic, feeling as he did so that he was somehow unclean. The man made an attempt to get back to his knees, but fell sideways to the ground again and covered his bloodied face with his hands. He moaned softly.

Evan's rage left him as suddenly as it had come, and he felt only revulsion at the thing he had done. He perceived somewhat dimly that the gift was involved in the feelings that had assailed him, and there abruptly welled within him what could only be a great compassion for the injured man on the ground.

He turned to face the line of grinning spectators. "I'm sorry," he stammered. "I shouldn't have done that. Will you help me please?" The others moved to his aid, although he had not expected them to, and together they lifted the man to his feet. His head hung down, and he turned his face away, resisting Evan's attempts to examine his injuries. One of the other men elbowed his way between them and they began to escort the man away. Another turned to Evan and spoke for the first time with a dismissing gesture. "Shove off!"

Evan stood numbly and watched them walk away, his aggressor stumbling limply, his head still hanging forward. He moaned again, and the sound cut Evan to the very soul.

"I'm sorry." He called after them weakly, but he was ignored. He watched the departing figures for a long time, until they were only faintly discernible against the shimmering haze that hung over the field. He was left in silence—a silence so great that it seemed he could hear the beating of his own heart. The incident had been quite inexplicable, yet it had profoundly disturbed him—not so much because of the strange behavior of these people but of his own. His rage was somewhat predictable, because that had been his problem before, but the agonizing regret which gnawed at him now was something entirely new.

Strange things had happened to him during the few months he had been here, and he was changing. Once he would have been flushed with triumph after such an incident but now he felt only a stinging sense of shame. He drew a deep, shaking breath and wiped his hands on his tunic again. His tormenters were gone, and he was still lost.

"Mister Westering?" The voice came from a little way behind him, and he turned slowly, hands hanging limply at his sides. A man was walking smilingly toward him—a large, dark man with a shock of frizzy black hair and an equally ostentatious black beard. He wore the clothing of a worker also, although his demeanor seemed to differ considerably from that he had just encountered. Farther behind him, on the road, was a huge earth-moving truck.

"Mister Westering?" the man repeated.

"Yes?"

The man reached a hand across the broken hedge. "My name is Jason. Are you having some trouble?"

"Yes," said Evan without elaboration. He accepted the proffered handshake gratefully, and his new acquaintance put a hand to his elbow to guide him back through the hedge.

"I've been watching out for you," said Jason, "but I almost missed seeing you—being so far off the road."

"So you know all about me too?" Evan spoke with an air of almost relieved resignation.

"No—not really." His companion shepherded him along quickly, glancing from time to time behind them.

"Do you know where we are?"

Jason was wryly amused by the question, but his answer was not condescending. "You have been descending the west flank of the valley of the Nile." He pointed back toward the line of distant trees. "That's the Nile over there; we are about one hundred kilometers above the old site of Cairo at this point."

"That's both bad news and good news to me."

"Why?"

Evan laughed shakily, his tightly knotted stomach beginning to unwind. "It's bad news because I'm quite a way from where I thought I was—but it's good news because I have less distance to walk."

"I don't know how much information you had," said Jason, "but you must inevitably become lost here, even if you once knew the territory. There are now inland lakes everywhere, as you have probably noted, while the seas contain many new land masses. Everything is changed, and without a guide you could never be expected to know your whereabouts."

They arrived back at the truck which seemed even more massive at close quarters, and Jason helped him up into the passenger seat. The cabin was unusually comfortable—luxurious, in fact—and he was once more made suddenly aware of the magnificent technology that lay beneath the surface of every man-made object he had seen so far.

They drove off so silently and smoothly that Evan could hardly believe they were actually moving. It could have been electric, perhaps, although there was not so much as even a faint transmission noise. He asked Jason about it as they continued, but even he did not know. He was, he explained, only a truck driver. All that he did know was that it seemed to be entirely maintenance free, requiring neither refueling nor repair—facts which seemed to be regarded (at least by Jason) to be not at all unusual.

234

As the countryside slid silently by, Evan began to enjoy the ride. It was an unusual experience to be riding in a land vehicle—something he had not done since before the mission. Eventually he began to notice other groups of workers in the fields, and they occurred with greater frequency. The Nile valley, Jason explained, was one great ecological recovery project, broken down into a series of smaller projects, each under the administration of immortals. There was a major site at the confluence of the two main arms of the Nile delta.

Evan felt a sudden tug of alarm at the mention of the word delta, recalling Lyddia's urgent instructions. He questioned Jason as matter-of-factly as possible. "Is there a site called Project Delta?"

"Yes," said Jason, "that's the one I mentioned; we're on our way there now."

"Oh!" said Evan limply. "Do you usually work there?"

"No...and I should hope not. Some of the most intransigent ones are there. Not all of them, but enough to make it a bit unpleasant at times. You know, people like those you met a little while ago."

Evan felt a small twinge of panic. He had not regarded Lyddia's warning seriously at the time, but now the forbidden place seemed to have been drawing him toward it quite without his realizing.

"I didn't want to go there.... I mean, I had intended to go up to..."

"To the Promised Land?" Jason interrupted him with a knowing grin. "That's on the other side of the Nile. You would have to get help at one of the projects along the way in any case." He gave Evan a cautious sideways glance. "You have already had some contact with some of those people. Would you like to continue with it?"

Evan sat in belligerent silence. The man was right; he could not continue now without help. Who would help him, and who would hinder? At least Jason had been watching out for him, and the realization was only slowly dawning that he may well have been under surveillance since the very moment he had set off...by means that he did not understand!

They drove for about an hour, and the country began suddenly to open up. The extent of the works began to become more apparent, with vast armies of men, women, and young people moving like ants on a gargantuan nest. Jason slowed down, for they were in the midst of them now, and the people walked back and forth across the roadway in their path, seemingly heedless of the truck.

Evan watched the faces of these people with growing concern, for they somehow disturbed him greatly. He was not quite sure why, except that he could detect a kind of benign insolence in their eyes, similar to the people he had met before. But with these there was something more—perhaps even unspoken hatred. He was afraid.

They made their way down a gradual curving incline, and the administration building came suddenly into view. It was an unexpected sight in this stark setting—a modernistic, mushroom-shaped building set back in an excavation in the hillside.

Characteristically, it was surrounded with newly

planted lawns and shrubbery. Men were working in the garden.

The truck drew silently into the cool shade beneath the building, and Jason dropped quickly to the ground and appeared at Evan's door. He helped him down and shepherded him, perhaps a little too anxiously, toward the glass-enclosed entrance foyer. Evan twisted to shrug off Jason's hand from his arm and stood looking back at the moving mass of laborers. Jason waited obligingly.

"Those people—they sort of resent me, don't they?"

Jason replied softly, as if anxious not to be overheard. "Don't take it personally. Many of them treat everybody that way...me too."

"Why should they?"

Jason shifted awkwardly from one foot to the other. "They are the rebellious ones—people from the nations that..." he shrugged, "that had the most to relearn, I guess."

Evan noted that word again. "They don't look to be from all that many nations to me. Most of them look like Westerners." He glanced at the group working in the garden close to them. "In fact, those people over there could well be..."

"Americans?"

The voice came from behind him, and he spun in startled surprise to find himself face-to-face with David Cohen who stood framed in the doorway, smiling as always. "Does that surprise you?"

David's mere presence was the biggest surprise, and for the moment, at least, Evan was at a loss for words. David gave a nod of dismissal to Jason, who absented himself with obvious relief. He climbed quickly into the truck, bidding Evan good-by with a quick, circular wave.

Evan was embarrassed. With Jason gone, he felt like the errant schoolboy, freshly delivered to the principal's office. He thrust his hands uncomfortably into his tunic pockets. "Hello, David. I didn't expect to see you here."

"Had you asked, you would have found that I work here." David continued to smile at him, and Evan felt compelled to drop his gaze to the ground in front of him. "I'm sorry," he muttered almost inaudibly.

"I'm sorry, too," said David. "I'm sorry that you didn't trust us."

Evan wished for the ground to engulf him. It would have been easier had David been annoyed, but he was only disappointed.

"It wasn't that I didn't trust you...I didn't trust myself. There were so many things I would have liked to ask but couldn't. I thought you would try to stop me."

"Don't you think we could have stopped you anyway had we wished to?"

Evan kicked at the dust beneath his feet. "Yes, I did know that...but it wasn't as if I set out to defy you. It was sort of my way of saying something when I couldn't think of any other way of telling you."

"Why don't you come inside and tell me now?" David stood aside and held the door open for him. They ascended the carpeted spiral staircase into a spacious and colorful lounge. There were people there, sitting quietly, but David led him through quickly

238

without introduction. He led the way down a broad passage and held another door open for him to enter. He found himself in a very large office, dominated on one wall by an immense transparent panel which afforded a view of the work project. Strangely, it looked somehow different than the view he had seen only moments before, and he stood looking at it, trying to decide what the difference actually was.

David noted this and laughed. "Don't worry, Evan, your eyes are not deceiving you. Watch this!" He sat at his desk and placed his fingers under the back edge of it as if to operate some kind of control. The view through the window began to move away from them as if the whole building had suddenly begun to move.

Evan spread his arms—momentarily disoriented by this strange illusion—to David's undisguised enjoyment. The scene continued to recede until the view was entirely as it should have been. He realized that the window was acting as a giant zoom lens, capable of giving the operator a firsthand view of remote areas of the site.

"Can you go anywhere like that?" asked Evan, frankly amazed.

David nodded. "It's mainly for the use of mortals assisting in the administration of the project. It extends their faculties a little, don't you think?"

"It sure does, but are you implying that you don't need devices like that yourself?"

"No, not really, although I was using it to watch how Matthew was making out over in sector sixteen while I was waiting for you. He's here, too, you know."

"Is he involved in the administration of projects like this too?"

"Yes," said David, "although you might say in an honorary capacity. All immortals have ruling responsibilities, but not all of us are engaged full time—that is, unless you don't want to differentiate between administration and ministry. Our ministry never ceases, you know."

He looked at Evan meaningfully and motioned toward a chair. "Won't you sit down?"

Evan sat facing David across the desk, the immortal resting patiently back in his chair, giving Evan a chance to speak. "As I said," he began, "I didn't actually set out to defy you, David, but I was rather hung up on this thing about being different. And I *am* different!"

David smiled and nodded slowly.

Evan felt free to continue. "Well, it wasn't enough for me to just tell you what I felt. I could see that there were many people around me here who were obviously more worthy than I, yet I seemed to be preferred above them and given higher status that I don't seem to have earned. I seem to have kind of 'jumped the queue' and I can't look back without feeling that everyone is glaring at me."

David nodded again, and Evan could see that he was being told nothing new to him.

"Now, I know very well that I could have asked about many of the things that troubled me before this, but something stopped me. Maybe it was the gift, or perhaps I was just plain scared of what I might be told—I'm not sure which. Either way, I had become pretty well convinced that you knew something about me—that *everyone* knew something about me—something that would be hurtful for me to know."

David nodded again before he answered. "All knowledge is not necessarily of value to all people, Evan, and the gift would defend you against this if it was expedient to do so."

Evan sat forward in his chair. "That's the way I sort of looked at it—up until the time I met Rufus, that is...."

"Rufus?"

"Yes, I met him on the path near the lake at the biological studies building. He was going to the center place, and I gave him some of my food." He grinned wryly as he recalled that the statement was not entirely correct. "He was so happy...he had no hangups at all! He just figured that he had only to go ask someone. I thought that if it was as simple as that for Rufus, why should I sit around getting all uptight when I could do the same thing."

"So you set off to follow him?"

"Yes. That's all there was to it. It seemed so easy, but I knew that if I talked to you first it might become more complicated. I knew that you were...well, responsible for me, but if I did this by myself there would be no one to answer for me—would there?"

"Did you fear that I would stop you?"

Evan grinned involuntarily. "No, I figured that you would let me take the consequences of my own actions."

"And you got lost...and had a bit of a brush with some people on one of the projects. By and large, the consequences weren't too severe. It could have been different though. . . ."

"There were a lot of things that I really didn't think much about." Evan slid back again into his chair. "For one thing, I hadn't expected to meet any people as overtly hostile as those men in the field. You seem to know about that too."

David's grin broadened and he continued nodding. "There are quite a few people still hostile to the idea of the Kingdom, Evan, in spite of all that has happened to them. They caught you off guard?"

"Yes. I was getting so used to the idea of Earth being a perfect place that I walked smack into it. I still don't really understand what happened."

"There are relatively few people living under these circumstances, although they probably seem a multitude when you see so many of them in one place. These are the ones who thus far have refused all offers of help. They are under a rather heavy hand now, and they resent it. Those men on the road took you for one of high status, and they set out to bring you down."

Evan felt another pang of remorse as he recalled the incident. "He didn't even fight back—that man. He just lay there and let me hit him."

"He couldn't do anything else. The law forbids him to strike another so as to cause injury. The punishment would have been very severe had he done so." He fixed Evan with a steely gaze before continuing. "But he was armed, you know. He was armed with a weapon which had power to harm you much more than he could have with only his bare hands."

"He did? What was that?"

"He had a greater degree of the gift than you. He knew that with a minimum of physical intervention he could bring you down, and he carried it off."

"Are you sure that you know what *did* happen out there? As I seem to remember it, he got the business end of my fist."

"Ah, yes," said David, placing the tips of his fingers together in front of him, "but who was hurt?"

Evan could see the point, but he declined to admit to it. "He was!" he replied doggedly.

David was undeterred. "His injuries will be gone in less than a week, Evan. How about yours?"

Evan relaxed in his chair and backed off. "You mean he *knew* what I would do, and he just took it?"

David nodded.

"But what good did that do him?"

"I don't know that it did him any 'good,' but there was what you might call a payoff. For a start, he had the satisfaction of proving to himself, his cronies, and yes, even you, that you were not what you first appeared to be. You acted in a way in which even he himself was not permitted to act. He received justification for his own position, and, believe me, that could make the physical suffering well worth while."

Evan stared at the carpet until David spoke again. "May I repeat the question then? Who was hurt?"

"It seems that all we are doing here is confirming what I have already been saying, about being different, I mean. If I extend what you are saying to a conclusion, it simply means that he should be here and I should be out there working in his place."

David smiled consolingly. "Not really. He caught

you out at a specific point, that's all. Then, of course, you are simply not in the same position as these people, and I know this troubles you. It is true that you are occupying a station somewhat out of line with your qualifications, but then your arrival was somewhat unorthodox also. You will come to understand all these things in time, but meanwhile I can only assure you that your position is neither unjust or unfair."

"Even Lyddia told me that, and quite frankly I didn't believe it. If you say it's so, I guess that has to be right."

"I'm not sure that you are being entirely charitable when you say that, Evan, but I am telling you the truth."

Evan spun his chair to look out over the work site. It was approaching evening again, and a slow procession of people was visible—tired workers returning to their homes for the night. His tormentor was still out there somewhere, probably nursing a sore head. He caught himself smirking quietly at the thought, and it struck him just how true David's words were. He glanced down at his blood-smeared tunic and felt a fresh wave of foolishness and shame. The man *had* hurt him!

"This business of the gift, David. It is somehow both good and bad, isn't it?"

"We can choose how we use it...yes."

"It isn't possessed only by 'good' people?"

"Of itself it is neither good nor bad. Even the father of lies is in possession of it, and to him it is hardly a blessing."

"And it's free?"

"Yes."

"Then I must have it." Evan turned his chair back to face David again. He was surprised at his own resolve. "I want to go to the center place and ask for it as Rufus did—and like Paul is afraid to do. I want you to let me do it."

"Did I say I would stop you?"

"But you don't want me to go . . . you don't approve, do you?"

"You have a right to that which you ask, and I have already made arrangements to assist you in it. I am going to accompany you to Jerusalem."

Evan was caught unaware by this revelation. He had fully expected David to oppose him. "You'll come with me?"

"Gladly. In fact it's almost a matter of necessity. The Promised Land is not a place where people come and go entirely of their own free will. Only certain ones are even permitted to go there."

"You mean I have to be chaperoned?"

"You could call it that."

Evan laughed thinly; he was beginning to see something funny in the picture of himself stumbling along on his impossible one-man mission. They had been observing him all along. They knew where he was and what he was doing. David even knew that he would end up sitting here in this chair. "You mean that while I was wandering around out there in the wilderness you were making preparations to escort me?"

David smiled. "Yes, you were not quite as lost as you thought. Sector 05 is only recently reclaimed, and we like to restrict movement in that area by humans for a short while after. That's why you couldn't find anybody. But we would not have abandoned you."

"If I had tried to cross the Nile higher up the valley, would you have stopped me?"

"Had it been high enough up the valley there would have been no problems, but if you had attempted it anywhere near this region, we would have been obliged to intercept for your own good."

"Lyddia warned me about going near Project Delta. Was that because of the people. . . I mean people like those I met?"

"No, there is a much more serious reason—one which I cannot even discuss with you at this time. But since you mention it, I want you to appreciate that the project is strictly off limits to you unless I am with you. Is that understood?"

David's tone was suddenly serious, and Evan found himself nodding hastily. "Of course, if you say so."

"We will have to traverse some of the site on the way to the ferry tomorrow morning, and I'm afraid that's all of the place you will be seeing."

Evan nodded again. It was obvious that from now on David was clearly in charge.

"Would you like some dinner?" David asked.

"Yes, I'd like that very much." There was a soft tap at the door at the precise instant he spoke, and a middle-aged woman entered, carrying a small notepad. Evan was curious as to how she had been so unostensibly summoned, but he decided not to ask.

"You wish to order dinner, Mister Cohen?" She smiled pleasantly at Evan. "And your guest also?"

David had arisen and Evan, lost momentarily in

thought, scrambled belatedly to his feet also.

"This is Evan Westering," said David rather grandly. "He is my very special charge. Evan, I wish you to meet Mrs. Myer. She has charge of our catering here at the project office. Your inner man is in the very best of hands."

The woman blushed attractively. She was a mortal, and she was succumbing to the compliments. They ordered the meal with Evan simply following David's suggestion. When the woman had left, he had a wry question to ask.

"Do you resurrected people *have* to eat?"

David raised his eyebrows. "Our survival is not contingent on it."

"I'm rather surprised that you *do* eat."

David sat back into his chair and spread his hands. "If you read your Scripture you'll find that one of the things the risen Christ did on at least one occasion was eat. In the upper room he ate fish and honeycomb... no one seemed surprised at that. In fact it was probably of some comfort to the others there to see just how 'normal' he was."

"Oh, I'm sure you're right...but it just seems a bit strange—that's all."

"What would you have me do then? Should I just sit back here and watch you enjoy a delicious meal? Maybe resurrected persons should have their sense of smell removed also—lest we suffer unduly."

Evan raised his hands over his head. He was beginning to lose his case. "Okay, then, I'll withdraw that last statement."

The meal was indeed a splendid one, as David had

promised. They sat on opposite sides of the desk to eat it and talked about what they would do on the morrow. David had made the arrangements for their transport across the site to the bank of the Nile, in spite of the fact that it was considered customary for pilgrims to reach the Promised Land on foot. They would be traveling by truck, and although David did not elaborate on his reasons for doing this, Evan sensed that he was more than a little uncomfortable about his mere presence on the site, and for reasons unknown to him would have him off it again with as much haste as possible.

It would be a long walk to Jerusalem, taking possibly some three weeks, but Evan was excited at the prospect. With David's blessing, things would go much easier, and he even found his own position in this radically changed world taking on new meaning and purpose.

David explained at great length the route they would take, but Evan was not particularly listening. In spirit, at least, he had already crossed the Nile and was journeying far ahead—pressing his imagination to its limits in an effort to picture the sights he would see, the legendary people he would meet, and answers to the burning questions that he longed to ask!

Chapter ten

The ferry moved at a glacial pace, slowly filling the gap between them and the shore with a plain of shimmering water. Jason was leaning against his truck back at the landing, raising his hand at intervals for sporadic parting waves. Evan could not help noting that David had singled out the same driver to take them across the work site, and except for Mrs. Myer he had been pointedly steered away from meeting people at the administration building.

While these things had not gone entirely unobserved, they worried him little, for he was quite content now with David's explanation that it was not good for him to be at this place, and he looked at the receding shoreline with some degree of relief. David was relieved, too, and it showed in his relaxed and friendly demeanor, which in spite of his efforts to maintain it had flagged a little during their preparations for departure.

Evan noted this also. It was fascinating that even an immortal being carried many of the old earmarks of humanity. David was still an enigma, and it probably would be some time before Evan could expect to understand him fully. In fact, there was a facet to

David's nature about which he was not at all anxious to inquire, and that was the strange power that he obviously wielded over those under him. There had been a small incident the night before that, although it did not involve Evan, had left him feeling slightly uncomfortable. Someone had come up from the site demanding to speak to David—a bitter, aggressive man who seemed to have some sort of ax to grind with him. He had been whisked off quickly, and David had gone to speak to him in private.

Evan would have disregarded the incident had he not seen the man again later in the evening. He was being ushered through the waiting room, and even though Evan saw him for only a matter of moments the dramatic change in the man was plainly evident. Brash and outspoken only a short time before, he appeared now to be completely subdued, his face considerably paler and his eyes lowered to the floor. He walked quickly, with his head down, as if anxious to be out of the place with as much haste as possible.

The magnitude of the change meant only one thing—that David Cohen had used on this man a part of his nature which Evan had no desire to expose. If David had been angry he evidenced no sign of it later, behaving as if the incident had never occurred. Evan was happy to leave it that way.

The ferry seemed curiously out of place here. He was a little surprised, in the presence of such mind-boggling technology as he had witnessed over the past few months, that such a crude form of slow transport would be used. David pointed out somewhat unconvincingly that in the Promised Land time was an item of diminished importance, and in any event it was a place to be approached with due reverence. Evan would have liked to point out that the monorail seemed to be a notable exception to that rule, but he decided to leave the matter unresolved.

The only passengers aboard, they walked to the leading edge and stood in silence, waiting for details of the distant shoreline to become more distinct. As they did, Evan became more appreciative of the manner of their approach, for it presented him with a scene of growing wonder.

The country ahead of them was of indescribable beauty, notwithstanding the incredible sights he had witnessed before. He looked upon a magnificent and panoramic garden, more formal perhaps than the ones he had previously seen but possessing a beauty unsurpassed in its very intensity. The colors alone were beyond imagining. It was as if every leaf, flower, and blade of grass was illuminated somehow from inside—creating within him a strange feeling of peace and satisfaction in just merely looking upon them.

He said nothing to David as they approached this wondrous setting, for indeed there was nothing to be said; it was all quite beyond words!

Myriads of blooms exploded against the lush green backdrop, cascading over the banks and extending in some places down to the water's edge.

There were people also—people of both sexes and of all ages. As they drew closer to the bank Evan could see that they were mostly immortals—he could pick them out quite easily now, even at some distance.

There was no landing on this side of the river, and

the ferry simply bumped softly against the elevated bank, its approach cushioned by the overflowing foliage. Smiling faces appeared above them, and strong hands reached down to assist them onto the bank. They were greeted warmly by many people, and it was immediately apparent that David was well known to them all.

The formalities were quickly dealt with, however, and they were soon on their way, striding together along a broad, white path under the bluest skies Evan had seen yet. It was as if even the air was different here—made fresher to permit one to be more aware of the multiple perfumes that surrounded them, and clearer to the extent that even the most distant hills seemed much closer than they actually were.

This was perplexing to him at first, because it tended to give the impression that they were walking in almost one spot continually, with the pattern of surrounding hills remaining seemingly unchanged. Nevertheless, they traveled quickly, and despite his desire to be at the center place, he was reluctant for these idyllic days to come to an end. David was ever ready to tell him about the places through which they passed, and they spent much time in deep discussion. When they camped at night they usually slept in the open, often talking together until deep into the night before retiring.

Sustenance presented no problem, for there were now many dwellings and at every one were people who seemed only too eager to attend to their needs. Evan quite forgot the difficulties he had had in the past, for in this climate it was impossible to regard any other living soul as anything but a warm, affectionate friend.

The homes—mostly rural dwellings—were comfortable and luxurious. In keeping with all of the examples of architecture he had seen in the Kingdom, they exhibited a rustic graciousness which was always in complete harmony with their natural surroundings.

The farms were unlike anything he had previously seen. There was no sign here of the experimental or corrective projects which dotted the regions from which he had come. Here were magnificent farming properties in full production, with acre after acre of fertile fields stretching in every direction for as far as the eye could see.

While Evan's knowledge of agriculture was meager in the extreme, even he was quick to notice that all the phases of production seemed to be operating at the same time, with harvesters alongside fields of newly sprouting grain, as if one harvest was literally following on the heels of another.

David explained that this was so, and that all agricultural areas of the promised land were fully productive, with the exception of those areas that were being rested according to the law. There were places like this outside the Kingdom, too, he said, and in particular around the Western center place, but for the most part men were just beginning to implement the new technology. More specifically, they were not as yet fully obedient. David spent some time on this point, as if to insure that it would not be lost on his protégé.

From this place, he explained, all knowledge spread

out over the earth, and man profited from it in proportion to the degree to which he listened. The process was a slow one nevertheless, but herein was the role and purpose of the Kingdom dweller—to articulate and demonstrate the laws and principles of the new order. David resisted Evan's suggestion that people were being *forced* to comply with the law, preferring to maintain that they were still free to act—even if they were not free to choose the consequences of their actions.

One of the ironies of the Kingdom was that the corrective projects were predominantly populated by Westerners, and Westerners from the most culturally favored nations at that! Here in the Kingdom it seemed that for the most part other races were represented, and this was a curious revelation. After all the Western world, by and large, represented the "Christian" nations and included many people who could be regarded as having been custodians of the gospel.

David's explanation was chillingly simple. While many of the less favored citizens could previously have been described as being pagan or uncultured (having much to learn) they did, on the other hand, have very little to unlearn. The greatest difficulty for most people in accepting the Kingdom was not the matter of learning the new ways—for this was demonstrably a joy—but of disengaging themselves from the accumulated misconceptions and false values of the advanced countries.

As David continued to explain, it became progressively easier to see that the Kingdom was a widely different thing to different people. To some, the dawn of the Kingdom was a welcome and liberating experience to be embraced and adopted with joyous haste. For others it was an unanticipated and traumatic cultural shock!

Evan was not anxious to pursue this point further, for he already had some vague suspicions as to the cause of his earlier difficulties, and the nagging unrest had not entirely left him.

He enjoyed the walk to the center place immeasurably. At times, others joined them on the road, always immortals, and together they discussed many things, until Evan began to share at least to some extent their vitality and enthusiasm. On occasions— but only rarely—he sensed something within these people, as if, through a chink, he caught a brief glimpse of the eternal fire that burned within them. It was too fleeting to make out any more than this, for he was obviously only sensing something which he well knew he could not yet encompass. When, one evening after nearly a month of travel, David announced almost matter-of-factly that they would enter Jerusalem on the morrow. He was struck by a feeling of disappointment.

Evan slept fitfully that night, suddenly in awe of the experience that now confronted him. Maybe it was fear, because as he lay looking up into the sky, he began to sense new feelings which caused him for the first time to seriously consider the wisdom of his pilgrimage. Paul's voice continually revisited him: "I don't do it because I don't *choose* to!" Paul was a lot smarter than that! Why wasn't he here too? There was no doubt that David would have allowed it, for surely Paul was better qualified than he. There was Rufus, of even lower status than Paul, and he had come here! Of course Rufus was an old man. Why had he not gone sooner? Were the reasons the same as Paul's? Evan squeezed his eyes tightly shut. What did all these people know that he did not?

He turned to look at the sleeping figure beside him, inexplicably snoring softly in spite of his resurrected state. Surely this person could mean him no harm. Evan felt curiously drawn to him—this big, kindly man who had given of his valuable time to walk all these miles in the manner of a mortal simply to guard his passage. Would he do all this to no avail? That was unthinkable! Yet the journey had not been undertaken at David's suggestion, but at Evan's. If it was best for him that he come here, why was it that no one had suggested it?

He gazed back defiantly into the heavens and hardened his resolve again. These problems were certainly no justification for turning back; they were the reasons for his being here, and he was determined now to see the whole matter through regardless of his misgivings.

Dawn came far too slowly, and when David finally awoke Evan was already impatiently pacing the ground. They were, in effect, within the suburbs of Jerusalem now, although the country still retained its rural appearance. This, David explained, was due to certain laws pertaining to domestic dwellings in the Kingdom which required specific minimum distances between homes.

The last kilometers were walked in silence, continually uphill now. Contrary to his expectations, Evan was feeling progressively more unhappy with each step. He was disinclined to mention this to David because he as simply unable to identify specifically what it was that troubled him. He wished now that there had been a few more miles to travel—more time to talk, and more time to think.

David's pace was quickening, as if he relished the opportunity to be at the center place again, and Evan found himself hard put to keep pace with him. When they came within sight of the heart of the Holy City it looked quite unlike anything Evan had imagined. Somehow he had always carried a picture in his mind of a little white city atop a bare mountain. It was elevated, for sure, but it rose out of a sublime landscape that literally took his breath away.

The magnificent buildings arose as gleaming spires, reaching higher into the clear blue sky than any buildings he had ever known. Standing as they were some three or four kilometers from the city gates, Evan had an immediate impression of having shrunk to the size of an ant, the sight so dominated his vision.

David stopped and waited patiently while his companion absorbed this fantastic sight, but Evan emitted only a long, low whistle. He had no words sufficient for this splendor! The terrain fell suddenly before them, creating a deep valley which looked as if it might surround the city, although distance

257

prevented his making that out. The city was much larger than he had expected also, and they were obviously viewing only a small part of it at that.

The air in the valley was as clear as crystal, and in spite of the distance he could make out many details of the city itself. It was bounded by a smooth, white wall in which there were gateways. One of them was particularly large, and from it flowed a crystal river. It did not flow through the valley ahead of them but seemed to follow another deep valley which headed off behind them toward the west.

Paths radiated from the gates and crossed the valley floor in different directions. People could be seen moving back and forth, walking briskly and confidently, greeting one another in a manner that suggested a festive atmosphere. While there was no traffic noise that he could discern, the air was alive with the sounds of many people, as if the very lifeblood of the city could be heard coursing within it.

David beamed broadly. "What do you think of it?"

"It's quite a spot!" Evan concealed his awe carefully. "I didn't know that Jerusalem was on a river."

"It was not always so," said David. "That river commences near the east side—from beneath the temple in fact. It flows in two directions—into the Mediterranean from this side, and away into what was the Dead Sea on the other."

"*Was* the Dead Sea?"

"Yes, it is now very much a living one. It overflows and empties itself clear down to the Gulf of Aqaba and into the Red Sea. There are no desert regions anywhere south of here."

David set off again impulsively, speaking back over his shoulder. "Just wait until we are inside. There are many more things I will show you."

Evan caught up. "I want to get everything over with first—I mean, let's go wherever you have arranged for us first."

David shrugged. "As you wish. That will be the temple—you can't see it from here, and it's quite a long walk."

"The temple? Is that where people go to ask for the gift?"

"Yes."

"Do I need to have an appointment?"

"Yes—in a way."

"Then I wouldn't have done very well coming on my own, would I?"

David laughed. "You would not even have been permitted this far, much less into the Holy City itself."

They covered the remaining distance quickly and were soon mingling with the people immediately outside the city. The seeming absence of other mortals made Evan feel uncomfortably conspicuous, although no one paid him any real attention. The gate through which they entered was a smooth white portal which did not seem to be provided with gates.

Once inside they stopped again to allow Evan to adjust to his first sight of what must surely have been the world's most fabulous city. There was much more space between the buildings than had first appeared from a distance, and this space was occupied by spacious gardens, bedecked with glorious foliage which overhung the smooth pathways leading off in every direction. Wherever he looked, his eyes feasted on an almost unreal scene of beauty, color, and exquisite design.

Every pathway was equally attractive and inviting, but David guided him onto one which led directly toward the heart of the city. It opened out eventually into a gently curved broad way, two hundred or so meters in width, in which was set at intervals trees, garden plots, fountains, and sculpture. It was entirely pedestrian traffic, although in the distance, through the trees, he caught the rapid movement of some kind of vehicular traffic.

Above their heads, curving gracefully among the buildings, was the monorail, and for the first time Evan saw one of the cars traveling at a speed which allowed him to study it. He asked no questions of his guide, for that would almost be to risk missing something of the incredible sights, sounds, and perfumes that surrounded him.

The buildings were every bit as striking in their appearance as those he had seen previously, but with an added impact of sheer size. David tugged at his sleeve. "You'll see the temple when we come to the next concourse. It's obscured for the moment by those buildings over to the right."

They approached another intersecting broad way, the concourse of which David spoke, and as they rounded a huge plot of fernery marking the corner, Evan gazed for the first time on his fantastic goal. It stood at the far end of what turned out to be an immense concourse, a gleaming dome-like edifice with the appearance of pure gold. It arose from within an outer wall, and the front of the building was served by a gigantic staircase, giving the lower portion of the building the appearance of an Inca pyramid.

"How far away is it?" said Evan.

"It will take about an hour and a half to get there."

Evan frowned. "It doesn't *look* that far."

David chuckled. "Everyone says that—but it's a bit of a trick of perspective. The temple is much larger than you realize, and the concourse widens as it approaches it."

David was, as usual, right again, and it was late into the afternoon when they finally drew near to the temple. The concourse was very much wider here, and there were significantly fewer people around them. Evan was unhappy with this, because with every step he found himself feeling more and more exposed and conspicuous, as if the building itself were gazing down upon his approach. He would have preferred even to have walked closer to the side of the concourse, under the shade of the gardens, but David had chosen a line that took them to the center. He noticed also for the first time that he was not the only mortal, and that others were traveling with him in the same direction. There were just three or four of them, and it was only the thinning of the crowd that now allowed him to see them.

He nudged David. "I can see other mortals."

"Yes," said David without looking at them.

"What are they doing here?"

"The same as you—going to ask for the gift."

"There aren't very many of them. Why aren't they escorted too?"

They have permission to make the pilgrimage alone."

"Not like me. . . ." Evan grinned humorlessly. David ignored the comment.

By the time they had reached the outer wall they were alone except for a few other mortals. They passed through one of the many unguarded portals and walked toward the first flight of stairs—stairs that were so wide they disappeared into the distance in both directions. No other person was within several hundred meters of them.

Evan became suddenly and unaccountably alarmed. They were too alone! "Why does it have to be so wide?"

David spoke gently. "It's like this all around the temple. It has to be wide enough to provide for all the people who *ought* to be here!"

"But why aren't they?"

David looked away up the stairs. "You have walked for many days that you may discover the answers to such things as this. Why is it that you now ask *me?*"

Evan followed his gaze. The actual building of the temple was no longer visible and they could see only to the first landing—quite a long way above them. David was right! He was simply trying to opt out of the duty ahead of him. He swallowed hard and consciously leveled his voice as he spoke—but it still betrayed him.

"Well. . .what do we do? Just walk in?"

"There is a little way to go yet, Evan. We must pass

over seven landings before we even enter the temple itself."

"You make that sound like quite an odyssey!"

David spread his hands. "It is!"

They began to climb the stairs slowly and, in Evan's case, somewhat apprehensively. As they did so, he became aware of a strange feeling within him. At first it was only a quickening of the pulse, which could well have been due to the extra effort of making the ascent, but it continued to grow until it approached a kind of excitement and elation. It was a pleasant feeling but at the same time deeply disturbing also. He said nothing, preferring to wait until he was entirely sure before commenting, but by the time they had reached the first landing he knew beyond doubt that something strange was happening to him.

They paused to rest, although he knew that in David's case it was hardly necessary. They had an elevated view back over part of the city now, and as he gazed on the scene he tried to analyze his new feelings. It was a curious mixture—a feeling of being more responsible, more mature, more joyous, yet tinged with a strange sense of sadness and foreboding. It was both exciting and frightening.

He glanced at David and found the immortal looking at him knowingly. "Are you ready to continue?"

It seemed an odd question, as if there were some likelihood that he was not. Evan nodded, and together they walked across the wide landing toward the next flight of steps.

They had no sooner commenced when the sensation

began to grow again, stronger and more persistent, becoming more intense with each step, until it seemed almost that something would burst within him.

His fear was now beginning to outweigh his pleasure, and by the time they had arrived at the second landing it amounted almost to panic. David was striding ahead, apparently unaware of Evan's faltering steps. He reached the landing first and waited to be joined. "Are you all right, my boy?"

"No!" Evan blurted, "I'm not!" He sat abruptly on the top step and looked back toward the city again. "What's happening to me, David?"

"You are being prepared."

"Prepared for the gift?"

"Prepared to meet the Master."

"But what's actually happening? I'm not sure that I like it!"

David sat slowly on the step beside him and placed an immense hand around his shoulders. "You know a little about the gift, don't you?"

"Yes, and I know that to receive it fully is to be immortal—as you are."

"Then you must realize also that there is an enormous expansion of the human faculties involved— a magnification of your discernment, your under-standing, your soul."

"Yes."

"That is what is happening to you now—by degrees."

Evan looked into the kindly face in frank amazement. "You mean I'm already receiving the gift?"

264

David nodded.

"But why so soon? Why not when I meet the Master?"

David shrugged. "It's rather a circular experience, you see. We come to the Master that we may receive of the gift, but on the other hand, we cannot even endure his presence unless the light of the gift first burns within us. We simply have to receive a measure of it before we can approach him for its fullness. Do you understand?"

Evan nodded. "I guess so—when I think about it. That also fits what I felt when I started up the steps, although it's different now—almost as if it's too much for me." He gesticulated despairingly. "I don't feel 'magnified,' I just feel exposed and foolish—even afraid!"

"Ah yes, but I must remind you again of what the gift entails. Once you have received it completely you will have a fullness of vision to the extent that you will see the reason behind every reason, the truth beyond every truth, the consequences beyond every thought and every action. No man will ever deceive you, and no facade will have the power to mask your discernment."

"I still don't understand!"

David continued. "You will look upon a good man and know that he is good, even beyond his own knowledge. You will look upon a wise man and know that he is wise, quite beyond that man's wisdom. And..." David lowered his voice significantly, "you will look upon the fool and know that he is a fool... likewise the liar and the hypocrite."

"So?"

"The fool is a happy man, for if he is fool enough he is truly innocent—being for a time, at least, unaware of his station." David looked directly into Evan's inquiring face. "But given understanding..."

Evan's mouth went suddenly dry, and as he spoke his upper lip trembled. "Then what you mean is that if I am to have this great, blinding searchlight of understanding..."

David nodded. "You must be prepared for its illumination to fall upon you personally."

Evan put his face into his hands. Of course! It was perfectly simple—the only problem being that it had never occurred to him in this way before! He lifted his head. "But why should it be all that bad? I mean, I *know* already that I'm not perfect, and I'm not afraid to confess that!"

"That is good—essential in fact. But how *well* do you know it?" David stood up and paced a short distance along the landing before turning again to face him. "Think back, Evan—think back to your baptism. How old were you then?"

"About thirteen I think."

"Think of your understanding and ambitions of that time. Think of your naïve ideas—all of those false impressions you had of yourself...the things you thought and said and did. Were they not foolish?"

Evan grinned. "I can hardly deny that, can I? But I grew a little...I think!"

"Of course you did—in a series of small hurdles which in themselves were not all painful revelations of your foolishness—more a matter of a growing awareness. You see, it's only as you look back across them all collectively that you become aware of the gulf and are ashamed of yourself."

"That's true—I suppose."

David moved back closer again and sat down. "Just imagine, then, that you were transported to the end of the race, denied the opportunity to take those hurdles one at a time, and found yourself looking back over that gulf which you had not of yourself bridged. What do you think you would then feel?" David's eyebrows raised expectantly as he watched his words slowly sinking in.

"So that's what is happening to me. I've sort of arrived here unprepared, haven't I?"

"Yes, although that doesn't necessarily mean the opportunity is withdrawn. If you continue, you may well discover that grace is sufficient for you...but I can't advise you on that!"

Evan clasped his hands on his knees. "I can appreciate my difficulty a little now, but I still can't see that this revelation has to be all that bad. I mean, I can be fairly objective if I wish to be."

David shook his head slowly. "To be truly objective is to be fully able to acquit 'them' of any complicity in our own evil, and I don't know that any mortal man faces the truth to that extent. Think back again on some occasion—any truly painful occasion—when you have said or done something supremely foolish. Do you visualize the experience again, trying to persuade yourself that with only a little modification the outcome would have been different? These memories are indeed painful to us, for in that instant we are truly objective, being capable, even against our will, of knowing ourselves as we will be known."

They sat together in silence, Evan looking unseeingly at the magnificent skyline. The feelings of alarm still stirred within him, except that he understood the problem a little better now, and his fear was beginning to subside. Perhaps he was even now a bit better equipped to continue!

Eventually he spoke with measured determination. "I think I'll go on now, David."

He sprang lightly to his feet and walked briskly across the landing toward the next flight of steps. He had already commenced his ascent before he realized that David had not moved.

"Aren't you coming?"

David rose slowly and shook his head. "No, Evan, I am required to stay with you only until you are fully aware of your own commitment. After that you must continue alone."

Evan felt his bravado crumble. "But can't you stay with me if I wish you to?"

"No, my friend, but I will wait for you here."

"But how will I know? I mean, it may turn out to be more than I can endure."

David gave him a kindly smile. "There will be many at the second resurrection who will be *obliged* to endure it. Right now, you have a choice, and the gift will not allow you to come to harm. Go on now...go on!"

Evan took two more cautious steps and turned back again, but David motioned him on. He continued, forcing himself onward and upward until every step seemed to require supreme effort. The feeling continued to grow within his breast, spreading up the back of his neck and into his head—a kind of exquisite pain which seemed to burst into his brain like a cascade of exploding lights. The distant horizon appeared to flee behind him, as if each step were lifting him disproportionately toward some new height.

Something was up there...not yet within his sight, but he could feel it calling him...a white-hot radiance that seemed to beckon him as a flame atttracts a moth. Yet it was at the same time desirable above anything else he could imagine.

The seemingly great height afforded him a view of something even greater than the surrounding terrain. It was as if he were conscious of every blade of grass and grain of sand within his field of vision. There was something else surrounding him also, for the sweeping panorama was overlaid with a closer view of himself, as if every yesterday was but a moment ago, closing in on him, rushing up behind him with a kind of solid presence which compelled him again to look back.

He did not look behind him but stopped short, and the wildly compressing time stopped also, hovering behind him like a terrifying being, breathing on his shoulder! He tottered momentarily, as if about to topple backwards, then regained his balance.

He dared not look back, for it was all there—a horror beyond bearing—yet in his mind's eye he could discern the eyes of people wronged, of friends betrayed. There were fleeting, shadowy images, too—of burned and broken bodies, of gnome-like figures of deformed and starving children, even the bloodied face of that man on the road.

There were so many of them! He never knew there could be so many of them! They were people that had nothing to do with him, or so he thought, and they all stood there behind him, waiting! What issue did they have with him? What issue *could* they have with him? Surely he was not answereable to all of these people?

The answers were still in front of him—up there, out of sight, and yet in that instant he knew that he could not take another step. They would all begin to move again, advancing on him until all his questions were answered in one blinding, burning influx of inspiration. He wanted to call out to Someone up there, but he could not, for the power behind him was not one of vindictiveness but of righteous judgment!

He detected a movement at the corner of his eye and turned to see another traveler striding up the steps a hundred or so meters away. The man looked toward him and Evan signaled desperately for him to come. The other, misreading the gesture, simply acknowledged the greeting with a short wave and continued on his way. Within a few moments he reached the next landing and moved out of sight, leaving Evan feeling more alone than he had ever before felt, worse even than during that lonely half-orbit behind the moon. He had a timeless sense of being lost beyond recall.

He fell forward onto his hands and then to his knees. His circumstance was becoming clearer with every passing second. He had miscalculated—badly, in fact! Throughout his journey to the center place he had been almost unconsciously steeling himself for the confrontation, he had thought, with his God! Now the bitter irony of it all swept over him like a flood. The confrontation was not with God but with himself!

His eyes stung suddenly with tears, not of sorrow, for his perception precluded that, but with rage—rage at his own failure, at his wasted effort, at his oversight, even rage at David Cohen, for surely he must have known all this. But no, it was not David's fault. David was his custodian and his guide. Evan needed him now more than ever before; David was the sole bridge between this state and whatever lay somewhere above him.

He crawled carefully forward one more step and felt the threat loom even larger behind him. Then he sank slowly back; it was no good—he could neither go forward nor retreat. He closed his eyes and called out weakly, "David, please help me!"

There was no reply, and he called again. "David, help me!"

There was a soft movement behind him, and he felt a firm hand descend comfortingly upon his shoulder. Then it all went away, and he felt himself being lifted to his feet. He experienced again the childlike humiliation he had felt when David first lifted him into the boat.

They stood for some minutes without speaking, the immortal supporting the mortal, and as they did so, Evan could feel a great load slipping slowly from his shoulders. His rage and frustration gradually gave way to a sensation of peace and assurance, as if the Presence up there ahead of him had touched him momentarily but lovingly before it departed. He had

271

failed in his quest, but somehow he had been forgiven for that. Now he was free to go his way!

"Are you ready to come now?" Evan nodded, and allowed himself to be assisted down the stairs. Not till they reached the bottom did he look behind him again.

"Why didn't you tell me, David?"

David shrugged and smiled. "Would you have accepted my word?"

"No," Evan said simply, "I guess I wouldn't have. Does that mean that you came all this way with me knowing full well that I would chicken out at the end?"

"Yes, but try not to think of it as a failure. It was something which had to be done sooner or later. There are reasons quite beyond your control which had a hand in your not being able to receive the gift fully. You will understand later on."

Evan was content to wait. His senses had been battered by more data than he wished to absorb right now, and he did not plan to expose himself to too much more!

They soon rejoined the crowds in the concourse, and he actually began to enjoy himself. The failure was not as disastrous as he had first thought, because he could now at least take comfort in the knowledge that he had attempted everything which was in his power to do. As they traveled farther down the concourse and the temple was at a more comfortable distance from them, he even felt free to ask more questions of his guide.

"You mentioned something about the second

resurrection back there—about some people not having a choice."

"Yes. You experienced but a small taste of the calamity which faces those of the second resurrection—their judgment."

Evan rubbed his chin thoughtfully. "I had already considered myself to be a 'Christian,' but I'm certainly not going back and face the walk up that stair again."

"Don't be so sure about that; you will not always have the opportunity to refuse, you know."

"Oh, I realize that; but I don't think that any amount of preparation would really equip me to face it again. I'm not going to be looking forward to my next opportunity!"

David placed a hand on his shoulder as they walked. "That's because you don't yet realize the efficacy of mercy, my boy. God isn't out to crush you with your own burdens. He asks only that you acknowledge them in honesty. Beyond that they are forgotten."

"I suppose you're right," Evan conceded rather ruefully, "but please don't ask me to go back there again soon." He turned to the other man awkwardly. "Look, David...thanks for what you did...I mean, for going to all that trouble...."

David patted his shoulder. "There is no need for thanks, my boy. It is my job...and I enjoy every instant of it!"

They remained in the city for another two days in order to allow David to show his protégé briefly around. They visited various administrative and cultural centers and took time to participate, to some extent, in the social life of the city. They ate in magnificent restaurants, took in a ball game, and attended a symphony concert at which, astoundingly, no one coughed!

In spite of the many things that drew his interest in the city, Evan began to feel impatient again, for there was other business to which he yet needed to direct his attention. He confided these promptings to David as they sat on the grass, feeding the swans in one of the gardens.

"It's not that I don't want to stay here, because I do! But I've just got to go out and tell people what I now know. I mean, even if I didn't make it back there, I know at least that the gift was truly there for the taking. I *am* different; I know that for certain now, but there are others who need still to be told about it, and I'm not going to be content until I've done just that. Do you see what I mean?"

David sat at the water's edge, idly throwing pieces of bread. He waited for several seconds before replying.

"You have someone in mind?"

Evan grinned. There was not much point in trying to lie to David. "Yes, I'm thinking of Paul Bernard. Perhaps it's not the best thing to admit to, but for the first time I feel as if I might have the jump on him. I asked him a question once about the gift, back when I first met him. He tramped me before I hardly got my mouth open. He said, in effect, that until I knew what was actually involved in the gift I should keep my trap shut."

"So now you're going to rub it in?"

"Of course not," Evan retorted. "I just want to go back and talk to him on equal ground, that's all. I would consider it much to his advantage to know what I now know."

David sat looking across the water for a long time, and Evan was finding it quite impossible to discern his attitude to the idea. He was not pleased, of that much he was fairly certain, but then, he was not necessarily opposed to it either. Finally he spoke. "So you want to go home, do you?"

"Yes—as soon as possible...if you don't mind, that is." He added the last words cautiously.

David spread his hands. "I am here on your behalf; my time is yours. If you wish to return, we shall."

"Can you arrange for us to travel more quickly?"

"You will be traveling alone, for you no longer require my assistance. I can grant you a little extra speed, but we are not permitted too much impatience in the Kingdom. I can arrange a horse for you if you like."

"It sounds as if that will have to do, but will I be able to find my way and keep out of trouble without you? I don't at all relish the idea of going back across Project Delta."

David responded sharply. "You will not go anywhere near Project Delta." It sounded more like a command than an item of information. "The horse we give you will show you the way, the way you should have come before." He relaxed slightly before continuing. "There is another Nile crossing above Aswan; it cuts a fair slice off the trip and avoids the areas which could be a problem to you."

Evan felt relieved. "That's great. May I leave in the morning?"

"Yes, whenever you like."

"When will you be coming back?"

David's eyes sparkled with wry humor. "I'm an immortal you know. I don't *have* to walk!"

Chapter Eleven

The horse stumbled slightly as it mounted the crest, causing its rider a moment of unconcealed alarm. Evan's prowess as controller of his mount left much to be desired, and he was not improving with distance. He reigned to a halt and turned to look back across the vast expanse of the Nile. Far below him the little ferry still nestled against the bank, the amiable ferryman's arm raised in a parting salute. Evan replied with a similar gesture.

He raised his eyes to look back even farther across the distant expanse of the Promised Land, savoring its beauty for the last time. The precipitous country ahead of him would soon mask the view, so it demanded a long departing look. He had enjoyed the ride on his own immensely up to this point, if only because of the sense of a crisis that had passed. The horse seemed to have chosen an interesting route too, completely shunning the pathways and weaving an intrepid course through a beautiful wilderness.

He had become suspicious, on occasions, that the horse was wandering aimlessly and in the wrong direction, but it reacted with extreme stubbornness whenever Evan attempted to interfere with its course. It was not until they had arrived precisely at the ferry that he realized the horse was to be entirely trusted.

The route had taken him farther south than before, skirting around the tip of the Gulf of Suez (the canal was no longer in evidence) and traveling southwesterly so as to reach the Nile at a point some distance south of the spot where Jason had first picked him up. This course took him well clear of the forbidden Project Delta.

He would have liked going farther north, because at one point he had had an elevated view in that direction and had seen an incredible sight in the distance. It was on the horizon, or perhaps even a little beyond—that was difficult to tell without knowing how big it was—a huge, seemingly transparent bubble, shining golden in the reflected light of the sun. It was immense—of that much he was quite sure. It appeared to be forty kilometers across the base.

The strangest thing about this sight was that at the time of seeing it, he would have been only around seventy kilometers from Project Delta, yet he had not seen it on the first part of his journey with David, in spite of the fact that it must surely have been close by. He had thought to detour and inspect it more closely, but in the resulting battle of wills between him and his mount he had come off the loser, and he was forced to abandon the attempt.

Later, when he stopped at a small farm dwelling for food, he asked about it, and was told that he had seen the space center. Evan was enthralled. So his profession *had* continued! The implications of this discovery beggared his imagination, and he was inclined even to attempt to visit it on foot. On more serious reflection he realized that this would be most unwise—and certainly against David's wishes. It was just another of those things that would have to wait!

Now he was outside the borders of the Holy Land, and the longest part of his journey was over. He waved again to the ferryman and wheeled his horse around, giving it free reign. Beyond this it remained only for him to hold on for dear life, for the horse was quite its own master. It needed no further bidding, setting off at a surprisingly brisk pace which carried him very soon into familiar-looking territory. They passed swiftly through the green valleys and broad, overshadowed glades which had required some few days of Evan's time to traverse previously. Evening had begun to descend by the time they approached the biological studies building area, and when they arrived at David Cohen's home it was quite dark.

He dismounted some two hundred meters from the house and looked at it for a long time. There were lights burning within, and it looked homey and inviting. He had not fully realized before this just how much he had come to consider it as his home. Yet it was much more than a home, for in spite of its size it possessed a kind of communal warmth, the like of which he had never really encountered before.

There was the sound of voices too. David was there, and he caught faint ripples of Lyddia's laughter, drifting to him on the still night air. He found himself wishing that she would come outside, for she was really the only one he felt he could talk to comfortably right now. He had not seen Miriam since his ill-conceived departure, and he still suspected that

David was not fully in agreement with what he planned to do. He was disinclined to meet Matthew, and felt even a little peeved at the thought that David had probably returned almost instantly, leaving him to make his own way back. Only Lyddia would understand, or at least would listen to his explanations without subjecting him to the burning spotlight of the gift.

David probably knew he was there, but if he did, he took no action. Evan was tired after his journey, but he decided, rather than face the family right now, to delay the event by visiting Paul first. It wasn't all that late yet anyway, and he could always return as he had left—with everyone else asleep!

He remounted and turned his steed back into the forest in the direction of the grains project. He allowed it to amble slowly; for some reason even the prospect of meeting Paul seemed less important, if not less desirable than before. The progress up the side of the valley was even slower, but the complex drew inexorably closer and eventually the horse drew resolutely to a halt several meters from the entrance.

There were lights burning here also, except that the place breathed an entirely different spirit than David's house; the darkness tended to make it seem somewhat colder rather than enhancing it. The gate yielded gently to his touch, closing again quietly behind him as he entered. There were people in the dimly lit walkway, although he had not noticed them on his approach. Some lounged in the doorways of their home units, while others stood in small groups, talking softly. He nodded to them cordially as he passed, and they responded in kind, exhibiting a restraint that left him feeling faintly uneasy.

As he approached Paul's unit his discomfort became more intense, and he recognized again the promptings of the gift. He ignored it now, because to a degree he was now accustomed to it. He had endured much, and he was confident now that he could recognize the point at which he should call a halt. That point was not yet!

The door to the unit was open, giving Evan the odd impression that he was expected. As he hesitated his suspicion was abruptly confirmed.

"Come in, spaceman."

Evan walked through the entrance hall and into the sitting room, feeling somehow as if he were re-enacting their first meeting. Paul even sat in the same chair, except that it was swiveled away from him. He stopped just inside the doorway.

"How did you know I was there?"

Very slowly Paul turned around. In the subdued light, his face looked unnatural. "I was just sitting here thinking to myself, 'Now what is the worst thing that can happen to me?'. . .and here you are!"

There was something alarming about Paul's voice and demeanor—and a strange smell too! Evan walked across the room and peered incredulously into his face. "Are you. . .are you drunk?"

Paul grinned stupidly. "Yes."

"But how could you be? I mean, you wouldn't be allowed. . .would you?"

Paul shook his head clumsily and waved a finger in

front of Evan's face. "Wine isn't forbidden, space-man."

"But you're drunk! That doesn't fit your 'responsi-ble' image particularly well, does it?"

Paul's expression darkened perceptibly. "You have all the answers, spaceman. Why don't you tell me? That's what you came here for, isn't it...to straighten me out?"

Evan became suspicious. "Has David been talking to you?"

"No, he hasn't. I don't need him to talk to me, because I *know* you, you see?"

It occurred to Evan that this was probably true; Paul did have some measure of the gift.

Paul pushed his chin forward defiantly. "Well, spaceman, what words of wisdom has the conquering hero brought back for me?"

Evan was dismayed. He had expected Paul to be somewhat difficult, but this situation took him completely off guard. He had known what he wished to say, but suddenly his train of thought was derailed. He felt his face flush with anger. "If you think you're going to get a rise out of me, Paul, you can forget it. Whatever you may care to make of it, I didn't come here for my own sake. I came to help you."

"Who said I needed any help, spaceman?"

"I don't need to be told that. I know that you try to paint yourself as the all-sufficient pillar of inde-pendence, but it doesn't work on me. It never did!"

Paul seemed to sober abruptly. He motioned to the chair opposite him. "Be seated, O fount of all knowledge, and let me drink of your wisdom."

Evan sat. He found Paul looking at him with a pious attentiveness which needled him almost beyond endurance.

"Well, speak!"

"I only came to tell you that I know what it is you should do."

"And what's that?"

You should go to the center place and request the gift...as I did." He saw Paul about to react incredulously and hastened to continue. "I know, I know. I chickened out; but I didn't really understand until I actually stood on the steps to the temple just how much of the system I had bypassed. I mean here I was in the center place, without either being resurrected or living through the indignation. I was different than any other person, and I just had to go away again."

Paul fumbled at his beard. "So you are telling me I should just go along there and walk in!"

"Yes. Look, I know I didn't go all the way, but that doesn't mean that nothing came to my mind. On the contrary, I learned many things. I know, for instance, that the gift *was* there for the taking. I know that the answers were up there...and justification...and forgiveness and grace. I wasn't chastened and sent away; I was only shown the reasons why I should not have been there."

Evan arose and began to pace the room. "But you...you have lived your prescribed time. You have obviously worked your way up through the new administration. You admit yourself to occupying a favored station, and you possess a large degree of the gift already—even if you try to deny it. You have as your counsel and advocate a man like David Cohen, who would happily guide you into any good thing you could wish for."

"I thought I explained to you before, that I don't yet *choose* to possess the gift. Did you think I was lying to you?"

"No!" Evan shot back irritably, "I think you say that just to extract the maximum satisfaction from your misery. You like to see yourself as the eternal angry young man, and you are prepared to keep acting out that role even if it means never growing up. Look, as I see it, you have absolutely everything going for you, much more so than I have, yet you fritter away your time here carrying on like some kind of martyr." He did not look at Paul as he spoke; he had gathered up the lines of his speech and he was determined to make sure that it was all said. "You carry a millstone around your neck in keeping with your self-imposed image of the persecuted intellectual. It makes you look like a tower of strength, while the truth is that you just don't have the guts to take the only obvious course. You have chickened out on your only opportunity to really live!"

He suddenly ran out of anything more to say. He looked at Paul, but the chair was turned away from him. There was no response—only an icy silence that warned him belatedly that he had again said too much. He shook his head suddenly and savagely. "I'm sorry, Paul; I must seem to be pretty hard on you."

The chair turned slowly. Paul's face had turned the color of gray paper. Evan was taken aback, thinking but for a moment that he must be ill, but it was silent rage which so transformed his appearance. Evan detected this, but it was already too late!

Paul sat silently for a long time, and Evan found himself rooted apprehensively to the spot, unsure now of the consequences of his words. When Paul finally spoke, his voice was surprisingly well controlled.

"Sit down, spaceman, and shut up!"

Evan sat obediently. "I'm sorry, Paul, I hadn't meant to hurt you. I got carried away."

Paul rose and left the room, returning a few moments later with his glass refilled. The color of his face was unchanged. He stood directly in front of Evan, regarding him with an expression of icy distaste. "Westering, you are a fool. You scamper off on a stupid little escapade, the result of which is a big, fat nothing; and then you come here and talk to me as if it has somehow furnished you with all of the wisdom of the ages."

Evan tried to speak but Paul quickly overruled. "Well, let me just show you how much you actually know. I will tell you how I came to be here, and perhaps if you can hear me out without offering any more 'advice' you might understand just how much of a fool you actually are."

Paul began slowly to pace the room before continuing. Evan dared not interject. "I am a Frenchman. I didn't come here because I wanted to. I came to the Middle East as a marine—part of a Eurasian force that arrived during the tribulation. I arrived during the assault on Israel. We were supposed to be an occupational force—you know, to keep the natives herded after the victory."

285

He laughed thinly. "Victory? Oh, yes, it was a victory!" He stood still, gazing silently into space for a few moments before continuing. "I arrived at Haifa—or at least what was left of it. Of course, you wouldn't know what it was like to enter a city after a 'clean' nuclear attack—to really be there I mean." He looked at Evan with a kind of stupid wonder. "There was nothing there—nothing to occupy! We had the job of what could be euphemistically called 'mopping up'!"

He laughed again and then continued, speaking as much to himself as to Evan. "I think it happened almost immediately, the breakdown in discipline I mean. We had nothing more to do than to stand and gaze at a silent horror! We were there for a month in what you might call a backwater of the war; the main assault had already passed. It still continued elsewhere, of course. The pall of smoke was so heavy as to create a continual twilight, with the sun showing itself only occasionally as a blood-red ball in the sky. It was so unreal we all just went slowly and quietly mad!"

He pulled himself up stiffly and continued to speak as if to the ceiling. His eyes seemed to have receded into the gaunt shadows of his face. They may have been closed...but Evan could not tell.

"Then we got orders, orders from another world, I think. There was to be a massive regrouping in Jezreel—something to do with the assault on Jerusalem. Jerusalem! Can you imagine that such a pint-sized city could even be capable of arousing the enmity of every nation on earth? Well, it did! We set off on foot toward the south, ostensibly obeying that order." He laughed coldly. "Of course, we were already defecting—right then. We didn't say it to each other in so many words, but we had no intention of catching up with the main force. We didn't need to speak, you see. We all looked on the ashes, and we felt them in our mouths. It's funny, you know, because that was about the smartest thing we did—defecting—all those people subsequently died in Kidron, and we weren't there!"

He continued to stand motionless, for the moment no longer aware of his audience, lost in a nightmarish reverie. Then he recovered with a mild start and continued his pacing again. Evan detected now that he was shaking. "It was a limited yield attack on Haifa, and it wasn't long before we began meeting up with survivors— mostly people who had been living on farms, or had been out of the city at the time. They were not of any consequence to us, being civilians, but we continued our 'mopping up.' It was a sort of diversion that allowed us to stall off that regrouping order."

"You killed them?" Evan found his voice.

Paul shot him a glance of fawn-like surprise. "What else?" Evan shrugged and sagged back into his chair. Paul waited for a long while before continuing. "We spent a lot of time routing them out and we did a bit of looting—not that we took anything we could ever hope to use. Mostly we were looking for women...."

He turned to look suddenly at Evan, as if defying him to ask for a further explanation, but Evan adroitly avoided his gaze and looked at the floor.

"That was something of a pastime in Israel during those days," Paul mused. "It became a sort of end in itself."

"What are you trying to prove, Paul?" Evan asked abruptly. "Are you trying to shock me with the picture of the kind of bad man you were?"

Paul looked at him with an expression that bordered on amusement, as if he enjoyed the fact that Evan was losing his cool. "Shut up, spaceman; I haven't anywhere near finished yet. The plot thickens even more if you'll just listen."

Evan rested his forehead on his hand and continued to gaze at the floor. Paul continued. "We did actually reach Jezreel, but there was no one there, of course. We were too late. We could both see and hear somewhat of what was going on farther to the south, but we just ignored it. You see, it wasn't real to us anymore. We lived like animals, enclosed in a tight little world where nothing but our immediate satisfactions existed."

He stopped pacing the floor and stood in the same place in front of Evan. As he began speaking again his voice wavered as if from some great inner turmoil. "Then there was this farm . . ." He stopped and drew a deep, shaking breath, consciously collecting himself.

"There was this farm—like a lot of others in Jezreel. Mostly they were deserted—looted; the occupants had either been driven out or killed by the forces that had passed through ahead of us. This one, for some reason, had escaped—although not from us! It was just a small house, a few empty animal pens, and a barn of sorts.

288

We didn't expect to find anything, but four of us went to investigate anyway."

He wiped the corner of his mouth with a shaking hand. "There were three people in there—a woman and two kids, a boy of about eight, I guess, and a girl of about three or four. The woman threw the little girl through a window just as we came in. We had surprised her, otherwise she would probably have got the other kid out too. He would have been a bit of an inconvenience to us, so we shot him."

Evan felt Paul look at him suddenly again, but he did not stir, frozen now by the horror which was being so carefully detailed. "You ever see someone get hit with a high powered automatic weapon, Evan? They don't just drop down dead like in the movies—especially a kid. It spread him all around the room!"

He waited for another space of time, as if to give Evan every opportunity to visualize the scene clearly. "Then when we had finished with the woman we killed her too."

Evan began to rise, but before he could gain his feet an outspread hand pushed roughly into his face, forcing him again into the chair. "Stay there, spaceman. I haven't finished yet!"

"No, Paul, I've heard as much as I want to hear."

Paul withdrew the hand slowly. "I told you to stay there. Now, you can either do as I say, or you can have me persuade you...."

The threat was obviously genuine, so Evan stayed.

"Then we went looking for the other kid—all four of us, would you believe? She was out of sight, but we figured that she was in the barn, about a hundred meters away. We never did catch up with her, because just as we got to the barn, we saw this battered old truck drive up to the house and went back to investigate. We were pretty cautious, and it was some little time before we broke back in."

He wiped his mouth again. "Well, there was this little Jewish guy, the woman's husband. Do you know what he had done? He'd gathered up what was left of his wife and son into a sort of heap in the middle of the floor, and he just sat there nursing them, rocking back and forth and crying. I knew all along that the things we were doing were indescribably horrible, but at that moment, for some reason, it sort of all caught up with me. We shot him, too, of course."

Evan screwed up his face incredulously. "He just let you do all this—without retaliating?"

"That's right. In fact he didn't even seem to be particularly aware of us. . .not that he would have been capable of doing anything anyhow."

"Why was that?"

Paul's eyes gazed at him from a face which seemed suddenly to have aged far beyond his years. "Because, you see, he was a hunchback!"

At first the reply fell without meaning on Evan's ears, but only for a moment—the time it took for the significance of it to reach home. He felt his own face drain of color now. Added to the horrors he had already heard, it shocked him beyond belief! He spoke with great difficulty, for his top lip seemed to have turned to leather.

"Then the little girl. . ."

Paul's face broke into an almost maniacal smile.

290

"Yes, spaceman, for the first time you know me—Lyddia's original man with the long hair. She came back and found them all later, and she remembers it surprisingly well."

Evan was stunned beyond feeling. He could think of nothing more to say!

Paul suddenly threw down his glass and leapt forward, grabbing a handful of clothing at Evan's collar and lifting him with almost superhuman force into a standing position. "Now do you understand, spaceman? Are you a fool, or are you not?"

Evan was powerless to reply. He was close to being strangled by the tightly knotted fists at his throat. He could feel the buttons on his tunic giving way.

"Do you know what, spaceman? I've got a wife out there someplace, on one of the projects. I haven't yet had the courage to go and face her, yet you come here to me, all awash with cheap wisdom, and tell me to go confront my God! You have the pompous effrontery to tell me that *you* consider me to have chickened out on life?"

He threw Evan back savagely into the chair and his voice became shrill. "Do you realize, Mister Know-it-all Westering, that I'm not *allowed* to die?"

Evan opened his mouth weakly, but no sound came. Paul clutched his hands to his face and stumbled backward, away from him. Then he screamed—a sound so ghastly that Evan felt his blood turn to ice.

"Paul, I'm sorry. . . ." His voice trailed off, for the words sounded futile and ridiculous.

Paul kept his face covered. "Get out!"

"Believe me, please, I *am* sorry. . . ."

"Get out!" Paul's voice had risen even higher.

Evan rose numbly and stumbled toward the door. Then he turned and tried again, but Paul had slumped into the chair, breaking into uncontrollable grief. "I'm sorry!" Evan called again across the room, but Paul seemed to be no longer aware of him. Instead, he gazed now with open-mouthed horror at some point above Evan's head as if he could see something there. Evan felt a cold chill grip his face, and he instinctively looked up. He could see nothing; whatever it was, it was for Paul's eyes alone, and he cried as he looked upon it—his attention now completely diverted by some grim specter of the past. Evan started back toward him, but Paul seemed suddenly to see him again. "Get out!" he screamed for the third time.

Evan stood limply for a few moments, rocking back and forth in indecision. Paul's grief was hurting him beyond bearing, but there was nothing left for him to do; he had nothing to give.

He spun on his heel and ran from the room through the darkened entrance hall and back into the walkway. It seemed cold and dank and somehow washed of color—a strange and terrifying place. He ran blindly along it, still pursued by the dreadful sounds which he tried vainly to block out. It wasn't just Paul's voice now but the sound of a thousand voices; they were all around him, emanating as if from within his own head.

The walkway appeared to have become unaccountably longer, holding him back and denying him escape, even though he was driving himself to a degree of physical panic which hurt his lungs as he ran. There were faces too...faces in every annex and door-way...gray, impassive faces unaware of the terrible sounds, unfeeling and devoid of warmth, watching him as he ran.

The gates loomed before him just as the cacophony became beyond endurance. He flung himself against them and, mercifully, they swung outwards, allowing him to stumble blindly into the night. In his headlong plunge, he lost his footing and fell forward onto the cool, dew-covered grass, sliding for a moment upon his hands and knees before plunging full-length onto his face.

The sounds stopped abruptly and were replaced by a silence so profound that he could plainly hear the rush of blood in his own ears. He lay still, hardly daring to move, flooded with feelings of intense relief at being out of the complex. He lay thus for several minutes, as one dead, recovering from this unexpected and traumatic experience.

When finally he raised his head he was immediately struck by the impression that it was unaccountably dark. He looked quickly over his shoulder, and with a strange pang of fear realized that the complex was entirely blacked out! It was silent, too, as if it had become inexplicably deserted.

He raised himself to his knees on the wet grass and flung his hands forward toward the open gateway in a futile gesture of remorse.

"I'm sorry!" he cried despairingly, and he heard his words echo down the hollow, darkened walkway, returning to him again in bleak, mocking echoes which decayed into a vibrating silence.

The sky was darker than he could remember it ever being before, and he could feel the enveloping mist around him, enclosing him in an oppressive, clinging blanket. His hair began to prickle at the back of his neck. He was suddenly and terrifyingly alone!

He climbed quickly to his feet. He could not see his horse, and he called to it softly, as if fearful of waking some sleeping horror within the complex. It neighed a soft reply, so close to his elbow as to startle him, and he felt his way toward it, grateful for its company.

Once Evan had mounted, the horse set off quite unbidden, as if itself appreciative of the opportunity to leave this place. He glanced quickly behind him on several occasions as they made their way across the fields, but there was still no sign of life.

He became aware of the tattered condition of his tunic, and he shivered slightly as he sought to draw it more tightly around him. Funny—it was the first time he could remember feeling cold since he had been propelled into the millennium. It must have been cold, though, because the horse shivered a little also. Even so, it was a strange chill, and he had the odd suspicion that it was not due to the climate.

As they progressed lower into the valley, the moon reappeared, reminding him again of the tranquil beauty of his surroundings. It was bright enough to penetrate through the trees to the valley floor, causing the mist to take on an ethereal, otherworldly light. This was quite wasted on him, for he noted it only in passing. The trauma of this latest experience was fading, but there was no peace to take its place. Why had David not stopped him? Could he not have forewarned him a little—given some small clue that would have deterred him from riding roughshod over a friend?

But then it could well have been another of those things which just had to happen—like the trip to the center place. He had a distinct impression somehow that the events of the past few months were anything but random—as if they were all intended to teach him something. But what? Where did he go from here? Were there yet questions that he could dare to ask?

He shivered again involuntarily, haunted anew by the specter of Paul's agony. He was not ready for this place, and yet he was here—not of his own choosing but through an odd quirk of circumstance and time. Was he really obliged to be here? He would have to think a bit more about that.

There were no lights visible when he arrived back at the house, and for this he was more than a little thankful. The horse stopped at the entrance to the courtyard, demonstrating remarkable intuition inasmuch as the animal had no way of knowing that he lived there.

After dismounting, he obeyed the instructions given him back at the center place, removing the bridle and stowing it in one of the saddlebags. He stroked his companion's soft nose for a few moments, then stood and watched it disappear into the mist, presumably returning to the Promised Land.

He felt his way cautiously through the house in the

darkness and emerged onto the balcony. A faint light came through the open doorway of his own room—the only light he had seen anywhere. There was no one inside, but the bedcovers had been turned back and his nightclothes laid out for him. The light came from a single, scented ornamental candle at the head of the bed, and he knew instinctively that this was Lyddia's work.

He pushed the door shut behind him, although not engaging the catch, and stood looking at the room. It seemed a warm and inviting oasis after the experiences which had so buffeted him since his departure, and he was beginning to realize that he was desperately tired.

He sat wearily on the edge of the bed and debated with himself as to whether he should change into the nightclothes or just simply lie on the bed as he was. He chose the latter, flopping limply onto his back, and lay watching the light from the candle play gently on the ceiling.

A cool breeze passed over him, fluttering the candlelight and causing the door to swing slowly and silently open. He raised himself to his elbows, assailed suddenly by the feeling that he was not alone. In spite of his tiredness, curiosity prevailed, and he arose from the bed to investigate. The balcony was awash with moonlight again, and he could see without difficulty.

At first he thought that he must have been mistaken, for the balcony appeared quite empty, but then a small movement caught his eye, farther along, at the sun deck. There was a figure standing in the darkness, light-colored clothing merging deceptively with one of the columns and the white balustrade.

He walked toward the figure cautiously, although the size left no doubt as to who it was.

"David, is that you?"

The figure turned toward him, and he felt the warm smile penetrate the darkness. "Yes, Evan."

"I thought you would be asleep!"

"No, I was planning to wait until you slept before I retired. Are you all right?"

Evan did not answer but took up a position on the balustrade alongside the other man and contemplated the garden below. There seemed no point in reply, for he knew now that his answer was already known... and yet there was a genuine and gentle concern evident in the question.

"David...there is something I would very much like to ask you."

"Yes?"

"I've been thinking about the accident, about what happened after it, I mean. It wasn't altogether miraculous, was it? I mean, we already knew back in my time about the theories of relativity—about the compression of time under sustained acceleration. What happened to me could be considered a quite normal, technical feasibility, could it not?"

David grinned. "I'm not sure about your distinctions between the miraculous and the technically feasible, but inasmuch as I understand your question, yes, it was a normal, physical event."

Evan took a deep breath. "Well, I realize of course, that my eventual controlled return to earth could never be attributed to chance, but assuming that all of the technicalities involved made use of ordinary physics..."

David raised a hand to bid him silence. "What you are trying to ask, Evan, in painfully abstruse language, is whether the process is reversible?"

"Well...yes!"

"And you wish to know whether or not you could return to your own time?"

"It's not as if I'm unappreciative of what I have found here...it's just that I feel somehow as if I have come in without a ticket, and it's important to me that I discharge that feeling. I would just like to go round again—that's all."

David turned to look at him, the moonlight catching the coppery smoothness of his skin and even the clear glint of his eyes. "You have every reason for feeling as you do, my friend, because the thing that you so strongly suspect is quite true."

"You mean, I could return?"

"More than that, you must! That has been intended and planned for since the very beginning."

Evan was engulfed in a curious mixture of feelings. On the one hand, he was disturbed by David's unexpectedly forthright reply, but on the other he was suddenly released from an inexplicable burden.

"You mean...I never really belonged here?"

"I'm afraid that is something you have in common with most of your generation, but it's true!"

Evan walked slowly across the sun deck and fell heavily onto the seat. Then he turned sideways and drew his knees up under his chin.

"You'll have to explain this to me. I'm not sure that I

understand. Do you mean that I have only been permitted here on the condition that I eventually return?"

"Yes. It was planned for me to tell you about it tomorrow, but you asked first."

Evan thought for a few moments, picturing the possibility of returning to his own time and knowing the things that he knew now. He felt a curious rush of excitement. "But how could I tell anyone? I mean, who would believe my story? I will be going back bearing possibly the best tidings the world has ever heard, but how would I get the message across?"

David sat beside him and sighed heavily before answering. "For one thing, Evan, it would not be new tidings. People have known about this time from the beginning. They haven't believed others, and they won't believe you either. Of course, they will *tell* you that they do, but most of those statements could never be taken seriously." He moved on the seat somewhat uncomfortably. "There is, of course, another factor which really removed all of these things from your concern. You see, you will have no memory of these events after your return."

Evan almost exploded. "What in blazes is the use of that?"

David was unperturbed. "It would be a bit too much for you to understand at this stage, Evan, so I'm not going to try to explain it to you, other than to say simply that it has to do with the integrity of time. I wouldn't want you to think, though, that we intended to send you back empty-handed, for indeed, that would be impossible."

"What do you mean?" Evan was trying to thrust aside his disappointment.

"I mean that while we must confiscate the memory of this place from your mind, we are quite powerless to diminish anything from what you may have become. We can take nothing from your stature as a person, and that must inevitably have been expanded as a consequence of your being here. You will therefore take it with you."

"Even my small measure of the gift?"

"Even that!"

Evan sat thoughtfully rubbing his chin on his knee. "Now that I know that I'm going back, I'm not sure if it's what I really want. . . and yet, I feel a lot happier now—more content even. Are you quite sure that I can't take just some tiny recollection?"

David smiled again. "If you did, you would be unable to distinguish it from the promptings that all men already have in varying degrees. But it is not meet that man should know too much about his future. Indeed, if you were given the opportunity to see your whole future laid before you, would you take it?"

Evan nodded his understanding glumly. "I suppose you're right, but I suspect that it would be easier to face than what I almost took on back there at the temple. I was glad to back out of that!"

"It has to be done eventually, you know."

"Yes, I *do* know." He suddenly sat upright. "That's it! That's what was different about me. I didn't *have* to go at that time! That's why I found myself so out of step with what is going on here. I had to come back and do it all again, and because of that, this period of time didn't really count—a sort of moratorium on my judgment!"

David nodded slowly. "What you say is true, but you're not entirely correct in saying that it doesn't count. I said that you would take with you what you had become, and that is not a thing of little consequence. You will take with you a breath of the Kingdom, and that may well be detected within you by many people. You will carry something of its spirit, and that will assist you in interpreting the expectations of the Kingdom to people in your time. You will spark their imaginations!"

Evan frowned. "That's all very nice, but if I have no memory of this time, I can't see myself contributing anything other than speculation."

"You are being unfair to the notion of speculation, Evan. If you think about it, you must realize that the ability to speculate is an important factor in the nature of man. Surely no great discovery has ever been made without some man first speculating about its existence. The space mission in which you yourself participated would have held no purpose had men not speculated that there would be more to discover than could be seen by other means."

"But surely any old flight of fancy could pass as speculation, couldn't it?"

"I don't think that anyone living in your generation could really deny the existence of *inspired* speculation, Evan. It doesn't have to be entirely correct in every detail. A thousand people might well speculate about the future, and they would all certainly be wrong, but people would *think*, and in thinking they would prepare. Inspired speculation furrows the mind and awaits the seed of truth. Fancy does not."

Evan grinned wryly. "Do *you* speculate?"

"Of course! I may have been resurrected immortal, but I haven't arrived at any point where the future holds no tantalizing mysteries. In your generation, you would have perceived this time only dimly, but there is a period even beyond the millennium which beckons me—and I don't fully understand it yet either."

"And you actually speculate about that?"

David spread his hands questioningly. "Could any intelligent mind dwell within an infinite sea of stars and not ponder its ultimate relationship to them?"

Evan felt a strange thrill, as if, just for an instant, he had again caught a glimpse of light through a tiny chink in his circumscribed, mortal mind—a faint sense of the intellectual fire that burned within the other man. But then it was gone...somewhere just beyond his grasp. An interesting thought occurred to him. "Have others been here too...I mean into the future, as I have?"

"I think you know quite well that they have. There have been inspired people since the earliest history of man who have reached across the years to this time and even beyond. You have ample record of that. The record is not always as clear as you would like it to be, for these people frequently lacked even the language required to communicate the wonders they had seen, but their ultimate testimony is revealed not so much in what they recorded but in what they themselves became as a consequence."

"And I could be like that?"

"You have the potential to be."

Evan rested his chin back on his knees. "It's funny, David, but I remember that Kurt made a rather prophetic sort of comment on the way out. I'm still not sure whether he was being serious or not. We were talking about the reasons for the mission and such, and he said something to the effect that if we should meet some great Power out there, we could find ourselves being advocates for the whole earth. He was right, wasn't he? In a back-to-front kind of way, I mean. When you think about it, you could almost say that I'm going back there now as . . . as an advocate for the future!"

"That could well be so."

Evan frowned again. "You seem to qualify all of your answers, as if you are not certain."

"I can't be certain, Evan. I can only assure you that there will be promptings within you which you may or may not heed. That's all in your hands, not mine."

Evan nodded resignedly and swung his legs down into a more conventional sitting position. "How are you going to do it?" he asked. "Send me back, I mean. Will you have to put me back out there—in space?"

"Yes, your command module has been retrieved from your landing site and is being prepared right now for relaunching back at the space center which you probably saw on your way back."

"Yes, I did, although it was rather a long way off. I had intended to ask you about that. I figured it was only a few kilometers inside the borders of the Holy Land—not all that far from Project Delta—but for some reason, I don't recall seeing it when we went past the first time."

"The protective bubble is erected only during launch preparation. When you saw it, it had been erected on your account, you know."

Evan laughed. "That makes me feel quite important. That's a feeling I haven't had much while I've been here." His brow furrowed again. "But how can you explain it to them? Surely I can't just drop out of the sky without people realizing that there must have been some sort of intervention?"

"We are quite aware of that. Your return will no doubt be called 'miraculous,' but men will have no real difficulty in arriving at a rational explanation for it all, you may be sure of that!"

Evan arose and walked slowly across to the balustrade, still deep in thought. "You say that people have looked into the future, David, even beyond this time. Has that happened to you?"

"To a limited degree it has."

"And you saw an even greater purpose there?"

"Yes."

Evan spun around abruptly. "Show me!"

David shook his head. "There is nothing to be gained. You would be too limited purely by your inability to understand."

"Not even a glimpse?"

David regarded him in silence for several seconds, obviously weighing his thoughts with great care, his head tilted to one side as if he were listening to advice from some unseen source. Then he rose to his feet. "Come with me," he said.

Chapter twelve

They made their way back along the balcony and down the external stairway into the cool, moist fragrance of the garden. David led the way at a brisk pace—so brisk in fact that Evan was obliged to run occasionally just to keep up. They left the garden and walked for several minutes up the wooded slope at the back of the house. In spite of the moonlight, Evan stumbled frequently.

When they reached the top of the hill, David turned and looked back, inviting Evan to do so too. The extra height afforded by the hill considerably enhanced their view back down the valley, and the moonlight reflected clearly from the distant expanse of water. David's house was immediately below them, in darkness, save the single light still shining from Evan's open door. There were other lights visible along the valley walls, however, and the biological studies building was also in view. Evan looked, but nothing of any particular significance caught his eye.

"Well," said David, "what do you feel?"

Evan shrugged. "It's very beautiful. . . ."

"I didn't ask you what you can see. I asked you what you could feel."

Evan looked again, not sure that he had caught

David's meaning. "Well, I feel rather small and insignificant. I mean, when I picture myself here against the great expanse of the sky and the sea. I just feel small!"

"But you have a part in all of this, Evan, and a more blessed part than anything else you now see, because unlike the natural creation you have access to the mind and will and love of your Creator. Does that affect the way you feel about it now?"

Evan looked again. "I feel differently, I guess, but I can't quite understand how. I feel kind of small . . . and then great. It's a bit of an enigma."

"And that is the problem. You see, man just cannot stand alongside something of immensity and fully comprehend it. By the time he retreats far enough so that he can encompass it fully, he is too far away! It's a problem of spiritual focal angle. We are unable to see God in his immensity on one hand and as a loving and personal entity on the other. He is both of these things, of course, but it will be a long, long time before you have sufficient of the gift to be able to fully perceive it."

"But how far can I go now?"

David touched his arm softly. "Look again."

Evan felt an odd sensation. The scene remained precisely unchanged, but he had the impression that the horizon was somehow rushing away, so as to continually expand his field of view. It was not altogether unlike the feelings he had experienced on the steps of the temple. It made him distinctly aware of much more than could be seen from this vantage point.

He was aware of the people also—almost as if he could see them all in front of him—millions of them—coexisting with him in this one instant of time. Something within him had enlarged sufficiently for him to accommodate a concern for every one of them, as if he could even name each by name.

David spoke again. "What do you feel?"

Evan understood the question this time. "I feel that what you said is indeed true—that I'm not a mere observer here; I am a great part of it all." He looked at David. "How am I doing?"

David smiled, but did not commit himself. He took a firm hold on Evan's arm, above the elbow. "Look again."

Evan was totally unprepared for what happened next. The view before him suddenly disappeared and was replaced by an incredible scene. He was standing out in space with the whole glorious orb of Earth visible before him. He was momentarily disoriented—panic-stricken in fact—until he realized that he could still feel David's hand on his arm, anchoring him to reality. He found that he could breathe comfortably, but except for this, the vision was as clear and as real as it could possibly be, in spite of all his efforts to blink it away. It was even more magnificent than anything in his previous experience, because his view was completely unencumbered by either spacecraft or pressure suit. He estimated the distance away as being around a hundred thousand kilometers, and he also noted quickly that it was Earth very much as he had left it, bearing even the milky-white contrail layer—the legacy of his own generation.

"What do you feel?" The voice at his side startled him.

"Would you believe...scared?"

"You have no cause for fear. What do you feel?"

Evan studied the incredible scene more seriously. There were many things that could be said, but he knew that they would not be the things David was seeking. His feelings were almost too complex to describe.

But he could feel something—it was that lump in his throat again! It was a familiar experience; he had had it before! And yet he understood it a little differently now. There was a sadness that seemed to have its origin somewhere outside himself, as if perhaps he were sensing Earth's own sorrow.

That was it! He was looking on the earth as a living thing which suffered and yearned, and he could surely feel its mourning!

"What do you feel?" The question came again.

Evan's eyes stung with tears. "I feel a great compassion. I feel that the earth weeps, and that I bear much of the blame. I feel that I want another chance—that I want to start all over again with it."

The grip on his arm tightened, and he felt himself being drawn backward. Earth was beginning to move away with such speed that he instinctively threw his free arm out as if to steady himself. The speed became still greater, and the scene began to change so rapidly that he found himself holding his breath in alarm.

The earth shrunk to a tiny speck of light and eventually disappeared. The sun hove into view, and then shrank rapidly also until it became only a relatively insignificant star, indistinguishable from the great white mass of stars that now appeared around it. This was rather a little frightening, for it seemed that all familiar things were suddenly taken away, and he was conscious of the vast, unimaginable void surrounding him.

The mass of stars continued to close down in front of him until they formed a milky blanket in which individual stars were progressively more difficult to single out. He glanced around him and realized that the stars did not fill his entire field of vision, and stark black areas were beginning to appear all around its edges.

Then he knew what was happening! Traveling at what must have been the speed of thought, he had backed away to a point where the whole galaxy could be contained within his view. As it continued to shrink, he found himself hovering over a huge, glowing disk of bluish-white light—stars massed so densely that they appeared to coalesce into one great, swirling, homogeneous mass—a wonder beyond his wildest imagining!

His speed seemed to be reducing gradually, and eventually he was motionless. He was at such a distance from the Milky Way now as to be able to view it against the abysmal backdrop of space. Other specks of light were visible against the blackness too—thousands of them.

"What do you feel?" David asked again, more gently now.

"It's...so beautiful!" said Evan, quite overlooking the fact that he was again not answering the question.

"Look upon it," David said. "It is just one star family among billions of others like it. If you were to count off the stars within it at a rate of about twenty-five every second, you would still be counting them seven hundred years from now. It is rotating about its axis, but if you were to come back here and look at it in a million years, you would be unable to detect any change, for that time would represent the merest blinking of an eye in its history. Light, traveling at one hundred and eighty thousand miles every second, would take more than eighty thousand years to pass from one side to the other. That same light would take somewhere around eight hundred thousand years just to travel to the next closest similar star family. And yet this giant galaxy of stars is but the merest mote when viewed against the infinite space around it."

Evan shivered convulsively and confronted the question again. His only feeling was one of chilling awe, but that was not the answer David sought. Then, as he looked upon the vision before him, something changed—not the actual scene, but something within his own mind. A whole revision of perspective took hold of him almost by surprise. The disk of light suddenly lost its mind-numbing magnitude, adopting the dimensions of only a large dinner plate floating less than a meter away from him, easily within his reach.

"What do I feel?" he said slowly, "I feel. . . I feel as if I should put my arms about it. . . ."

There was no answer. The grip relaxed and was gone. He turned his head abruptly, but there was no one beside him—only the awesome void. The galaxy began to recede once more, growing rapidly fainter and fainter as sheer distance engulfed it. The chilling immensity returned.

He cried for David, but no sound left his lips. It was there within his head, but beyond that it was lost in a terrifying eternity of emptiness. But David was gone, he knew why, in spite of the cold shock of panic that had seized him. This was farther than even David could go. His wish was being granted!

But that was unthinkable now—he had seen enough! He drew a frantic breath and poured all of his remaining strength into a desperate, soundless scream, "No . . . no more!"

The star-field underwent a subtle change and became somehow less distinct, twinkling softly instead of being stony white. It was above him now, and he was looking up at it. The pattern of stars was familiar! Something moved at one side of his view. "Are you all right, my boy?"

He moved his head to look into David's face, and as he did so became aware of the damp grass against the back of his neck. He raised a trembling hand to feel his forehead. "Yes, I think so." Then he grinned. "Wow!"

David put a hand under his shoulders and helped him into a sitting position. He tried to rise, but quickly realized that he was almost totally drained of strength. "I feel as if I must have walked all that way," he said.

"You will be well enough to stand in a few moments; just rest until you feel able."

David was right. He felt a warmth begin gradually to move through his numbed and shaking limbs, and within a few minutes he was able to stand, his tiredness fading rapidly as his mind began to be crowded with new questions. "I've been asking about all of the wrong things, David—things that I didn't really need to know. I can see that now. But now that I know where I stand here, there are still so many things that it seems expedient I should know, though I may not be able to recall the answers later."

David smiled and took his arm again. "I understand how you must feel. There are some things you should know, and others that you should not, at least not at this time."

Evan chuckled nervously. "I am well aware of that fact, now, and I'm certainly not going to subject myself to any more experiences like the last few. I just want to talk for a while, that's all."

They began walking slowly back down the hill. "For one thing," said Evan, "I still find Paul's position very difficult to understand. I mean, knowing what I know now, I can't see why he enjoys such an apparently favored position in the Kingdom. He seems better off than many people who are out there laboring on the reclamation projects."

David nodded. "He is. But you must appreciate that this whole business of judgment is handled from a vantage point well outside your field of view. There is that matter of complicity you see...whether he was fully responsible for all of his actions or not." He laughed softly. "Actually, Paul will be all right, I'm quite sure of that, but there is still the problem of the consequences, and that is his problem alone—as you have no doubt observed."

312

"He still has to face them?"

"Yes, but he has much to learn about grace. That will take a long time, because he has yet to learn to be gracious himself. He sees himself pretty much as he is though, and that is nine-tenths of the problem completed, even if he doesn't realize it."

They arrived back at the garden, but Evan hesitated to go in. "Couldn't we just keep walking a bit farther? Down the valley perhaps? I don't feel much like sleeping now. Would it trouble you?"

"No, of course it would not. Did I not walk to the center place with you?"

They walked and talked, strolling slowly through the beautiful valley, its radiance clearly visible in the gentle glow of the moonlight. They were an unusual pair: one, a young and relatively naïve astronaut—a visitor only from a mortal past; the other, a miraculously resurrected being in possession of greater knowledge, insight, and understanding than any mortal could accommodate, yet a man so endowed with humility and compassionate regard as to consider it a joy to counsel his young protégé.

They walked thus for the remainder of the night, until long after the moon had disappeared and its light had been replaced by the soft gray-and-pink haze of dawn. They paid no heed to the progress of time, for they talked of many things that were now commonly dear to each of them . . . of justice and judgment, of wisdom and knowledge, of joy and pain, and of eternity. Evan heard things which normally would have stretched his mind far past the point where it could discern monumental fact from pure fantasy. Yet all this was tolerable to him, if only because he now knew that he could not be judged at this time according to the things he was being told. They were to be taken from him and given again at a later time.

But it was not without purpose, for Evan knew as they talked that even when his memory was erased there would remain within his expanded soul a cavernous space which would forever remain restless until it was refilled. This would be his only legacy of the Kingdom—a hunger for the spirit of this marvelous place that would surely haunt him until his return!

Their wanderings brought them again to the garden, and as if to delay the inevitable they continued to walk there too. The morning was cold, touched by the lightest carpet of frost, but Evan was entirely unaware of it. His heart beat rapidly, and his body coursed with a warm flush of excitement as he drank in the incredible joys of which they spoke— things far more wonderful than he could have believed...things far beyond even this place! All his doubts, his fears, his misgivings had fled.

It was David who pointed out that he would still need rest, and suggested that he return to his room and sleep. "I don't think I shall ever sleep again," Evan said. "I might wake up and find it all ended!"

David eventually prevailed, and it was not until Evan had slumped back, fully clothed, upon his bed that he realized what a heavy toll the events of the night had exacted of him. "You're right," he mumbled, eyes closed, "I think I just might sleep forever!"

"You may rest for as long as you wish," said David. "There is nothing more required of you."

Evan opened his eyes. "How long do I have? Before I go back, I mean."

"About a week yet; we have a few more preparations to make. You should go on a special diet for a while if you don't mind."

Evan shook his head drowsily. "That's okay." He grinned. "I suppose I should catch up on some of my work at the biological studies center—after going AWOL I mean. . . ."

David laughed. "I think we can afford to overlook that small detail; in fact, your remaining time here is quite your own. You will have to think about any other things you may wish to attend to before you leave."

Evan closed his eyes again and sighed deeply. "I'm probably about as ready to leave at this very instant as I will ever be. . . . There's really nothing left to do that can't wait. After all, I guess I'll have to leave myself *some* things to do during the millennium!" He sighed again; his mind was beginning to cloud comfortably in preparation for sleep.

"Rest well," said David. "We won't disturb you further." He turned to leave and began closing the door behind him.

"David."

"Yes?"

"There is one thing I would like to do before I leave."

"And what is that?"

Evan opened his eyes and grinned sleepily. "Do you think I might have a ride on that train?"

Evan stared with unseeing eyes at the rapidly fleeing landscape. He was not enjoying the trip in the slightest, and neither was Lyddia. He glanced at her, sitting at the window seat ahead of him and looking out with an expression that was probably remarkably like his own.

It was all too fast! The remaining time had fled, and he wished now that it had been much longer. He was not ready to leave, as he had first felt, and now the onrushing time of his departure was upon him, unbidden and unwanted. He and Lyddia had traveled several hundred kilometers to the south just so that they could pick up an embarkation point on the monorail and allow him to ride back to the space center on the train.

The bus ride had been magnificent, but again, too fast! Motorized transport, however sophisticated, was still somehow foreign to the life-style of the Kingdom, and for that reason it was rare and obviously discouraged. Evan would have been happy to walk had the program allowed him the time, but this was not to be.

Now this fleeting, fifteen-minute ride back to the space center only served to magnify his feelings over so rapid a departure. He would be gone in less than an hour!

The acceleration had ceased for only a few minutes

when he found himself being pressed forward firmly into his seat harness as the braking run began. The trip was actually remarkably unexciting, probably because the illusion of great speed was almost totally lost in the extreme comfort and silence of the cabin. The braking force increased rapidly, and Lyddia turned and forced a smile at him over her shoulder.

"We're almost there now."

The car began to bank steeply as it entered a wide, sweeping curve, first one way and then more gradually the other. The sensation was not unlike the landing approach of an aircraft. The final sweep brought the space center suddenly into view, and it was a breathtaking sight! The entire perimeter of the center seemed to be defined by a low, curving wall, from which at intervals there arose delicate-looking pillars some thirty meters or so into the air. They arched over gracefully at the top until they touched lightly on the smooth, golden surface of the enormous bubble. The pillars were somehow involved with supporting the incredible structure, but Evan was quite unable to discern just how it was done.

It occurred to him to ask David about that later, but even as the thought crossed his mind, he knew that he would not. There were yet so many questions. He was completely surfeited with questions now, and after all, there would be another time.

The car slid to a silent stop immediately outside the main entrance. They were down at ground level, and the hostess assisted them out of their seat harness. It took them an embarrassingly long period of time to leave, as each of the passengers insisted on shaking his hand and wishing him well before he could disembark. He acknowledged them numbly, wishing they would just let him go, for he was now feeling uncomfortably close to tears.

Viewed from inside the center, the golden bubble was not visible at all, and they were afforded only a view of the brilliant blue sky. Evan wondered idly whether, when he first looked skyward on his return to his own time, he would not be aware of the difference. Some small things like that must surely be remembered!

They walked together along a broad, white way which he now accepted as a typical Kingdom-type landscape. Scattered around them in the garden setting were several large buildings, apparently housing the offices and support systems required by the center. Evan marveled silently; after the things he had already seen in the biological studies building, what wonders then must surely be within these walls!

In the distance, directly ahead, sharply outlined against the deep blue of the sky, stood a slender white needle, pointing skywards.

Well, they still used rockets! It appeared from this distance as if it was constructed as one integral unit, lacking any evidence of staging. It was rather thin, too—its outline continuing in a smooth, unbroken line until it enlarged suddenly at the nose to a gray bubble which presumably housed his old command vessel.

It took a long while to walk there, but they walked in silence, for this very setting spoke eloquently enough of the things that were already within their minds—the pains, the misgivings, and the finality of his departure. They approached a wide, low blockhouse that he readily recognized as the launch control center. A small group of people were gathered around the entrance, and as they drew closer, Evan could pick out David, Miriam, and Matthew among them. The others, clad in white suits, were technicians.

After a minimum of introductions and greetings, he was whisked away into the building by the technicians and quickly reunited with his old clothing and pressure suit. The men worked silently and efficiently, and he realized with somewhat of a sinking feeling that no smallest detail was being overlooked. He would be returned to his own time in exactly the same state in which he had left. He could feel that technological barrier again, a lonely sense of being ignored. It was beginning to frighten him!

When they re-emerged into the sunlight, an astounding sight met his eyes. Extending from immediately in front of the blockhouse and sweeping majestically up to the very tip of the distant rocket was a smooth white ramp, supported, it appeared, on the most delicate-looking tubular supports and looking incredibly as if it had always been there!

The others waited for him—an uncomfortable group clustered around the bottom of the ramp. It was at this moment that the full strain of the parting began to descend upon him. It was all happening too quickly!

He walked toward them with as matter-of-fact an air as he could manage, feeling a bit ridiculous and cumbersome in this antiquated garb of an astronaut from a vastly inferior technology.

The good-byes were quietly restrained, with few words spoken, for indeed, Evan was almost unable to speak, being too afraid of betraying the childlike insecurity which assailed him. He bent low to kiss Lyddia, an operation made doubly difficult by the ungainly bulk of the suit, and as he did so, he could not help noticing how much paler her small, grown-up looking face had become. David approached him last of all, tousling his hair with an enormous hand in a final, affectionate parting gesture as he began the long walk up the ramp, flanked by the two close-out technicians.

The ramp was unexpectedly firm and solid, giving no hint of the ostensibly flimsy supports, although as it became higher he was increasingly more appreciative of the escorts on each side of him. The gray bubble at the top of the ramp was transparent, and within it he could make out the outline of his old spaceship. He was astounded to see that not only was his command module there but anchored in its correct place behind it was the service module and plasma engine! They must have recovered it separately. That was surprising indeed, for it was in no way equipped for a normal reentry and descent!

They arrived at a small platform at the top, and on closer inspection Evan found that his old craft looked remarkably unsafe. In any event, its design now seemed relatively utilitarian and crude, its coarsely fitted panels and ugly stenciled instruction plates contrasting harshly with the glistening, unbroken lines of the beautiful craft which held it there. It was damaged, also, still bearing scars of the accident.

On the other hand, the descent chute covers looked as if they had never been removed, and he knew instinctively the carefully folded chute inside would bear not the slightest evidence that it had carried out its task once already. Even the heat shields were intact, showing no sign that they had weathered the forces of reentry.

He turned for one last look at the tiny group in the distance. It was too far now to discern features, but he could identify each one with ease. He raised his hand in a silent, sober salute, and as he did so, he caught sight of yet another figure standing beside the blockhouse, well away from the others. The thin, angular build was obvious even at this distance, and he knew who it was. He extended his hand in that direction also, and the figure acknowledged him briefly.

One of the technicians touched his arm gently. "You'll have to keep moving, sir; launch time is very close."

Evan paused deliberately, and scanned the scene around him in a full circle, determined to absorb every detail of this extraordinary place, as if trying to force upon himself some last impression that would not be forgotten. Then he turned abruptly toward his craft.

The technician merely raised his hand, and the protective cover became less distinct and then seemed to simply melt away, leaving his ship looking perilously exposed and most unprepared for its journey.

He should have felt at home, back in his central, contoured couch, amid the familiar sights and odors of the command module, but he did not; it felt strange and otherworldly.

A technician approached with his helmet. "I'm afraid we are going to have to anesthetize you before lift-off, Mr. Westering—if you don't mind. It's not the kind of launch you would be accustomed to." He felt a small, cold touch at the side of his neck, and he realized that something had been administered to him, probably with a tiny air syringe. Then the technician lifted the helmet carefully over his head.

"It will take a few minutes, and then you will begin to feel drowsy," said the other man, "but if you relax, it will have no unpleasant effects."

Evan nodded through the glass. He was much less concerned about possible side effects than he had been on that first occasion. The men worked quickly, fastening his harness and reconnecting his life-support systems. The craft was obviously fully operational.

A face appeared above him. "Are you comfortable, Mr. Westering?"

Evan's senses reeled slightly. Hearing that same question again had given him a sudden, strange feeling, as if he were back on that launch pad in Florida, about to leave on a mission that had not yet taken place. He nodded again.

"Good-bye then, God speed!"

Then they were gone, and he heard only the sounds of the hatches being secured. He was alone. He was beginning to feel drowsy, as the technician had promised, and with all contact with the Kingdom gone it already seemed to him as if it had never been.

With some effort he thrust the tiredness aside and

pictured again the group of people outside. He felt the sting of tears in the corners of his eyes. He did not try to suppress them, for it was safe to cry now...perhaps. Even in the absence of all those biological sensors and telemetry, he still experienced something of that feeling of nakedness he had had at the very start of the mission.

A tear ran back toward his ear. He didn't want to go! He wanted to climb out of this mindless machine and walk back down the ramp to the most valued friends he had ever had. He wanted them to take him home! But he knew that that way was not open to him. He had a different path to walk, and as he considered it, it seemed to stretch out into the distance before him—longer and more difficult than he could ever have imagined it to be.

But he would be back...

A thin pall of dust hung over Project Delta, merging in the distance with the shimmering haze rising from the hot, bare earth. Unlike the densely forested areas elsewhere, most of Project Delta lacked the leafy cover which served to moderate the surface temperature. Work on the site had slowed accordingly, particularly for those engaged in heavy manual labor.

From a rocky excavation in a bare hillside, there emerged a very old man, laboriously pushing a loaded wheelbarrow. He was perspiring profusely, and wiry muscles stood out boldly on his thin frame as he maneuvered his load carefully down the slope.

Then he stopped suddenly, dropping the feet of the barrow into the broken earth to bring it to a halt. He drew himself upright—not fully upright, for his body was permanently bowed due both to his advanced age and the legacy of so many years at this type of work.

He dusted his hands vigorously on his worn tunic, stealing a furtive glance as he did so in the direction of the project administration building. There was a strange sound, and he shaded his eyes against the white glare of the sun to peer anxiously around him.

A second figure issued from the fissure behind him, similarly laden. This was a younger man, somewhere past middle age, and bearing obvious family resemblance to the first. He drew his wheelbarrow easily to a halt. "What's the matter?"

"I don't know. . . . There was sort of a noise. . . like something thumping on the ground . . . only a long way off. I felt it rather than heard it. It's still there. Can you hear it?"

The younger man lowered his barrow to the ground and instinctively glanced toward the administration center. "Yes—I hear it."

"What do you think it is? We wouldn't be having an earthquake again, would we—not like before?" The old man's voice quivered slightly.

The younger man's eyes narrowed, and he turned to look to the southeast. "It's not an earthquake, Dad; it's a rocket launching!"

"It doesn't sound like a rocket."

The other showed some slight irritation. "Well, I should know, and I'm telling you that it's a rocket launching. It's one of those old liquid propellant things for some reason. They haven't sent one of them off since before the millennium." He raised a hand slowly to point. "See—there it is!"

The old man shaded his eyes with both hands and squinted into the distance. A thin white pencil had appeared slightly above the horizon, enthroned on a brilliant plume of yellow flame.

It rose very slowly at first, as if pondering its course, but then began to accelerate rapidly, growling majestically upward into the enormous pantheon of the heavens.

"Wonder if anyone's in it?" muttered the old man. His companion made no comment but frowned a little—as if the remark had disturbed some dusty corner of his mind...something just beyond recall. The two men stood side by side watching, faces upturned to the sky, their labors for the moment entirely forgotten—father and son in times past, now brothers in judgment...watching.

They watched until the unexplained spacecraft was far from Earth—until the white flame of its engines was no longer discernible against the vast, bright blue canopy of the sky, and nothing remained but the gentle murmur of a distant thunder.